Above Average

Praise for *Above Average*

'I like the honesty and truthfulness of the story; I like the understated quality of the emotions, and I particularly appreciate the simplicity and directness of the prose style.'

—Amitav Ghosh

'Bagchi's biggest asset is his language. He moves smoothly from funny desi similes and Delhi-speak to lyrical description.'

—*Tehelka*

'These are authentic characters with authentic dialogue.'

—*The Hindu*

'[The novel's] many set pieces—riffs on entrance exam madness, a rock competition gone madly awry, a first kiss by an old well—are lovely.'

—*Outlook*

'Bagchi has an honest candour in realizing that IITians lead a hermetic, rarefied existence and so frequently brings in events of the outside world. Sensitive to issues of gender and caste, he attempts to address these concerns through allusions to the problems that SC quota students [...] face.'

—*DNA India*

'The pure desiness of the novel brings to you the smells, sounds and sights of Delhi. The uncles and aunties of Mayur Vihar's society are people whose parallels you'll find in your own neighbourhood.'

—*New Indian Express* on Sunday

'Amitabha Bagchi's debut novel recalls Joyce's *Portrait of the Artist as a Young Man* and Marcel Proust's *In Search of Lost Time*.'

—*The Tribune*

Above Average

A NOVEL

Amitabha Bagchi

HarperCollins *Publishers* India

First published in India by HarperCollins *Publishers* 2007
4th Floor, Tower A, Building No. 10, DLF Cyber City, DLF Phase II,
Gurugram, Haryana – 122002
www.harpercollins.co.in

2 4 6 8 10 9 7 5 3 1

This edition published by HarperCollins 2025

P-ISBN: 978-93-6569-983-8
E-ISBN: 978-93-6569-004-0

Typeset in 11/14 in Simoncini Garamond at
HarperCollins *Publishers* India

Printed and bound at
Thomson Press (India) Ltd

MIX
Paper | Supporting
responsible forestry
FSC® C010615

This book is produced from independently certified FSC® paper
to ensure responsible forest management.

For my parents

'Mujhe maloom hai uska thikaana phir kahaan hoga,
parinda aasman chhuune mein jab nakaam ho jaaye'

– Bashir Badr

'I might not be good looking but I
am definitely above average.'

(overheard in IIT Delhi,
circa 1994)

1

Photocopy

STUDY CIRCLE CLASSES ARE HELD IN THE TAMIL SCHOOL INSIDE Lodi Estate. I take a bus or sometimes get a lift to Pragati Maidan and change buses there. The road leading into the school is lined with whitewashed bungalows. Names from newspapers are painted on the nameplates: a famous police officer, a cabinet minister, a high ranking naval officer. Outside one or two of the gates stand policemen with carbines slung from their shoulders, protected by small sandbag fortresses. Really important people live in these houses.

People are milling around the school gate. It's five, class is about to begin. There are at least five different batches, about two hundred and fifty students. They are all about to file past a large photograph of President R. Venkataraman into high-ceilinged classrooms with impossibly small desks.

I go to the first floor classroom where my section will meet today. It's the room in which I had taken the screening test to get into Study Circle; a test to prove that I was good enough to study under their guidance for another test. They don't want to waste their talents on people who don't stand a chance of getting into IIT. I go to the back and wait for Bagga and Karun to show up. Mumbler comes in. People settle down.

Mumbler is a short, curly-haired fellow with a dark pockmarked face. His narrow eyes make him look cunning. He isn't. People say he is an ex-IITian. It's hard to establish this by looking at him. He is in his late twenties. There's a pack of Charms visible through the synthetic material of his shirt pocket. It sits next to a box of Ship matches.

Bagga and Karun trundle in, climbing over desks to get to my seat. Mumbler gives them a cursory look and carries on. He says something that sounds like: 'Mome uf ersia zz tigra uf emar de arr.' Luckily for us, he also writes down what he just said: 'Moment of inertia is the integral of m times r times d r.'

'Nice colour, yaar,' Bagga whispers loudly to me. On a whim I have bought turquoise ink and am writing with it. Several years later I will get an email from Bagga saying he remembers the strange ink I used back in Study Circle.

Every now and then Bagga and Karun ask Mumbler to repeat himself. He's getting annoyed. He decides to strike back by asking us questions. 'Hey,' he says, pointing at Bagga. 'Wazz mome of ersia uf hoo?'

Bagga stands up slowly with a wide grin on his face. 'Mome of ersia, sir?' he says.

There are a few scattered snickers.

'Yus, yus,' says Mumbler. The pack of Charms wobbles up and down in his pocket as he bounces on the balls of his feet.

'Uf hoo, sir?' asks Bagga.

Some people laugh out loud now.

Mumbler splutters at this impudence. It's becoming impossible to understand anything of what he is saying now but he seems to have cottoned on to the fact that Bagga is making fun of him.

He moves toward Bagga who coolly puts up a hand as if to stop him and says: 'Shall I derive it, sir?'

Mumbler halts in his tracks. 'Yus.'

Bagga draws a hoop on the board. He then navigates the derivation from 'let us consider an infinitesimal' to the inevitable 'm r squared' with practised calm. He underlines the answer and tosses the chalk out of the window with a flourish.

I must have decided at some point in my time at school that I should try to get into one of the IITs. But when I made that decision, if I ever made it consciously, I could never remember. It was not my parents who suggested it, it was not my teachers. I never talked about such things with either. It may have been the people I studied with, it may have been the friends I played cricket with in the government colony we lived in before we moved to Mayur Vihar. It could have been anyone, or it could have been no one in particular.

My father had retired from the government a year before I took my class ten board examinations. We had stayed in the government flat for that entire year. Eviction notices came and went, but we stayed on. It was too important a year for my studies to be disturbed by the trauma of a move.

I did well in the exams and took Science – physics, chemistry, mathematics, English and computer science – in class eleven. It was the obvious choice. All the intelligent students took Science. And once you entered the tall grey Science block there was only one important thing to talk about, only one important goal to work towards: getting into IIT

It was one of my Science block friends who told me about IIT Study Circle. It was the best of all the Delhi coaching classes he said. 'You know Vivek Mittal, two batches senior, top hundred? He went there.'

I knew who Vivek Mittal was; we all did.

Bagga, and his constant companion Karun, were identically thin and wiry. Their long sculpted faces always seemed to gleam with a mischievous hunger. They would sit at the back of the class, their pens at alert, their heads cocked, like predators hunting for fundas. Every so often they would swoop on their notebooks and scribble something, then jerk back up, their thirst only partly slaked.

I'd gone up to them one day after class. The pretext was that I wanted to look at their notes, but the fact was that in that section they seemed to be the two guys having the most fun.

'Hi,' I began. 'I am Arindam.'

Bagga was fumbling inside his bag for something. He looked up. 'So?'

I was nonplussed. Karun burst out into laughter.

'Umm, I just wanted to take a look at your notes for the Mechanics class. I think I missed one or two things.'

'Why should I give you my notes?' asked Bagga. 'What have you given me?'

Karun sniggered.

'Uh, okay, sorry,' I said and turned to leave.

'Wait, wait, yaar,' said Bagga. 'We're just joking. Here, take the notes.'

While he retrieved the notes, Karun introduced himself and Bagga. He asked me what school I was from and told me what school they were from. Then, as we walked towards the bus stop, the real questions began.

'So, which book do you use for maths?'

'M.L. Khanna,' I said, feeling a little unsure of myself.

'Waste of time,' said Bagga as Karun nodded wisely. 'Bring it to me, I'll mark out the important questions. Just do those.'

'Have you done Loney?' asked Karun.

'The trigo Loney?'

'No, the *physics* one,' said Bagga in the sarcastic tone I was to hear often in the coming months, and exploded with laughter, slapping palms with Karun.

'I thought that was only for class ten,' I said.

A mock sad expression came over Bagga's face. He looked at Karun. 'We'll have to look after him,' he said.

'He needs it,' Karun replied.

Then Bagga turned to me. 'The last few chapters are advanced. All the really hard trigonometric identities in JEE come from Loney. If you've done Loney then ten per cent of maths is yours.'

'Do you know how much difference ten per cent can make?' asked Karun.

I shook my head.

'Ten per cent,' said Bagga, 'can be the difference between Computer Science in Kanpur and Electrical in Bombay.'

'Or Mechanical in Kharagpur and Metallurgy in BHU,' said Karun.

'Have you taken Brilliants?' asked Bagga.

'No, I was thinking of taking Agrawals next year.'

'Good,' said Bagga. 'Brilliants sends too much material. Agrawals is concise and good. Just make sure you get hold of Brilliants' YG File.'

'YG File?'

'Young Genius File,' said Karun. 'Just problems. Best problems.'

'How will I get that if I don't take Brilliants?'

We were at the Max Müller Marg crossing now. I realized that they had been walking me away from my bus stop all this time.

Karun ran up to a car standing at the light. 'Faridabad,' he said, yanking at the door. The man waved him in. 'Bagga!' Karun shouted. The light changed to green. Bagga ran to the car. A scooter missed him narrowly.

'But how will I get YG File?' I yelled to them, feeling bulldozed by the conversation, my first intimation of what a massive task getting into IIT was.

The car had crossed the traffic light and was speeding away down Lodi Road towards Nizamuddin when Bagga stuck his head out the window, turned back towards me and shouted:

'Photocopy!'

The class finishes at six.

'I'm off,' I tell Bagga.

'Chem, maths, bunk?' he asks.

'Yes.'

'JLT?'

'Just like that,' I nod. It'll take too much time to explain.

Hurrying out of the school, I turn right. It's dusk now and the streetlights have just come on. There is a small crowd outside the auditorium – the usual suspects – kurta-wearers of both genders. I feel awkward, slightly nervous. No one here looks like me. It's hard to imagine that less than five hundred yards away there are two hundred and fifty boys cramming for an exam. Finally the doors open and we drift in. Some people look at me quizzically, others look through me. The lights go down and the video begins; Rossini's *The Barber of Seville*, a 1988 production. It's grainy, the sound quality is poor and there are no subtitles, but I am thoroughly enjoying myself. I have to leave at eight, before the end. I don't want to explain this to my parents. Explaining it to myself will be hard too. I will wonder how a love of opera squares with a diligent application towards going to engineering school. What confused compost of these two have I become?

I pass the Tamil school on my way back to the bus stop. A knot of boys is standing around a slightly older-looking guy. Bagga is among them. He detaches himself and comes to me. 'Where had you gone?'

'Nowhere,' I shrug. 'Who is this guy?'

'He taught us maths. He's in his fourth year at IIT Delhi. Computer Science.'

'Wow,' I say. We go up and join the phalanx of admirers.

'Sir, what was your JEE rank?'

He is a thick-mustachioed fellow, his well-oiled hair is combed over to one side. His faded jacket has USA written across the front.

'Hundred and thirteen,' he says.

I notice he is wearing green polyester pants. Some years later I will find myself in the throes of an internecine friendship with Neeraj, whose green polyester pants and mathematical brilliance will challenge and confuse me. But I have Rossini playing in my head today and no clue of what the future will bring. So I slip out of the group and continue on my way to the bus stop.

'Bagga,' I said, one day, early in our acquaintance. 'I don't know where to study Physical Chemistry from. What do you use?'

'Yaar, I want to get Bruce Mahan. *University Chemistry.* Kartik uses Bruce Mahan. He showed it to me once. I was totally blasted, couldn't understand a thing. Only Kartik can read that book.'

'Who's Kartik?' I asked.

'I haven't told you about Kartik? Oh shit. This guy is a total Bond, yaar. Ever since he came he's been the topper in our school. He's a sureshot top-hundred guy.'

'Do you know he taught himself differentiation and integration in class ten?' chimed in Karun.

I had taught myself differentiation in class ten. But I had balked at integration, so I kept quiet.

'He finished all of S. L. Loney in one week,' said Bagga. 'He borrowed it from me one day and then a week later he brought it back. Done, already? I asked and he says, done. Fuck, yaar, that guy is just too much.'

'Tell him about the Irodov Mechanics problem,' Karun said.

'Oh shit,' said Bagga. 'He just cracked the scene that day.'

'What happened?' I asked.

'It was about a month ago,' he said. 'I had just got my Irodov from the Soviet Book Centre and I was trying to solve the Mechanics chapter.'

'Irodov?' I cut in.

'Don't know Irodov?' Karun said, shaking his head.

'It's a Russian book with physics problems,' said Bagga. 'Only problems. Lots of JEE problems come from Irodov. You can get it from the Soviet book place in Connaught Place, just thirty rupees. I'll show it to you. Anyway, I came across this problem, number 243 in the Mechanics chapter. Some trolleys and blocks, you have to find the acceleration. Lots of those in Irodov.'

'I haven't done Mechanics yet,' I said.

Karun sniggered. Bagga slapped my back. I felt mildly reassured.

'All morning we had been trying to do 243 in school. All the guys in the class tried it. Fourth period was physics. We asked Bhatkande, our teacher, as well.'

'Bhatkande is not like the other teachers,' Karun said. 'He knows things. He can solve problems.'

'But Bhatkande also got fucked,' Bagga continued. 'He tried for ten minutes then said, you boys keep wasting my time with JEE problems. I need to cover the board syllabus. Everyone is not taking JEE, you know.'

'Bullshit!' said Karun. 'Everyone in our class is taking JEE. No one cares about the boards.'

'Finally, at break-time Kartik returned.'

'From where?'

'There was music practice,' said Bagga. 'Some competition coming up.'

'He plays guitar,' Karun said.

'He missed physics for music?'

'He doesn't need to sit in class to learn physics, yaar,' said Karun. 'He can teach Bhatkande physics.'

'So, I went to him,' said Bagga. 'Kartik, I can't solve this problem. Can you take a look at it? He took the book from me, sat down at his desk and took out some paper. He wrote a line or two, scratched his head once, then said, haan, done. He had done it less than two minutes!'

When Bagga spoke of Kartik's academic exploits, his eyes would gleam with unreserved hero worship. Hyperbole would pile on hyperbole and I would think that either this Kartik was a figment of his imagination, invented to gull me, or he was some kind of savant, the new Ramanujan.

*

One afternoon, after class at Study Circle, Bagga and I had gone to Nirula's together where we had run into his friend from school, Kartik. The second time Kartik and I met it had been on the train to Bombay.

Kartik and I had both taken Agrawals Classes for the IIT exam and we had both made it into the top hundred. And so it was that along with ten or twelve others we had found ourselves waiting on the platform at New Delhi Railway Station for the Rajdhani Express which would take us to Bombay for our all-expenses-paid two-day vacation, courtesy Agrawals Classes.

'Arindam, right?' he had said, coming up to me. 'Bagga's friend? I'm Kartik.'

'Of course,' I said. 'We met at Nirula's.' After all the stories Bagga and Karun had told of him I would have recognized him even if we hadn't met earlier.

When we entered the train compartment in which Agrawals Classes had booked all of us, one of the Papas decided to ensure that we all sat together. 'Please bhaisahab,' he said, hectoring one passenger after another, 'adjust a little, all these boys are travelling on their own for the first time.'

'Let's stay here,' said Kartik, his seat and mine having been assigned together by chance. When the proactive Papa offered us two seats he had arranged for us near the others, Kartik demurred.

'Look at all these guys,' he said pointing at the other people who were part of Agrawals' group. 'Such shadys.'

They looked very much like each other, these entrance-exam toppers, their expressions amalgamating baby-faced innocence with worldly-wise arrogance, a combination I was to see in many variations in my time at IIT. Many of them would be my classmates in a few weeks' time, some of them would become close friends.

When I thought back to the time we met on the train I would imbue those school-leaving wispy-moustached boys with the qualities that would make men out of them. Even after years of being in class together I would be able to recall with clarity each one of their faces as I saw them on the train that day. But clearest of all I would remember Sheikhu, who, three years later, dragged me kicking and screaming into the world of research and then left it himself. Whenever I would think of all that went between us and all that it meant, a picture of him sitting by the window which looked out onto the platform would slip into my mind and I would imagine him lost in a mathematical reverie, drawing figures in his head.

These seventeen-year-old lives of ours, first brought into physical proximity on a platform of New Delhi Railway Station, were to become intertwined with each other like harmonic lines in a musical composition, point sometimes and sometimes counterpoint. We would measure ourselves against each other for years after we graduated just like we would measure our grades against each others' in the four years we were to spend together. But at that time I had no inkling that this bunch of shadys were my future.

'Ya,' I said. 'Such good boys.'

'All come with their Mummy-Papa,' he laughed.

As the train pulled out of New Delhi Railway Station, he turned to me and asked: 'So, which bands do you listen to?'

Our first semester at IIT was a period of bonding for Kartik and me, living next to each other and hanging out a lot even as we followed different paths. He successfully struggled to establish his place at the top of the academic ladder while I was happy to float and enjoy my newfound freedom. In the process I had forgotten all about the guy who had first told me about Kartik, our first mutual acquaintance, Bagga.

Later, when Kartik and I became good friends, I asked him about Problem 243 from Irodov's Mechanics chapter. 'I'd done it a few days earlier,' he said. 'I pretended that I'd seen it for the first time, just to psyche them.'

At first I was puzzled by how an obviously intelligent guy like Bagga had been unable to see through the simple lies that Kartik told. It dawned on me much later that Kartik's incredible stories were part of a performance that he was expected to give for Bagga and Karun's benefit; a performance they wanted to watch as much as he wanted to give. He was, after all, their topper, the one person they were all supposed to look up to.

We all lied in one way or another. Some lied brazenly like Kartik, others went about it more subtly. Some lied just to others, some to themselves as well. In the years to come, as I slowly began to unravel the truths and falsehoods of my own life, I realized that it was not enough to catch a liar in his lie, it was much more important to figure out whether he believed the lie himself.

Unshakeable self-confidence was key to winning the battles we fought. The battle for grades and academic achievement was just one small part of the larger war, the others being the battles to appear unconcerned, in control, well rounded, cultured, self-confident. Accustomed all our lives to being lauded as exceptional, we were all scared that the true measure of ourselves, our unremarkable selves, would emerge one day. Each difficult task carried the potential for failure. But attempting simple tasks was complicated too. We knew that if we took a soft option, or even if we failed at something difficult, the scorn of our peers – or, worse, their pity – would pour down like napalm and burn us down to our bones. If we lived past that assault we had to face our parents' disappointment. And, finally, burnt and beaten, we had to answer to ourselves.

My fear of being unexceptional was inextricably linked to a deep desire to be accepted as ordinary. The averageness that I was ashamed of showing became my most intimate friend. I started thinking that those people who were in touch with their inner ordinariness even while they went about the business of self-aggrandizement, which was the business of survival itself, were fundamentally okay. Those people were, somehow, more likely to survive the trials life was to bring.

I realized later that Kartik, the Institute topper, and Neeraj, the self-proclaimed future Turing award winner, both became close friends of mine because I sensed that their struggles with their own self-image were closer to my own than anyone else's. And although it was several years before I asked myself why they became my friends, I was forced to eventually realize that perhaps their reasons for being my friends were more or less the same.

Neeraj and Kartik were both people whose legend entered my life before they did. But there were many times in my four years at IIT with Kartik when I felt he didn't believe the image of himself he had projected to Bagga and Karun. And perhaps that is why I could make some sort of peace with him. But Neeraj believed he was the illusion. Or maybe I could never convince myself he did not.

Bagga stopped attending Study Circle six months before the IIT exam. Karun came alone a few times but his heart wasn't in it without Bagga around. Finally he stopped coming too. 'Yaar, have to study for the boards as well,' he said, at the last class he came for. 'Who knows if I'll get into IIT. Board marks are important.'

This was a strange sentiment coming from him. He, and Bagga, had always been so focused on the IIT, so well organized, that I had simply assumed that they would take the board exams lightly. I knew I was treating them like a minor annoyance. It wasn't as if I was certain I would do well at the JEE but I pooh-poohed the board exams because everyone in school did. JEE was the big one, the real challenge.

'The boards!' I said, disbelievingly.

'Yes,' he said, averting his eyes from mine. 'Can't take a risk with the boards. In all other engineering colleges your board percentage matters.'

Nine eventful months later, sitting at the bus stop outside IIT hostel, I said to Kartik: 'I can't believe Bagga didn't take the exam. JEE was his whole life.'

'He played cricket as well,' said Kartik.

'Yes, yes,' I said. 'But with me all he talked about was physics this and chemistry that. This book for geometry, that book for trigonometry.'

'It was strange, yaar,' said Kartik sitting up. 'I met him when I went to school to get my board result. He said that he had gone to submit the form on the last day and there was a problem in it, or with the bank draft, and they had refused to take it. By the time he went with a new draft the place was closed. Something like that.'

Through my time at IIT whenever I thought of Bagga, and it was infrequently that I remembered him, I would shake my head at the cussedness of the bureaucracy that had denied him an opportunity to do what he had so badly wanted to do. It was only much much later that I realized Bagga had told one more unverifiable story that I had, for all these years, unquestioningly believed.

One day many years later, in Baltimore, I got an email from Bagga. He was coming to the US. He had got my email address from Kartik. He remembered the turquoise blue ink, he said, and he remembered one class in which there had been an optics question, an eagle and a tortoise swimming in a stream, something to do with refraction. Before anyone else could even figure out what was going on, before Mumbler himself, I had cracked it. As usual, he said. As usual.

I could hear Bagga's voice: 'Fuck, that Arindam is some guy, yaar. Give him any optics question, he can solve it without using pen and paper, all in his head.'

It was like seeing myself in a twisted mirror.

2

Parachute

MY GRANDFATHER WAS A TERRORIST AND A SHAKESPEARE scholar. He left home in his teens to study English Literature in Calcutta. The extensive landholdings he left behind were among the biggest in his part of what subsequently became Bangladesh, my father told me. They had been part of a talukdari granted by one of the Mughal emperors. I often wondered, especially when I had a particularly hard exam to prepare for, what my life would have been like if my grandfather had not chosen to leave home for Calcutta, if he had not chosen to exchange his hereditary privilege for a modern education.

In Calcutta, the story went, he got involved with a revolutionary group. My father did not remember the details but there was something about a stolen shipment of guns, an assassination in the Maidan. Whatever my grandfather did in Calcutta was not serious enough to get him hanged or put in jail, but it was bad enough to ensure that he had to travel the breadth of India looking for teaching jobs.

'He went all the way from Rangoon to Peshawar,' my father told me one weekend when I was fifteen, as we sat waiting for my mother to serve lunch. 'But no job lasted more than a few months. His police record would always catch up with him.'

Finally, he decided to look for a job outside British India. That was how my father's family reached Gwalior, the capital of what remained of the Great Scindia's greatness.

'Things were not easy in Gwalior on a professor's salary with five children to feed,' my father said, pulling at his earlobe as he often did when he was thinking. 'We never went anywhere in the holidays. All summer we stayed in Gwalior. There were two jobs Baba did in that time. One was examinership for the Ajmer board. I remember, it would be our job to take sheaves of corrected papers and sew them up in gunny bags, then go down to the post office and register them to Ajmer. That was what we did in the summer, that, and study Bangla, one hour a day, five days a week. The other job Baba had was to annotate Shakespeare's plays for publication by Gaya Ram and Sons. Gaya Ram, with typical bania sharpness, had taken Baba on and grown from "Booksellers" to "Booksellers and Publishers". Every summer, Baba would annotate the play that was in next year's syllabus. My friend Radheshyam told me that he was at Gaya Ram's once and some chap came in and asked for *Hamlet*. Which one do you want? the man had asked. Shakespeare's *Hamlet* or Chatterjee Saheb's?

'He never talked about home. All we knew was the name of the village, the subdivision and the district,' my father told me. And whenever he would say that I would feel a twinge of pity for him. I had what he did not have: stories of my father's childhood.

'Maybe he fought with his father before leaving,' my father said. 'I know he never went back. In any case, travelling up there is so difficult. You remember, I had gone to Dhaka for three months in '88? This youngster called Khorshid Ahmad was the liaison officer from the Bangladesh government. Very nice chap, he called me to his house for dinner many times. And he still writes from time to time. I said to him in the very first week, Khorshid, can I go up to Netrakona? My ancestral village is there. He said, Chatterjee Shaheb, this is not the right season, all the rivers are in flood. Half the ferries will not be running. It will take days to get there. That's the problem, travelling in Bangladesh, he said, too many rivers.'

By the time my father and his brothers finished college, India was independent. They all ended up joining the Central Services, except Choto Kaku who moved to Bombay and took a job in a company that made sinks and toilet seats.

In the early Seventies my father was posted to the Centre after several years of being in the Field. I was born in Ram Manohar Lohia Hospital, it was called Willingdon Hospital at the time, in 1974.

For the first fifteen years of my life I lived in the heart of the newest Delhi – the British Imperial capital, built not more than fifty years before I was born – speaking English, Hindi and Bengali with an unmistakably Punjabi accent.

I caressed the stippled stone of India Gate and ran my fingers over the engraved names of Indian soldiers who died fighting for the British, picked jamuns off the roads and ate them till my tongue turned purple, walked on the red sand up Rajpath to the Secretariats then walked through North Block to Kendriya Terminal and took a bus home, watched the sun rise over Purana Qila and National Stadium and India Gate. I knew all the lines that Lutyens and Baker had drawn and I traced them lovingly, on foot or on cycle, whenever I got the opportunity.

Then my father retired and we had to move east of the Yamuna, to Mayur Vihar.

*

Roses bloom twice in Delhi – December and February. On a weekend in one of these seasons we would go to Rose Garden in Chanakya Puri.

It would always be a Sunday. Saturday mornings were busy ones. They were reserved for trips to the bank in Connaught Place and the shops of Shankar Market. I would sit in the car waiting for my mother. She would go and fight with the plump, bald man with a K. L. Saigal moustache and sly smile, whom we referred to as Mod because his shop, a tiny rectangular affair with its back to the railway station, was called La Mode. 'The blouses were supposed to be ready two weeks ago,' my mother would say. 'Next week, madam,' he would reply looking at a point somewhere above my mother's left shoulder. 'You always do this.' 'Next week, one hundred per cent.' The argument would go on for a bit, moving from his tardiness to his shoddy workmanship and back. I would sit baking in the car near Indian Oil Bhawan waiting for my mother to return.

But on Sundays there was nowhere to go. Sundays were for sitting at home and eating omelettes and reading the newspaper and watching TV. Except on rare occasions, like the weekend in December, or February, when we made a trip to Rose Garden.

It meant dressing up, of course. That was the part I liked least. I would have to put on one of my nice shirts, like the grey one with navy blue stripes. The family photograph was taken on one of those trips by my uncle who used to live near Rose Garden. I stand there on the right, my arm linked with my mother's, my wispy moustache bent into a grimace, my body slightly stiff at the sudden tug that always follows the photographer's exhortation to pull closer. I am wearing the grey shirt with the navy blue stripes. Then there were the pants that always seemed to have become a little tighter than the previous time I had worn them. At the end of the whole process, I would have to comb my hair rigorously. But no matter how much I combed it, my mother would always run the hairbrush through it once again before we left the house. She herself would be dressed in a starched sari, her hair freshly hennaed, her neck visibly powdered. My father would wear a T-shirt; one of the few times he did.

We would take our places in the car: I sat behind the driver's seat – my mother's seat – my sister sat next to me, behind my father. I learned how to drive in this car, which my sister later bought from my mother. After I got my licence I often drove my parents around, always feeling proud when my mother handed me the keys, always feeling like I didn't deserve the privilege.

My mother would navigate the roads leading up to the nala bridge very deliberately, honking at every turn. But once she reached the main road we would feel the car roar, the air would rush in through the open windows. Liftoff.

When we got our first Maruti my mother had touched seventy kilometres an hour on the Mayur Vihar to Rose Garden trip. Her 1966 model Standard Herald had hardly ever crossed forty. I remember the delight on her face, the muffled roar of the engine, the giddy feeling we had all shared.

Each bed had a different breed of rose – Lucille Ball, Pride of India, Morning Glory – a different colour. There are no blue roses, my father would always say. In nature roses are always red or yellow or in between. We would walk slowly from bed to bed, reading the strange names, oohing and aahing at the flowers. Sometimes we would pose in front of them. My father rarely took photographs of the flowers alone, one of us always had to stand by them. There were enough photographs of flowers on calendars and postcards.

Afterwards we would go to the Chinese restaurant on Malcha Marg. My father would order the food. He liked to get steamed rice with the dishes. I would want noodles or fried rice. We would always get one of each. There was never any food left. I always overate.

On the way back I would try and stretch my legs, try to make room for myself in the back seat. As we headed east, the trip back always seeming shorter than the journey out, the deeper yellows of the afternoon would settle on trees and traffic lights. By the time we reached India Gate I would have dozed off. When I awoke, drool at the edge of my mouth waiting to slip down my chin, we would be back in our covered parking space in the Society. I would drag myself out of the car and stagger towards the stairwell, belching chicken manchurian as I went.

I tear the page I have just written from the notepad and slip it into Lakhmir Singh's *Guide to Board Chemistry, Class Twelve.* Sliding the writing surface back into the table, I rise, pick up my jacket off the bed and come out into the drawing room. The sound of seeds sputtering in oil comes popping out of the kitchen.

'Going for a walk,' I call.

Onions explode into oil. I go out through the front door into the dimly lit landing.

It is almost sundown in Mayur Vihar. A large Ambassador trundles by, a foot away from me, its horn screeching. Clouds of dust linger in its wake. Stray dogs trot about purposefully, dodging stones being thrown at them by small dark children in torn vests and coloured shorts. The shop directly opposite our gate has the words 'departmental store' emblazoned on it. At the counter inside sit two moustached men listlessly watching television. Next to the shop is a small lane leading inwards, away from the road, at the very centre of which is a narrow open drain. With two spindly bamboo legs in this drain sits the paanwala's makeshift shop. Two or three men are hanging around near it. The paanwala sits inside, head bent over the counter, slathering a leaf with lime.

Kar Uncle walks up to him, blue plastic bag in hand, spinach poking out from the top. 'How is business, Ramesh?' he asks, proffering a twenty-rupee note.

Ramesh shakes his head, making a grunting sound that is partly a giggle and partly a sigh. He reaches back and picks out a pack of cigarettes, the correct brand, and puts them on the counter in front of him. In the same action he sweeps the note out of Kar Uncle's fingers.

I can't decide whether to greet Kar Uncle or to put my head down and keep walking. The Bangla greeting 'Nomoshkaar' starts off in my head as the Hindi 'Namaskaar' and has, in the past, come out as 'Namoshkaar' at least once and 'Nomashkaar' several times. A small set of syllables does battle in my head. The correct ones emerge victorious, but weakened. 'Nomoshkaar, Uncle,' I mumble into the lapel of my jacket.

Kar Uncle does not hear me. He has put his bag down, and is busily filing away at the cellophane covering of his ten-pack Goldflake.

The oblong stretch of land next to the Society had been designated a park in a long-forgotten plan. It is just a large patch of dust now, one side lined with shanties made of cloth and discarded sheets of corrugated metal, cemented together with wet mud. There is a huge crater in one corner of the park. Mud for the shanties has been taken from here. The rest of the park is being used by overlapping cricket games, at least three, probably more. As the sun begins to set these games are heading towards their raucous conclusions.

A bowler is running in to deliver. As he heads towards the crease I turn my neck to keep him in view. The batsman is a little boy, not much bigger than the bat he wields. It is not easy to tell which of the thirty or forty people standing around on the field are involved in this game.

The ball sails across the pitch. I have to stop to watch it. The boy swings the bat. He misses. The ball hits the ground and does not rise. Scurrying past the batsman, missing the wicket, evading the wicketkeeper's half-hearted attempt to collect it, rolling and bumping, it reaches the edge of the crater and falls in.

I turn and keep walking along a covered drain. Every so often it peeks through where a slab of cement has been removed. It flows with the grace of a village stream in the plains, carrying empty packets of potato chips flecked with drops of black water.

I pass the crowd at the 'foreign' liquor shop. I turn and walk towards the bridge. The temple at the foot of the incline that leads up to the bridge is ringing with the sounds of evening prayers. Hawkers begin to light their lamps in anticipation of evening shoppers. I walk up the incline. The road to NOIDA and the embankment beyond it and the flood plain even further beyond come into view slowly.

On the bridge I pause and, resting my elbows on the cement railing, look down into the large open drain that marks the western boundary of Mayur Vihar Phase 1.

If you had been atop Humayun's Tomb on a particular day in 1803, for whatever reason, you would have seen guns lined against each other in the green fields east of the Yamuna as the Marathas battled the British. The British won the battle of Patparganj, subsequently establishing themselves as a presence in Delhi for the next century and a half. The Marathas were beaten back to Gwalior.

A hundred and seventy years after 1803, the sight that would have met your eyes would have been more or less the same, except for the cannons, the British and the Marathas: fields and villages, a road or two.

Within the next few years, however, several waves of people were to spill out of Delhi to what is called Trans-Yamuna by those who live west of the river and East Delhi by those who live east of it. The first wave was the 'resettled' slum dwellers of Delhi, housed in the riot-prone warren called Trilok Puri. The second was of people certified to be part of the 'middle-income group' by the Delhi Development Authority. This certification was accompanied by the privilege of inhabiting one of hundreds of dirty yellow concrete boxes that the DDA collectively named Mayur Vihar. The third wave was the Society dwellers.

All you had to do was form a group of creditworthy people who needed a place to live. Sixty dwelling units per acre was what you promised to put up, at your own cost, to your own design, within certain guidelines. A hundred such plots were carved out north of the National Highway 24 bypass. Just south of the bypass, sandwiched between the road and the DDA flats, were another fourteen plots. The Society we moved to was one of these.

Three hundred gazetted officers, or former gazetted officers, of the Government of India had come together to form our cooperative group housing society. Many of them were Bengalis. Consequently, a construction company from Calcutta was engaged. They built four grey towers, blocks A through D, each eight storeys high, and three strange, interconnected four-storeyed structures, E block. There were two oblong patches of grass near the south end of the Society. Trees were planted all along the periphery; one of the members had some connection with the horticulture department. In the centre of the Society was a water tank. It was an underground structure, the roof of which was about a foot above street level. This water tank was closer to a square, geometrically and otherwise, than most people in Delhi could hope for.

The Society had two kinds of inhabitants. Members and Tenants. The Members were a more homogeneous group: retired government servants mainly, the occasional family of a serving officer who was posted outside Delhi or one who had decided that he did not want to risk renting his flat for fear he might not be able to get his tenants out. The Tenants were a more mixed group: young professional couples whose current salaries did not permit them anything fancier than a flat in faraway Trans-Yamuna, rich businessmen hiding from income tax amidst the resettlement colonies, musicians waiting to make it big, unmarried MBA-types living three to a flat. And many others, too few to classify or too hard to pin down. It was expected that in the course of time more and more Members would retire from service and move to the Society, tilting the ratio of Members to Tenants towards the former. It was an expectation that was, on the whole, satisfied.

My mother heard from someone that my school had finally relented and decided to run a bus to NOIDA, and that it would pick up children from Mayur Vihar on the way. If the driver recognized my school uniform he would stop. If he didn't I would have to trek across the city like I had done each day the previous week; 327 to Kendriya Terminal, 680 from there to Sangam Cinema. Each journey took almost forty-five minutes.

I took my position on the nala bridge at six in the morning. People walked past me on their way to the DTC bus stop. Rickshaws rolled by carrying women immaculately dressed in salwar kameez, their hair combed down, a little bit of colour on their lips, a purse slung from their shoulders.

The bus would come from NOIDA mode, the huge T-junction where Nizamuddin Bridge's approach road began. A 364 lumbered by, people spilling out of it. It wheezed and grunted as the driver took the turn onto the NOIDA road at full speed. As it came to a halt at the bus stop I spotted a van scooting past in the opposite lane. It had my school's colours and a big crest. It sped up to the crossing. Heaving my bag onto my shoulders, I walked right into the middle of the road and put both hands up. The brakes screeched, the van skidded and came to a halt two feet away.

The driver was still fulminating when I got on. The conductor was telling me what he thought of my mother and my sister. The other children were staring and the one teacher on the bus had her finger raised and wagging.

'It's a new stop, ma'am,' I said, hurrying to the back before she could say anything.

By the end of the month four students and one teacher were taking the school van from the nala bridge. I often heard them talk about being pioneers of that bus stop. But I knew it wasn't so. They had started coming at least three days after that April morning when I first stuck my neck out to stop the bus on the nala bridge.

The engine took on a laboured roar as we ascended the Mother Dairy flyover. It was a Vijay Super, Bobby's scooter. They had stopped making them some years back. The throttle was turned open to the maximum, both our bodies leaning forward urging the old machine on. The exhaust behind us was billowing black. We were going to get a quarterly pollution check.

'Mandawli is over there,' shouted Bobby turning his helmeted head to the right.

'Where?' I shouted back.

'There,' he said, taking his right hand off the accelerator and pointing over my shoulder. The scooter wobbled.

'Bobby!'

'Relax, yaar, I have it under control.'

My heart racing, I gripped the side of the seat, tearing its already ripped cover a little more. We were up on level ground now as the road crossed the railway tracks. He took his right hand off the throttle again, pressing the clutch with his left as we began to coast down into Shakarpur.

'Scared?' he said. He was laughing.

'What were you telling me about Mandawli?' I asked.

'Have I told you about the doodhwalas of Mandawli?'

'No.'

We pulled up at a red light. Buses and handcarts jostled for space as the road narrowed, its sides eaten up by fruit and vegetable vendors.

'There isn't a single virgin left in Mandawli,' announced Bobby rather loudly. The man on the scooter next to ours turned his head sharply.

'What nonsense!' I said.

'I am telling you, Arindam, believe me. There isn't one virgin left in Mandawli – the doodhwalas don't spare a single girl.'

Mercifully, at this point the light changed. We crawled into the intersection, then balked as two or three stragglers decided to risk life and limb to make it across. Finally we sped forward, to the extent that Bobby's beloved contraption could speed forward. He had taught me to ride on it. 'No matter how much raise you give, this scooter won't jump.' It hadn't.

We drove in silence till we reached the service station. Bobby parked the scooter outside and walked into the glass cabin while I waited. He came out a minute later with a scrap of paper in his hand. Leaning against someone else's scooter he resumed his narration.

'They are horny bastards, those Mandawli doodhwalas. Whenever a new girl appears in the colony they get after her. They don't rest till they have taken her virginity. You can't take a panga with them. They can be really vicious. There was this girl in Preet Vihar ...'

'Bobby?' announced a balding man in overalls. He looked around as if it were not obvious to him that we were the only people at the service station. Bobby stepped forward and the process began.

He kickstarted the scooter. The bald man inserted some kind of metal probe into the sputtering exhaust pipe. I was left to contemplate the frequency with which unnamed girls from Preet Vihar, the posh area of East Delhi, made an appearance in Bobby's stories.

The numbers on the digital display increased with a rapidity which the bald guy had evidently seen rarely. When the ascent finally halted he looked up at Bobby. 'This is too much. Such a high reading!'

Bobby said nothing.

'Never,' the man muttered as he went about removing the side panel which covered the engine. 'Never, since the checking started, has a scooter given such a reading. I have seen trucks which pollute less.'

Eventually he uncovered the regulatory screw. Putting the end of the screwdriver into the groove he started tightening it.

'Arré, arré! Will you cut off the petrol completely?' exclaimed Bobby.

The man looked up at Bobby and then, very deliberately, turned the screwdriver once more.

'The government gives them a little power,' Bobby mumbled, 'and they start behaving like they are DCPs.'

The bald man was unfazed. He kickstarted the scooter himself, inserted the probe, took a cursory look at the meter and then scrawled something on a piece of paper.

'Here is your certificate.'

Bobby snatched the document from him, folded it carefully and put it into his wallet. He put his helmet on and got on to the scooter.

'Sit,' he said.

'What about the girl in Preet Vihar?' I said.

'What girl?'

'The doodhwalas of Mandawli and the girl ...'

'Oh, yes,' he said, putting the scooter into gear. 'There was this girl in Preet Vihar. Very beautiful. Really beautiful. Some guy from her colony fell in love with her. He used to stand beneath her balcony every evening and try to make eye contact with her.'

We had pulled up around the corner from the service station. Bobby got off and parked the scooter. He retrieved a toolkit from the compartment beneath the handle.

'But this girl gave him no lift. Everyday he would stand there and she would not even look at him, forget about smiling at him. Then one day he saw another fellow in the street. She was looking at him and smiling and he was looking at her and smiling. So he, the first guy, got very angry. I'll show them, he thought.'

Bobby was removing the side panel now. The scooter's greasy entrails came into view for the second time that day.

'This guy happened to know someone who had the backing of the doodhwalas. So the very next day they came.'

'The doodhwalas?'

'Yes. They came in a Maruti van and waited outside her house. As soon as the other fellow arrived they dragged him into the van and drove away to some remote place.'

'And then?'

Bobby had reached the regulatory screw. He put the screwdriver on it. 'And then they gave it to him up the ass.'

'What?'

He looked up at me and laughed, his thin frame shaking with delight. Then he turned back to the engine and began systematically undoing the bald man's work.

'Each one of them did it to him twice. He couldn't walk straight for the next four or five days. He never went back to Preet Vihar.'

'What are you doing, Bobby?'

'I am just increasing the flow of petrol to the engine,' he said, getting up and dusting his hands. 'The scooter doesn't idle properly if the screw is too tight.'

We were on the bridge again on our way back to Mayur Vihar when he turned his head once more and bellowed into the wind: 'Arindam, if you are ever in trouble, tell me. I know the doodhwalas of Mandawli.'

When we shifted to Mayur Vihar, the Society had a TT table. It was an old uneven table, its surface blotched and bloated. There was no TT room, just an unused parking spot on the ground floor of C block with no walls on two sides. When I went down there for the first time, a day after we moved into our new flat, two people were using it, knocking the ball back and forth in the manner of rank beginners. My heart sank at the sight.

I had been playing table tennis since I was six. It was the only game I was good at. All the government colonies we had lived in had at least one good TT table and several very good TT players. Some of them played state-level tournaments, a few had even played in the nationals.

One summer I managed to get selected for the summer coaching camp at Nehru Stadium, the one attended by seeded players on the Delhi table tennis circuit. Many of them had rich parents who bought them imported rackets and shiny gym bags and pushed them to do just one thing: play table tennis well. The very first morning I met a short Sikh boy. His father watched us play, badgering him after every knock, pointing out how my topspins were really strong and how I held my racket correctly while returning his shots. Many years later, when table tennis had long receded into the past for me, I saw the same little Sikh fellow's face, older and with wisps of hair on it, in the newspaper. He had become Delhi's state champion.

It was at the camp that I found out that my racket – the precious Butterfly racket an uncle had brought from Dubai – was not a very good one. The problem was it had Tackiness rubbers on it. They were slow, for defensive players. I was an attacker, I could trade loops with the best. But with a racket like mine I would never be able to stand my ground. Everyone said that the best racket you could have was a combination of the attacking Yasaka Mark V rubbers on a steady Juic blade. But it was very, very expensive.

There was a guy at school who wanted to sell me one of his faster Sriver rubbers. He was going to buy a new Mark V. It was a battle to convince my parents that this was a good deal. They thought I was out to spoil my imported racket. But I fought and I fought till, finally, they gave in. I loved showing off my slightly tattered Sriver, explaining how the fast forehand coupled with the slow Tackiness backhand really balanced my game.

It was this Sriver – Tackiness racket that I stood clutching in that parking space, almost in tears at the thought of having to spend the rest of my life playing on a dead table with people who didn't know a topspin from a flat. Then, hesitantly, I asked them: 'Are you playing a game?'

'Yes,' the boy said. 'Best of three. This is the first game.'

It was an old trick. Tell the new guy you are playing best of three and have just begun. I wasn't going to fall for it.

'Let's play winners to continue.'

The girl on the other side sniffed and caught the ball. The boy looked across at her and then back at me. He was about my height, but thinner. He wore cream coloured trousers which fell smoothly – making him look just a little gangly – and full sleeves. It struck me as strange, I was wearing jeans and a T-shirt. His hair was slicked down and looked a little greasy. His narrow eyes at the top of his thin-lipped pockmarked face commanded attention. He looked sly.

'My name is Arindam,' I said, holding out my hand.

'Bobby,' he said, putting his hand in mine. I pressed down on it like I had been taught at school only to find it limp and unresponsive.

Much later Bobby told me: 'When I first saw you I thought, where has this bookworm kid come from?'

I didn't tell him but my first thought about him had been: This guy is a bully.

*

Bobby and I became friends; I never quite figured out why. The friends I made at school or the people I came to know when we lived in New Delhi were, like me, the children of government officers, class 1 officers at that, or of professionals or academics or rich businesspeople. My falling in with them was, somehow, natural. But with Bobby I often wondered how it was that we came to be so close.

With most of his other friends he got into some kind of situation or the other, but he and I never got into trouble together. There was just the one time we tried to sneak into another society and play table tennis in their recreation room on their new tables. The man who caught us was a short fellow wearing black-rimmed spectacles. He must have been on his way back from the market when he saw the light in the recreation room and decided to investigate, he was holding a plastic bag full of vegetables. This incident was a joke compared to the drinking, smoking and vandalism that Bobby participated in with his other friends.

At first I thought he made me his friend just because of the maths tuitions I gave him for his class twelve board exams, but our relationship only grew when I went away to college and our meetings became relatively infrequent. At other times I wondered if I was just the respectable face he wanted Abhilasha's parents to see him walking around the Society with, but he kept coming even after he had moved to a different part of Mayur Vihar and Abhilasha was no longer a possibility. I was able to think of many reasonable, if not entirely convincing, arguments for why he would want to be my friend but I never really had a theory for why I liked him so much, why I enjoyed spending time with him while being acutely aware that I would never be able to introduce him to my friends from school.

Bobby's jijaji was a stockbroker. Around the time I entered my fourth year at IIT, Bobby was to start working with him in the brokerage after they got a card for the new National Stock Exchange. It was really prestigious, he told me, very few brokers got a seat on the NSE. I took his word for it although I had spent most of my newspaper-reading life jumping straight from the editorial page to the sports page. Everything in between was Commerce.

In my school, when you cleared your class ten board exams you went into one of three streams. The smart students went into Science, the rich kids went into Commerce and the rest went into Humanities. The people in the Humanities section were okay, we Science people felt, they just did not have good enough marks in their board exams to get into a Science section. The people who were not okay were the Commerce people. The girls were all 'fast', make-up wearing types, skirts dangerously high above the knee. The boys were all goondas who wore stylish clothes and gelled their hair and drove around in cars after school with the stereos blaring. Bobby was in Commerce.

Maths was the hardest subject in the Commerce stream. At his request, I tutored Bobby for the class twelve board exams. For me and for my friends at school who were also studying for the engineering entrance exams, board maths was a joke. For Bobby, on the other hand, it seemed really difficult. I was always surprised at how little he knew. It appeared as if he didn't attend classes at all. But I persevered. He had a copy of *Ten Years' Papers*. We went through the whole thing, year by year, all the way from 1982 to 1991. I took him through every type of problem, step by step. He would sit at my little desk with his notebook and the unwieldy Manjit Singh *Guide for Class Twelve Mathematics* open in front of him and I would sit on my bed and prompt him as he struggled through the problems. I even showed him my *U-Like* problems book, which, unlike Manjit Singh, had no solutions. I would get him to solve a problem and then check his solution. He trusted me to be right. More, perhaps, than I trusted myself.

When we met after the exam he was smiling. 'The questions were just like the ones you showed me, Arindam. I did them just like you told me to. I think I am going to pass. I attempted a lot of problems.' He didn't ask me how my exam had gone.

He scored sixty-five in the exam. Across the phone line, the evening of the results, I could feel his surprise and his happiness. He forgot to ask me how I had done – ninety-nine out of hundred – and I forgot to ask him how he had fared in his other subjects. Many years later I would be one conversation away from a lifetime as a teacher, walking down a hallway to a conference room to give my first job talk for my first faculty position, and I would hear Bobby's excited voice in my head: 'Sixty-five, Arindam! My parents are shocked. My jijaji has said he will buy me a new scooter. All thanks to you, Arindam. Where do you want to go for dinner, tell me?'

In return for my teaching him maths, he taught me how to ride the scooter. My mother had taught me how to drive a car but no one in my family had ever ridden a scooter before. Bobby had brought an old blue Vijay Super from somewhere. 'They don't make these anymore,' he had said.

The first thing to learn was how to let go of the clutch without the engine stalling. The second thing was to make sure that the scooter didn't jump because of too much acceleration when the clutch was released. 'That's why I brought this gaadi,' he had said. 'No matter how much raise you give, it will never jump.' He had been right, it never did. It was late afternoon the first time I actually got the scooter to move. He had parked it behind C block. The sun was slanting into the back of the Society from over the jhuggi next door. The scooter shook as I rode it, the engine now sputtering, now roaring, but never stopping. And Bobby sitting behind me – the sound of his long sleeves fluttering in the hot slipstream – his body tense, his words encouraging.

Bobby's own scooter was a white LML Vespa. The LML was a smoother ride than a Bajaj, he told me repeatedly, but harder to maintain. The Bajaj had better resale value, it was hardier. After my first year in college when my parents agreed to buy me a scooter, he suggested I buy a Bajaj. At that time, as before, he told me his riding philosophy. Always ride at forty kilometres an hour. Never take the scooter over sixty. Speed is not important, he would say. A smooth ride is. Besides, the scooter's life increases if you ride it within sixty. And the many, many times I rode behind him, I never once saw him doing any different.

He told me that he never let anyone else ride his LML, not even his jijaji whom he respected more than his father. It could have been that it had grown old by the time I first rode it, that he didn't care that much any more, but I still remember how happy I felt the day he first allowed me to ride it.

Sometimes in the evening, instead of taking our usual leisurely stroll around the Society or running down to the market on his scooter, Bobby and I would play cricket with the others on the front lawn. He was not very good at it. Once he had batted his fill he would usually leave. When he was at the crease he would swing his arms at every ball, trying to hit a six every time. His arms would flail awkwardly, the ball would usually go through to the keeper or squirt away to the square fielder. But people were afraid of him so no one ever laughed.

He talked about his notoriety as if it were a relic of a bygone era. He told me that in the old days he and a friend of his called Winky, who had moved away since, used to be quite a team. 'We did everything together, Arindam, everything,' he said. 'Winky taught me how to smoke, he gave me my first drink on the A block roof. What a guy Winky is, all the girls would sneak looks at him when we walked past. He's fair, tall, and his muscles, huge! He lifts weights every day, every single day. He told me, Bobby, I can miss eating or shitting one day, but I can't miss weightlifting.'

'What about you, Bobby, didn't he teach you how to lift weights?' I asked.

'No, yaar,' he laughed, flexing his slender biceps. 'With him around there was no need for me to build my muscles. Did I tell you about the time Winky broke Ghosh's windshield?'

I'd heard the story several times but I didn't stop him.

'We were walking in the Society, just like you and I are walking right now. Ghosh, the guy who lives in E block, thinks he's very smart, was driving in. We were in the way. He started honking loudly, rolled his window down and said a few things. Winky just stopped, right in the path of the car. What are you doing Winky, I said. He turned slowly and glared at Ghosh through the windshield. Why are you looking at me like that Ghosh said, get out of the way. Chowkidaar, chowkidaar, he started shouting. Winky grabbed my hand and pulled me in front of the car. Stand here, he said, and walked to the side of the road. He took hold of one of the bricks stuck into the ground along the border of the Society's nursery and started pulling it out. The mud was dry, Arindam, it took him almost a minute. His muscles were swollen with the effort, his face turned red. Ghosh was shouting, move away, move away, who do you think you are? I was stuck there, not knowing whether to move or to stay. Finally the brick came loose, a hunk of earth coming out of the ground with it. Winky brought it to where I was standing and, without saying a single word, drew his hand back and threw it straight into the windshield.'

He finished the story, like he always finished it, by shaking his head and saying: 'Winky is crazy.'

Bobby claimed he himself was different now, he had given up that life. Nevertheless, certain stories would come up from time to time.

'The other day I went and parked my scooter near my block in an empty space. This chap comes to me and tells me I can't park my scooter there, it's his spot. I told him, this is the only place available. I am not going to move it from here just because you say so. He caught hold of my collar and said show me some respect. I didn't say anything. I just pulled his hands off my shirt and walked away. A couple of days later I had gone to the Pocket 1 market. There I met some of the boys. Do you know Pandey? No? Well, everyone in Pocket 1 knows Pandey. He saw me and said what's going on, Bobby, we don't see you much nowadays. I told him I am studying, I have to make a career. I told him I have a friend called Arindam who is helping me with maths. He said come, drink some tea. Tell me if there is anything we can do for you. At first I didn't say anything but then he kept insisting so I told him about the guy in my new Society. He said you should have told me earlier, I would have straightened him out. Anyway, the next day I was in my Society, starting my scooter and the same guy comes up to me with his hands folded. Sorry Bobby, he says, I didn't know who you were. I told him forget all this sorry-vorry, just don't do this kind of thing again. Chutiya, saala.'

There were many stories like this one. Some featured him in a starring role. Others, like the famous Mandawli doodhwaalas story, had unnamed characters. These stories often revolved around a girl who lived in upmarket Preet Vihar. The men were normally from the dirty and densely-populated areas of Shahdara or Lakshmi Nagar or Seelampur.

But panga stories were not the only ones he told. He would often tell me about the share market. Once he told me that I should invest in LML. 'Our guy who goes on the floor told me, it's at 80 now. It has a rally up to 150. These fellows have their own network. They know.' A few weeks later I was back in the hostel at IIT sitting in the common room when my eye fell on a newspaper open to the stock prices page. I remembered what Bobby had said and looked up LML. It was at 72.

One day he asked me: 'Do you know which is the best coconut oil in India?'

'Which one, Bobby?'

'Parachute. It has the largest market share. Which oil do you use?'

I didn't use Parachute. I used a brand called KMP. I told him so. Some weeks later we were talking and somehow coconut oil came up again. 'Arindam, do you know which are the two best brands of coconut oil in India today?'

'Which ones, Bobby?'

'Parachute and KMP.'

On weekends we ate fish for lunch. Sometimes it would be mustard fish, sometimes tender whole pabdas in a watery gravy. I didn't like fish curry so, just for me, there would be fried fish. Every weekend my mother would say, 'Try some, it's good,' and my father would back her up by mixing the curry with his rice just a little more vigorously and bending just a little further into his plate. I would make a face and that was normally enough for her to put the ladle back into the dish, pick out two of the largest pieces of fried fish and dump them on my plate. My sister would take the opportunity to proclaim to no one in particular that she liked fish curry.

At some point, I am not sure when, I started eating mustard fish; the right amount of curry mixed in with rice, the way my parents did. I ate with my hands, putting down the spoon for once, because it was the best way of picking bones out of fish. It meant that I had to wash my hands before and after lunch, but it was worth the effort. My mother still said, 'Try some, it's good,' and always seemed surprised when I silently nodded. My sister would now point out how in the past I had never liked fish curry.

We didn't sit around the table, we sat on three sides of it. The fourth side was against the wall. My father sat at one of the ends and I sat at the other, cramped into a corner between a cupboard and the wall. My mother and sister sat at the long side of the table, my mother next to my father, my sister next to me. The dal and curry were always placed in front of my mother, to make it easier for her to fill everyone's plates. The rotis, or rice, depending on which meal it was, sat in front of my sister. It was her job to dispense those. During the week when my mother and I ate lunch alone, my sister and father being out to college and work, I would sit in my father's place, always feeling thrilled, and a little guilty.

But on the weekends, I enjoyed sitting in the corner at lunch. Almost as soon as the first round had been dished out my father would start telling one of his stories.

I knew all the characters by heart. There was Captain Poltu Mukherjee, commandant of Gwalior's Victoria Cadet Corps in the Forties, whose self-importance and naivete made him the butt of several jokes. There was Ghono, the dashing Fiat-owning, mustard-fish-cooking man about town, whose bachelorhood in Delhi in the Sixties had coincided with my father's. There was John Williamson, the uptight Australian telecom specialist who had accompanied my father on a UN assignment to the South Pacific in the late Eighties and only just managed to redeem himself, in my eyes at least, by convincing my father that he should buy a recording of Faure's *Requiem* for me in a Sydney music store. And many, many others.

Every turn of every plot was etched into my memory: 'But the problem, you see, was that Mr Kasturi Rangan, Srini's boss, was right there sitting next to us in the movie theatre. With his wife and daughter-in-law!' I anticipated every nuance of recitation: 'His Highness Raj Rajeshwar Maharaja Sawai Shri Sir Man Singh II, Maharaja of Jaipur.' And I lay in wait for the punchlines, laughing loudly when they came: 'Just take it, he said, you don't have to pay anything, and he walked away muttering: God knows where these people come from.'

The smallest thing, the most fleeting reference, could trigger off a story. 'Oh, I forgot to water the kadipatta,' my mother would say. 'No, no,' my father would say. 'You shouldn't forget the kadipatta. I don't think you understand the importance of kadipatta. Let me tell you. When I was in the UPSC, one day my friend Srini – you remember Srini Uncle? – said, I say, let's go to Corbett Park. Okay, I said, let's go. So we went; Srini, his wife, his sister-in-law and I. We stayed in that lodge, what was the name? ... hmmm ... you know that one where we had stayed when we went in 83?' He would fall into thought, then say, 'Just the other day someone was telling me that it burned down in a fire. All these lodges are made of wood, nothing was left. And nowadays, with so many tourists this sort of thing is bound to happen. When Srini and I had gone, tigers used to come up to the back gate of the lodge. Nowadays you can spend a week in Corbett Park and not see a single tiger. Anyway, we stayed at that place.'

Sometimes, after lunch, when we were sitting in the living room, he reading the newspaper, my sister and I scanning our halves of the Sunday supplement, my mother clearing the dishes, he would suddenly say, 'Dhikala, that was the name of the lodge. Dhikala.' And we would all feel relieved that at least the name of the burned down lodge still remained.

In school we had read of Jim Corbett and we had read Norah Burke's stories of the Himalayan foothills. I thought of my father whenever I read these stories of man-eaters being shot, hardy children trekking miles in the forest, poachers skulking in the night, rhino carcasses rotting in the humid day.

'Anyway, we stayed at that place. Near there, across the Ram Ganga, a leopard had been spotted. We went on elephant back, the four of us, one mahout and one guide. Sahib, the tendua – they call it tendua – has been spotted just last night very close to here, the guide said. People had heard it roaring in the area. Leopards have a distinctive roar, it sounds like someone is sawing wood. Once when I was in Mussoorie I was walking home late at night and I heard the sound of wood being sawed. I thought, this is strange, why are these fellows sawing wood at this time? I asked my orderly the next day, do the timberwalas work at night as well? Why do you ask, Sahib, he asked. I told him. His eyes grew big. You are lucky to be alive, sahib, he said, it was a leopard. But anyhow, the six of us were on the elephant going through the forest. The guide told us to remain absolutely silent, any noise would scare the leopard away. He had his gun at ready in case the leopard was in one of the trees. Suddenly the two women, Srini's wife and sister-in-law, screamed. The guide swung around thinking that the leopard had pounced. What happened, what happened? Kadipatta, they said and pointed at this huge tree with the biggest kadipatta leaves I have ever seen.'

We would all burst out laughing and he would round off the story by saying: 'We never saw the leopard. All that talk of kadipatta must have scared it away.'

It was in Mayur Vihar, finally, that my parents decided to open the crates their books had occupied for twenty years. The government flats they had lived in since moving to Delhi had been too small, and when they had been big enough there was not enough time left before retirement to justify the effort of breaking open large wooden crates. So it happened that series of Time-Life books on ancient civilizations, illustrated encyclopedias on world art, hardcover editions of the *Reader's Digest Condensed Books*, leather-bound writings of Maupassant and Hugo and Stendhal, all emerged and populated the bookshelves my father had designed especially for them. As did an illustrated coffee-table edition of *Song of Solomon,* which was kept hidden behind mountains of old government papers in one of the cupboards, probably because of the naked women and bunches of grapes that made up its illustrations.

There had been books around the house in the years before we moved to Mayur Vihar but they were paperback bestsellers and wildlife encyclopedias and big compendia of fairy tales. These were books that went to work everyday, unlike the delicate treasures that emerged from the boxes. These were the books that had been, up to that point, my window into my parents' mental life. Suddenly, it was as if the camera had zoomed out and revealed that what I had been looking at was just a small corner of the canvas.

Along with the decorative books, which took their place in the drawing room, came another slew of paperbacks. These were stacked in my room. Some of them I read – mountaineers' autobiographies, Jim Corbett's man-eater stories, Ruskin Bond's unfussed accounts of boys running away from school – and others I avoided – biographies of World War II generals, accounts of famous battles of World War II, books on the great ships of World War II. I had no real reason for not reading the World War II books. In fact I liked reading their titles, rolling *Rommel: The Desert Fox* around in my mouth or spitting out a gunshot *Patton*, but, occasionally, when I did open them and scan a few pages, I was bored quickly.

I bought my first bookshelf at a yard sale in Baltimore and spent an evening picking books off the floor and arranging them on it. When I finally stepped back to inspect my handiwork and saw my own books forming patterns on the shelves, exchanging associations with each other, reminding me of the places they had been bought and the people they had been shared with, I suddenly found myself thinking of my father's collection of World War II books. It was with a shock that I realized that the evacuation from Dunkirk, the battle of Stalingrad, the bombing of Pearl Harbour – historybook-distant as they were to me – had inhabited my father's childhood with the same immediacy as Indira Gandhi's assassination or the collapse of the Soviet Union had inhabited mine.

'We were all cadets in Gwalior,' my father had told me. 'There was no NCC then. But our college had its own Victoria Cadet Corps. Every weekend we would have drills. Ma was very much opposed to us joining, because that was her first reaction to everything: No. But Poltuda, Captain Poltu Mukherjee, came home and said: Mashima, you have to let the boys join the Cadet Corps. And he kept coming till she relented. In the winter we would go for a two-week training camp. The Maharaja's Fourth Light Infantry would be conducting Winter Manoeuvres and we would be attached to them, with our own camp, fenced off with its own guard post, some distance away. Choton, your Choto Kaku, was the most dedicated cadet I knew. When he was not on parade he was at home polishing his kit. He rose to the rank of Senior Under Officer and even represented the VCC at national and Commonwealth meets.'

I thought back to this story that evening in Baltimore and I wondered why neither my father nor any of my uncles had joined the army. And as I stood there in front of my first bookshelf my eyes fell on a tattered old paperback copy of H. P. S. Ahluwalia's *Higher Than Everest*, its spine held in place with cellotape. My father had given it to me when I was eight, at a time when every other book I had read was by Enid Blyton, and I had gone through the entire book in a week and then read it twice again the next week. At one time I had known the exact altitude of each one of the seven camps established by the 1965 Everest expedition, the first successful one put on by India. I had known the composition of all four summit teams, the different approaches to Everest and their relative hardness, the names of all the great mountaineers who had climbed the mountain in the twelve years between 1953 and 1965. I gently picked up the old white paperback and flipped through the pages wondering why I had never ever thought of becoming a mountaineer.

That winter when I visited Delhi I finally asked my father about his World War II books.

'You see,' he said, 'the Second World War was going on while I was in school. We brothers followed the whole thing through the newspapers. Your Choto Kaku was a fanatic. He used to maintain a daily war diary. Everything went into it: the collapse of the French army, the retreat from Dunkirk, the naval battle of the River Plate and the aerial Battle of Britain, the German invasion of Soviet Russia, the opening of a new theatre in the North African desert against the

Italians, the Japanese invasion of European colonies in East Asia. He and I would discuss the war situation every evening. Choton followed the progress of the different campaigns with the help of the newspaper's sketch maps and Baba's big atlas. I helped him fill up several scrapbooks with newspaper cuttings, sketches, photographs. It was an exciting time. I remember once the two of us were travelling by train with Ma, and Choton was talking about the African desert campaign. There were two Australian army officers sitting in the next compartment. One of them came up to Ma later and said: That young man will become a general one day.'

'Why didn't Choto Kaku join the army, Papa?' I asked.

'He was very keen on it,' he sighed. 'And he was sure he would get in because of his brilliant Cadet Corps record. But when he went for the physical they found he was flatfooted. It was such a slight defect that no one had noticed it. He was heartbroken, didn't leave the house for days. He did really badly in all the exams as well, that's why he didn't make it into government service. Ma shouted and shouted at him about it. He never said a word in response. Why would he care about getting into the government? That wasn't what he had wanted in any case.'

'She's the one I was telling you about,' said Bobby.

'Which one?' I asked.

'The dark one near the sabjiwala.'

She was lovely. Ebony dark, long straight hair, wide hips and large breasts. Her face was sculpted, regal and commanding even when bent over a pile of ragged green beans: a face used to receiving attention, contemptuous of those who conferred it.

'It's a thousand rupees a night,' said Bobby.

'What?'

'One thousand. Full service. Upstairs, downstairs, forwards and backwards.'

'How do you know?' I asked.

'She lives right here,' he said pointing to the society next to ours. Proof enough.

She paid the hawker, gathered her bags and turned to walk into the society Bobby had pointed to. We stood there watching her hips move slowly from side to side under her salwar.

'You know, Bobby,' I said, 'I have decided to never have sex with prostitutes.'

He smiled. 'Never?'

'Ummm, well, the first time I have sex it won't be for money.' I had just made this rather momentous decision.

Bobby said nothing but his eyes held an amused affection. He knew me well enough to sense that the vow I had just taken would actually turn out to be a long sentence of celibacy.

Bobby's sex life, on the other hand, seemed to be fairly hectic. Among others there was the girl who lived two doors down from his jijaji's place, the one who had invited him in to help her fix her cycle. There was the college girl in Preet Vihar whom he had met at the bus stop one day when he had taken a friend's motorcycle out for a ride. There was the girl in Kanpur whose father wanted him to be a stay-at-home son-in-law. The girl herself was not particularly interested in getting married but she did have other uses for Bobby.

The stories that really caught my fancy, however, were the ones which revolved around people I saw in the Society every day: the sexy aunty Bobby had spotted through an open bathroom window, brushing her teeth without a blouse on;

the maid servant whose seventh floor room he had looked into from the B block terrace; the sweeper he had seen adjusting her blouse behind the generator; the couples he had seen fondling each other behind the water tank on top of C block. These stories were less lurid, less fantastic, than the others, perhaps because he knew they were, in a sense, more verifiable. But they turned me on much more, they transformed so-and-so aunty into a saucy topless teeth-brusher and made an uninhibited rooftop jeans-crotch fondler out of so-and-so didi.

Sometimes in the mornings as I sat on the pot, or on the bus back from school in the afternoons, or in the evenings when Bobby was nowhere to be found as I walked around Mayur Vihar alone, I would make up stories. It would always be afternoon in these stories, or late forenoon. I would have missed college that day (the fictional me was always a college boy). Lounging by the water tank, I would see one of the sexy aunties in my harem walk by (in my fantasies the news of my sexual prowess had made the rounds of the Society). Maybe it would be the slim fair one who lived in A block, or the short buxom young mother who had just moved into E block. She would see me sitting there, my big hard cock outlined against my pants. Her eyes would linger on it for a while, then she would give me a meaningful look, perhaps run her tongue deliberately over her upper lip, as she walked past. I would linger for ten minutes or so, then look this way and that as I slowly got up and followed her. I would ring the doorbell and wait. She would take her time to get to the door. When she opened it she would be wearing only a wet sari, her dark nipples prominent on her chest. 'Yes,' she would say, smiling suggestively. 'Can I help you?'

*

A crowded bus stop sits a hundred metres away from the crossing. These people are headed south to NOIDA, having spent their day working in Delhi. On their faces I can see the grime of a long, partially completed journey home and the anticipation of its last leg. As one they crane their necks to look at the buses standing at the crossing, waiting for the signal to let them go, or at the vehicles coming from the other side of the road, hoping to spot the familiar outline that takes them home every evening.

This intersection is a huge one. The road that comes across the river is the National Highway 24 bypass, heading east to the towns of western UP. NOIDA's link road to Delhi bites into the bypass at the point where the cultivated land of the river valley needs to be differentiated from the urban outgrowth of Mayur Vihar. On the other side of the bypass is the historic village of Patparganj. There is no road to separate it from the fields that line the river bed, just an embankment that runs alongside the open drain, the northern leg of the one that runs by Mayur Vihar Phase 1.

Exhaust fumes have brought a premature dusk to this place. Beggars stand with me on the divider inhaling lungfuls of noxious air that blackens their clothes and darkens their skin. They will get off the divider along with me when the traffic stops and scurry to open windows, while I pick my way through cars, buses, trucks and lorries to the other side.

I cross finally and make my way to the path on the embankment. Cutting through sparse thorny vegetation I come to the point where the drain reappears to the east and the river comes into view to the west. From the foot of the sloping mud wall to the river in the distance there is a patchwork of fields. Some lie bare, dust brown and furrowed, some are green with tomato and yet others have thick crops of sugarcane standing in them. Beyond this patchwork lies the river glowing dully in the light of the setting sun.

On the other side of the river bits of New Delhi stick out over treetops. I used to live there, I think. A feeling of serenity follows that thought.

Reaching the dairy built at the foot of the embankment, I survey it from above. Bullocks stand in neat rows along the insides of a square enclosure, their home, tied to their posts, feeding at their trough. Next door is the house, a hut really. A small fire burns outside it. The little courtyard has a smooth mud floor. A cycle leans against the wall of the shack, black and chrome, more black than chrome.

As I walk north I come to a clump of ugly eucalyptus trees, malnourished and shabby. Their bark has scabbed off in places. Some boys are collecting this dead skin for kindling. They don't look up as I walk by. East of the path, Patparganj runs along, bordering the drain and then ending abruptly. A few stunted trees later are the tracks.

I step through the wicket gate. Two pairs of rail tracks lie here. Having just crossed the river, they look impatient to hurry into Uttar Pradesh, to connect the capital with its domain in the east.

The sun has set now and its afterglow colours the sky. The clouds form strange shapes. Up there in the sky I can see an island with its ashen grey beaches, protecting a small lagoon which is turning gold in the rays of its own setting sun.

On the other side of the tracks the embankment loses its definition and becomes a path. The eucalyptus grove lies level with it now. East of the path the embankment still falls away but at its foot lies a pool of dirty water. The drain has disappeared underground, or rather I have just gone upstream of the point where it comes overground. The houses that crowd each other beyond the pool, Shakarpur, cast dark shadows into the water. They are just hulking shapes, with no detail or colour left in this fading East Delhi dusk.

Afternoons in the Society were luminous, languid times. My mother would come back from school before me. We would eat lunch: dal, rice, yesterday's sabji, chicken or fish if there was any left, or chicken gravy with boiled eggs in it to make it a meal. We always ate rice for lunch and rotis for dinner. I never thought to ask why.

After lunch my mother would watch TV for a while and I would go to my room and listen to music, or read, or just sit around waiting for her to go to bed. When she went to her room it was like the whole house was at my disposal. In the summers the curtains would be down in the drawing room. They would glow incandescent with the heat of the summer sun. The occasional car would pass by on the road outside. I would walk from one room to the other, tiptoeing. Every creaking door, every rusty hinge would echo through the silence.

I would think of the summer holidays I used to spend with my cousins in my grandfather's house in Meerut, before he died and my uncles sold the property to a builder. In the afternoons we would all be put in the third room on the north side. It would be darkened, except for the ember glow of the line between the imperfectly fastened old shutters. Outside, in the lane, a goat would bleat, dogs would bay, while inside we lay on old beds and talked and played and wrestled as quietly as we possibly could.

In the Society, though, I would be alone in the little flat, sliding the kitchen door aside to go and get myself cold water from the fridge. I would drink it straight from the bottle, standing right there with the fridge open, the chill running like an arrow down the middle of my body on the inside, and sometimes, if I was not careful, on the outside.

I would watch MTV – U2, Tammy Wynette, Dr Dre – with the volume turned really low, sitting on the uncomfortable sofa with the remote clutched in my hand, my finger hovering over the mute button, ready for the slightest sign of movement from my mother's room.

At four o'clock sharp the afternoon would come to an end. The maid servant, the one who cooked, would ring the doorbell. My mother would come bustling out of her room, as if she had been crouching behind the door waiting. The maid would come in and head for the kitchen. She would chop and shave, the frying would come later. My afternoon glass of milk, with a little bit of instant coffee in it as I grew older, would be brought out, always a little hotter than I liked it, cold in the summers. The sprightly old dwarf who fetched our milk from Mother Dairy would ring the bell twice, once when he came to pick up money and the stainless steel bucket and then, fifteen minutes later, when he delivered the milk. It was my job to open the door these times, my mother being busy in the kitchen.

The light outside would have grown softer. I would go into my room and put on my shoes, ready to venture out. As I would head for the door, I would call out to my mother. In response I would hear the dramatic splash of raw chopped onions hitting hot oil. The afternoon was officially over, the evening had begun.

I leave the dank pool behind. My step quickens as the trees begin to clear. The smell of slums hits my nose, the smell of stale wheat rotis cooking on wooden fires. The slums near the Society smell like this as well. I am almost at the eastern end of the ITO bridge.

The beaten path becomes an unpaved street. On both sides are small cloth, wood and tin dwellings, black-brown-green as always. I have seen them from the safety of the road many times. This is the closest I have ever been. Self-consciously nonchalant, I stride forward.

There are people standing around. They look at me with an idle hostility. I feel the stones embedded in the path digging into the padded soles of my shoes. Children are playing with old tyres, running up and down, pushing the tyres along. I walk a little quicker, not looking at them but avoiding their path.

I walk out of the stench and into the car exhaust of Vikas Marg, turning right towards Shakarpur. It is dark now. The hum of people and traffic is gathering strength with the night. Vendors and shoppers are here too, uneasily sharing the road with buses and cars. Signboards advertising computer courses and sound systems and high fashion and deep fried samosas have their lights turned on, adding to the evening glow of kerosene lamps resting on pushcarts full of fruit and sodium vapour streetlights.

A flyover looms ahead, carrying me back over the tracks. This is that phase of the walk in which my thighs throb and my gait steadies in anticipation of the return home. But home is still at least half an hour away. Over the hump of the flyover I stride, not even stopping to look down at the tracks as I would have if I had decided to start the walk by coming this way. I almost run down to the other side, where Ganesh Nagar meets Mandawli.

A fruit juice stall catches my eye. Its front is coloured with barely recognizable portraits of film stars. But it is the display of oranges shining in the neon light that makes me look. I walk up to the side where the aluminium juicer is installed. 'One glass. Orange. Large.'

'Chotu,' the man inside says. 'One large here.'

A boy appears from behind the shop wiping his hands on a rag. He starts picking up peeled oranges from a bucket lying near the juicer. He switches the machine on and puts two into the opening at the top. Straining his muscles and standing on his toes he reaches up to press the oranges into the whirring blades. There is a brief roar as the fruit is consumed and pulped and then it subsides into an even growl. The boy pops in another orange.

I step away with the glass, sipping the juice as I move away. Across the road is a bus stop and behind that is an orthopaedic hospital, a small multistoreyed place with a large white board posted outside. Involuntarily I read off the names of the doctors who staff the hospital, their specialties and their timings.

One last sip of juice remains. Salt has accumulated at the bottom making it bitter and undrinkable. I gulp the remainder down, grimacing at the taste. Leaving the glass on the counter, I start for home.

Buses are crowding out cars at the traffic light. They want to turn right. The cycle-rickshaws want to go straight, into Mayur Vihar under the overpass. The highway lies on it, it has been built higher than the surrounding areas, and the right turn leads up to it. The road ahead leads under it. I decide to walk straight, go through the market and the narrow streets and get home that way, through the gateway made of mud and road.

The last leg of the walk is a blur. I speed past pushcarts, stray dogs, rickshaws, schoolchildren buying stationery, a watch repair shop, the new car dealership, a gift shop. The pavement booksellers gesture to me but I am not interested. Young men standing in the shadows, following pretty girls with their eyes, hardly register. The smell of the corner where the numerous Bengalis in the area buy their fish does not disturb me.

I fly up the stairs and burst into the house.

'What's the hurry?' my mother asks.

'Nothing, Ma.'

'Bobby had called some time back.'

'Bobby? Thanks, Ma.'

I pick up the cordless and take it into my room, shutting the door behind me. My fingers remember Bobby's phone number, punching it out on the keypad without my having to repeat the digits to myself. I drum the table as the phone begins to ring.

'Hello, Mr Chatterjee!' exclaimed the bald man with bushy salt and pepper eyebrows, his thick spectacles jogging up and down as he pumped my father's hand. Then, taking hold of his daughter by one of her thin, bony arms: 'This is my daughter, Abhilasha.'

'My son, Arindam,' answered my father.

It was a few months since I had first seen Abhilasha playing TT with Bobby. I was struck again by how thin she was. Her hair, like her father's eyebrows, was thick. It made her face look bigger than it was. But it was dry and lifeless, unmoving. She had expressive eyes, but she kept them shaded and neutral, in the way girls were taught to. I could see why Bobby thought her beautiful. Her face was pretty. But the way her arms hung by her body – loose, stiff, lifeless – made her unattractive to me.

'What class you are in?' asked Abhilasha's father, beaming at me.

'Eleventh,' I said.

'Science stream?'

'Yes.'

He nodded approvingly and gestured toward Abhilasha: 'She has Science too, with computer science as the fifth subject. What is your fifth subject?'

Abhilasha looked up when he said this. Her eyes flitted from my father to me. She must have recognized me but she didn't show it. When I looked at her, she looked away.

'Computer science,' I said.

'But she is in class twelve,' said the man with the salt and pepper eyebrows, and smiled like he had just smashed the ball across the table.

By then, thanks to Bobby, I already knew what class Abhilasha was in, what her subjects were, what school she went to, where she caught her school bus and several other facts about her life.

Abhilasha's family had been among the first to move in to the Society, as had Bobby's family. The difference was that Abhilasha's father was a Member of the Society while Bobby's father was just a Tenant. It would have been impossible for someone like Bobby's father to be a Member. Membership was restricted to gazetted officers of the government of India, or former gazetted officers. Besides, Bobby and Abhilasha had very little in common. She did well in school. He barely got by. She studied in an old reputed South Delhi school. He went to a place in Preet Vihar that had opened two years ago. She was considered to be a sweet, quiet girl. He was thought to be a hell raiser, a troublemaker.

But the Society was sparsely populated in those first three years – the prehistoric period in my reckoning – and so they became friends. She had helped him out with his class ten physics, he told me. That's when he fell in love with her. She was so soft spoken, so polite, so feminine and demure. He had decided then that she was the one for him. 'You'll see,

Arindam, I will marry her one day.' And he always framed the sentence in Hindi, with himself as the subject and marry used as a transitive verb.

If Bobby was to be believed, that tall thin girl, always clad in loose-fitting salwar kameez outfits that imperfectly hid the fact that she was gangly, her dull hair framing her pretty but unremarkable face, was the most beautiful woman ever to set foot on the soil of East Delhi.

I never really heard her speak, or even if I did, her voice left no residue on my memory. All I knew about her were mundane facts gleaned from conversations with my mother: 'Mrs Sethi was saying that her daughter is learning Japanese at Delhi University' or 'Did you see the big rangoli in front of the lift in A block? Mrs Sethi's younger daughter, that Abhilasha, she made it.' And, of course, from conversations with Bobby which normally began as reminiscences of their brief dalliance and ended up as an extended set of conjectures on what she now thought of him or what his chances with her were.

She rarely walked the circuit around the Society in the evening with girls her own age. I think we all understood that the evening was a sexually charged time. Sometimes at night, however, when I took my dog down for a walk, she would be walking with her mother. I would see her then – and whenever I thought about her in the future – walking with her eyes downcast, listening to her mother speak.

On reflection I realized that her anaemic lankiness, her insipid beauty, her slightly hunched walk did not connote a person to me; they were just a blank white screen on which the feature film of Bobby's hopes and desires was projected, preceded by my mother's newsreel.

*

The one time I met Winky was a coincidence. It was the summer after my first year at IIT and I was back home making my rounds of the Society on my cycle in the late afternoon. Behind C block, near the generator, I saw two guys talking. One of them was a friend of mine, a couple of years younger than me, who lived in B block. He flagged me down.

'This is Arijit,' he told me. And turning to Arijit he said, 'This is Arindam, he is doing engineering as well.'

We shook hands, Arijit looking away from me as he did. He had a wild look in his eyes, as if he were drunk, although I couldn't smell any alcohol on his breath. He held his arms curved, like he did weights regularly. I felt a little unsettled.

'Where are you studying?' I asked. He named a college in the south, one of the places where you could buy a seat.

'And you?'

'IIT, Delhi,' I said. He looked at me, a quick appraising glance, and then looked away again.

'I have a friend there. Bhats. Do you know him?' he said.

'Yes, yes, of course,' I said. 'How do you know him?'

'We were in school together.'

A thought struck me: Bhats had said something about a guy from Mayur Vihar called Winky who he knew at school. I had wondered if Bhats' Winky was the same as Bobby's Winky but had dismissed the possibility. Too bizarre, I had thought.

'What course?' he asked.

'Computer Science,' I said. 'And you?'

'Mechanical.'

The comparison of our engineering affiliations was increasingly in my favour. I wanted to change the topic. And I wanted to know if this was the famous Winky.

'Do you live here?' I asked.

'I used to,' he said.

'In C block,' I blurted out.

'Yes, how do you know?'

'Someone had mentioned you once,' I mumbled. Later I wondered why I hadn't told him that the someone who had mentioned him was Bobby, and that he had mentioned him more than once. 'Do you have summer holidays now?' I added quickly.

'Yes,' he said.

He was growing increasingly restless, as was I. The realization was seeping into me: this was The Winky, Bobby's Winky.

At school I'd had friends who were known goondas, who would beat up guys for no good reason. Winky's reputation was no worse than theirs. But his presence was, somehow, much more intimidating. Standing there in front of him I could easily visualize him, full of a quiet vicious anger, unleashing a brick at Ghosh's windshield. I could hear the brick smash through the glass, I could see the blood and shock on Ghosh's face. It had taken weeks of pleading by Winky's parents to hush up the matter. My mother said that both Ghosh and the police were paid off, that's what the woman who cooked in Winky's house had told the woman who cooked in our house. Winky's father had put his foot down and sent him south for college. Those places knew how to deal with people like him. And even if they didn't, whatever he did there would stay there, far from the ears of Winky's father's colleagues in the IAS and their wives.

But it was much later, when I looked back at this moment after what happened to Bhavna, that I realized that the source of the debilitating unease that gripped me by the stomach as I stood talking to Winky was not the story of the brick and Ghosh's windshield. In his physical presence I realized instinctively, and physically, that this guy was capable of anything. I eased my weight onto the cycle's saddle, involuntarily signalling that I wanted to leave. Immediately his shoulders straightened. 'I'll see you around,' he said putting his hand out. I shook it, hoping he wouldn't notice that my palms were sweating.

Riding away I didn't look back. When I turned the corner of D block I suddenly realized that the guy who had introduced us had vanished at some point and I hadn't even noticed.

Apart from a reputation as a goonda, and an ardent follower in Bobby, Winky had also acquired a girlfriend during his stay in the Society. Her name was Bhavna. Bhavna's brother and Winky's sister, both in their late teens, were an item in the early days of the Society. Winky's relationship with Bhavna was a natural corollary.

Bhavna was around my age, still in school when we moved to the Society. She was very friendly, always a smile on her face. She was, to use the Mayur Vihar term, a Society girl. She was good at school without being brilliant. She always had a namaste and a friendly word for the aunties and uncles. She was universally liked. My mother would often mention the time her car had broken down outside the Society gate and Bhavna had helped her push it all the way to our parking spot. 'Such a sweet girl. So quiet and so helpful.'

Her brother, despite having a girlfriend, was one of the 'Society boys', one of those who sat around near the water tank in the evenings with his friends, ogling the girls and the young married women as they passed by. He was the prime mover of all Society parties, and a permanent fixture at them. These normally involved turning the lights down in someone's house or in the recreation room if one could get permission, putting the stereo on at full volume, buying a lot of cola from Om Departmental Store, spiking some of it with alcohol, and then dancing and drinking till some uncle or aunty couldn't take it any more and came down from their house in their vest and dhoti or nightie and shouted till everyone went home.

When I moved to the Society, Bhavna was just reaching the age at which her parents would allow her to attend Society parties. I always noticed her first, at these parties: snug jeans, tight T-shirt, a glowing smile on her face, her hair bouncing and billowing as she danced. She was the only one there making an effort to get the shy ones onto the floor.

I was invited to some of the Society parties but not the really major ones, because I wasn't thought to be 'that sort of guy'. This emerged when one day Bhats came to one of these parties along with a friend of a friend of someone in the Society. He came to my house around the time we were all ready to turn in. There was a small plastic cup in his hand with some cola drink in it. He stank of rum. I introduced him to my parents and quickly took him into my room.

'Rindu, chutiye,' he said. 'I asked these people why they don't call you. Do you know what they said?'

'What?'

'They said, he isn't that sort of guy.'

Bhats laughed so hard that he almost threw up. Finally when he was leaving he asked, 'Who is that girl with the light eyes?'

'Which one?'

'You know, the one with the hair to her shoulders. Light eyes.'

'Oh yes,' I said. 'That's Bhavna.'

'She is really something, isn't she? Total maal item.'

'Fuck off, Bhats,' I said, slamming the door behind him. But it wasn't as if I disagreed with him.

The truth was that I liked Bhavna a lot.

My first year in the Society, Bobby either spent the evenings walking with me or with Abhilasha. This was before the incident that led to the break between the two of them. Occasionally we would meet Bhavna on our rounds, although I did not know her then. I only knew, thanks to my mother, which aunty's daughter she was. We never talked to her, although the way she smiled hello at Bobby often made me think they knew each other well. Bobby would nod at her and I would return her smile with a polite half-articulated hi. It was after one of these encounters that Bobby told me the story of the time he had seen Bhavna and Winky on the roof together.

'Do you know this girl?' he asked.

'No.'

'Do you know Manoj? The guy with the moustache? Hangs around by the water tank?'

'Yes, yes. He's in college, right?' I said.

'College shollege nothing. He's doing his BA by correspondence. Every now and then he takes the U-special to North Campus so that he can maaro line on the girls. Everyone knows he's a fraud. In the Society he acts like a big dada but outside he's nothing. You should see him at the Pocket 1 bus stop, wagging his tail in front of Pandey and the others.'

'What's that got to do with the girl, Bobby?' I asked.

'She's Manoj's sister. Actually Manoj had a setting with Winky's sister. This was before you came to the Society. At that time I would see her walking around with Manoj.'

'Who? Winky's sister?' I was getting confused.

'No, Bhavna. Manoj's sister. When Winky's sister came down, Manoj would shoo Bhavna away. Winky and I would go and talk to Bhavna, try and get her to walk around the Society with us. She always refused.'

Just then a clique of uncles passed by. My father was with them. Bobby's expression changed from sly and gossipy to ingratiating and cheerful. 'Hello, Uncle!' he said, hailing my father.

The uncles, my father included, were in the middle of an intense discussion being conducted entirely in Bengali. He nodded absently at Bobby.

'Then? Then what happened?' I asked.

We walked for a few more steps. Bobby glanced backwards and, satisfied that we were out of earshot, continued, 'Around that time some of my friends at school had taught me how to smoke,' he said. 'I don't inhale, yaar, just take it into my mouth and blow it out. Cigarette, gutka, it's all good for style. I don't want to be a charasi, can't do without a daily fix. Anyway, I had brought home a cigarette, hidden in my school bag. In the evening I thought I'd go and smoke it with Winky. Winky was an expert smoker. I went down around seven and walked round and round waiting for Winky to appear. An hour passed but no Winky. Finally I thought, fuck Winky, I'll go and smoke it myself. I went behind D block to the corner near the jhuggies. I was about to light up when three walking aunties came speeding by. I realized that everyone would be out at this time. I had to go to the roof.'

The roof. I thrilled with anticipation.

'The C block roof on your side of the building was the one Winky and I used to go to regularly, especially when we had some daaru or something. Three of the four flats were empty at the time so no one would notice us. So, that's where I went. It was dark by the time I got up there, past eight o'clock. The lights on the seventh floor landing were on but not the ones above that. I opened the wooden door and went out. It was really dark. I stepped across two of the water pipes and put the cigarette in my mouth. Just as I was about to strike a match I heard a noise from behind the water tank. The cigarette dropped from my lips. I bent down to pick it up. Behind the water tank I saw two pairs of feet. Very close to each other, rubbing each other.'

'Who was it Bobby?'

'That's what I wanted to know. Very carefully I stepped across to one side to get a better view. It was a boy and a girl. The boy's hands were right there.' He gestured upward with both hands. 'And the girl's left hand was right there,' he said, reaching down in a sudden motion.

'Oh, shit!'

'What can I say, Arindam? One hundred per cent full masti was going on. He was trying to slip his hands under her T-shirt. She was trying to stop him with one hand while she kept stroking him with the other. All the time their mouths were mashed into one another's.'

'So, you didn't get to see who they were?'

'Of course, I did. It was Winky and Bhavna. That bastard! I had gone to Kanpur for two weeks just before that. He must have pataoed her then. They had already progressed to the roof stage and I hadn't even known.'

3

Rocksurd

'THIS PLACE HAS NO ROCK CULTURE, MAN,' JOHRI SAID. 'IF YOU want to see real rockers go to IT BHU. That's the place to be. Just like we have toilets on every floor here, they have a rock band on every floor there. Every floor! Guitarist, drummer, bassist, man. On every fucking floor! Do you know why?'

'Why?' I asked.

'They make their fuchchas rock addicts, that's why. When a fresher arrives, a senior takes him to the music room. He locks the door and puts on rock. Full volume, hard rock. Megadeth, Metallica, Slayer. For five, six, eight hours the fresher has to listen to rock, rock and more rock, till he's almost unconscious. Stop, stop, he keeps shouting, and they just keep raising the volume and putting in one tape after the other. And then, you know what happens?'

'What?'

'The next day the same fuchcha comes to the senior and says: Sir, please give me more rock. Please, sir, I want to hear some rock. Please, sir, give me rock.'

Sometimes in the morning, before class, when there would be a line for the bathroom, Kartik would say thank god this isn't BHU, at least we have toilets on every floor.

Johri and Rocksurd both came from Dehra Doon. They had been in the same school, Johri two years senior to Rocksurd. Johri had made it to IT BHU in his first attempt at JEE. He stayed there for almost a year before he came away. Why he left, I don't know. It was not the sort of question one asked. But I had heard that by the time he did, it was too late to take the JEE again. So he dropped a year and then finally, two years out of school, made it into IIT Delhi where I met him when he came to my hostel to see Rocksurd.

Rocksurd and I were on the same floor, in the same wing of the same floor, in our first year. I met him sitting near the parking lot at the Institute one afternoon on my way back to the hostel for lunch.

'Not going back for lunch, Mandeep?' I asked him. The nickname was yet to be coined.

'What do those fucking seniors think? I'll do whatever they say? No way. Do you know what that Goel did to me the other day? He made me wrap my legs around a pillar and then he kicked me in the ass, really hard, ten times.'

This seemed very unlike my own mild ragging experience. The worst that had happened to me was being made to stay up all night and periodically knock on one senior's door. I hadn't even been slapped. In the second week now I was almost beginning to enjoy it, except, of course, for the jogging in the morning.

'Those bastards, they think they'll break me. They don't know what I am made of.'

I heard subsequently what the problem was. Rocksurd, it seems, would not stop smiling. This face he was showing me, sitting here in the safety of the Institute area, this troubled face was not what the seniors saw. A few days after this meeting I was ragged along with him and I saw the violence with which the seniors reacted when he started grinning. We had all been told, during class or in the canteen while we were away from the hostel, by other freshers who had been told by other freshers: the first rule is, appear to be really, really miserable. I applied this rule unfailingly, often getting sympathy when I deserved none. Rocksurd too realized the logic of the rule, and used it in the opposite way, often with terrible consequences.

After the ragging period ended, and with it all the hostilities, I was coming back to my room one evening when I saw that Rocksurd's light was on. I could hear MC Hammer's You Can't Touch This playing in his room. Even before I metamorphosed into a true IIT rocker, even when I was just a schoolboy in Delhi, I had realized that MC Hammer was too popular, too common, to be played out loud. The fact that Mandeep, who had begun to show indications that he might one day wear a name like Rocksurd as a badge of honour, was listening to MC Hammer at high volume right here in the hostel seemed to put him in dire danger of being laughed at. I decided to investigate, and, if possible, initiate the ridiculing.

Rocksurd had an entire bookshelf full of photos of the Sikh gurus. There were incense sticks burning in front of the photos and a neat stack of little booklets with Gurmukhi writing on them, lying to one side. On his table was the stereo and next to it lay the open cover of the MC Hammer tape. All the other cassettes in his room had portraits of Guru Nanak on them. Rocksurd stood facing the shelf. He had his hands folded and his eyes closed. I came away.

In the weeks and months that followed that evening I didn't meet Rocksurd much. I was spending all my free time in the carrom room. I would come back at three in the morning. He would either be sleeping or his room would be locked. The weekends I spent at home in Mayur Vihar. We had no classes in common so we rarely met in the Institute.

It was our first encounter with freedom, this dizzying flurry that was our first year at IIT, our irreversible entry into an academic world where our parents couldn't help with our studies, and the two of us were busy running, tumbling, rolling down different tracks. By the time the second year was half over, Mandeep had become Rocksurd. The nickname had come when he announced one day that he was learning to play the drums and someone had remarked: 'What's the point? You'll never be a rockstar. The best you'll be is a rocksardar.'

Near the end of the second year's summer I was walking towards the Institute one day – I had been doing a summer project with Sheikhu during the holidays – when I saw someone coming from the SAC waving at me frantically and shouting: 'Rindooooo! Rinds! Okay! All right!'

I couldn't make out who it was. He came closer and closer, but I still couldn't identify him. 'Saalé, Rindu, it's me.'

It was Rocksurd. Only, he wasn't a surd anymore. He had cut his hair.

By the end of our stay in IIT, of the three or four Sikhs we had in the hostel only one of them still had his turban and beard. All the others had, sooner or later, got rid of them. This process was inevitably followed by a switch to leather shoes, new jeans and printed shirts. It didn't take much getting used to for the rest of us but that first time was always a little strange and the first conversation always a little strained.

'Wow, Rocksurd, you're looking really good!' I said.

He grinned and pumped my hand happily.

'But why did you ...?'

The grip on my hand went a little slack. In all the other cases this unwelcome question would provoke a sheepish grin from the former surd and an attempt to dodge the question. With Rocksurd it was different. The smile disappeared and his face grew dark.

'It was very difficult, man. All those sardars on the street. People would just come up and start swearing at me. Because of the cigarettes.'

Rocksurd had taken to smoking. I had met him once at KLS and he had excitedly told me: 'I can make smoke rings, Rindu. Here check this out.' He had taken a deep drag, thrown his head back and started the complex process of wrapping the smoke around his tongue and pushing it through his lips. The rings were weak but they were rings nonetheless. 'You need total mastery of the sutta for this, man, total mastery.' I had seen him often, since then, at rock shows, sitting by the side of the stage or near the sound guy, his head thrown back, sending tiny smoke signals to no one in particular. Standing at the roundabout near the SAC, I couldn't understand this strange reason he was now giving me. 'People would just come up to you?'

'Yes,' he said. 'Sikhs are not supposed to smoke. They would threaten to beat me up, they would grab my cigarettes and break them. It was too much, yaar. I thought, fuck it, let's just cut it off.'

I remembered the time when I had met him a day or two after the big Rendezvous rock show. There was a band of longhaired rockers from Pune who had stayed at our hostel. Rocksurd had met them at the show and hung out with them while the other bands were playing. 'I had my hair open, yaar, total headbanging scene and all. So that Sanjay, you know, the guitarist, he asks me: how long have you been growing it? And I say, nineteen years. Totally psyched, like, wow this guy has been a rocker for nineteen years. But then I said, I am a sardar.'

Now with his hair cut, headbanging would no longer look as impressive, I thought. But I could see from his expression that the loss he was contemplating was a bigger one.

'You're looking great man. Really good,' I said. And then, seeing him brighten up a little, I asked, 'So, what did you do all summer?'

He had spent the summer working on his drumming. Taking lessons and trying to learn how to play along with songs. 'It's all improvisation,' he told me. 'Once you can play a four beat, the rest is just improvisation.' I didn't tell him that I too had taken drumming lessons that summer.

'But, do you know how all these rockstars become really great?' he asked.

'How?'

'Devil worship,' he said. 'You have to make a sacrifice to the Devil. Do you know that Robert Plant's son died mysteriously when he was just four? It wasn't an accident. It was only after that Led Zep became great and Plant's vocals became so powerful. All the great drummers, the Devil gets into them when they play. We think it's Bonham or Keith Moon, but actually it's the Devil. You see them in practice and they're nothing, but in the show they are massive, doing all sorts of fundoo things. The Devil doesn't come in practice, only for the shows.'

'Well,' I said, 'I have heard that if you play Stairway to Heaven in reverse it is some kind of chant for the Devil.'

'Exactly,' he said. 'All rockers worship the Devil.'

A few weeks later I met Johri at KLS.

'So Johri,' I told him. 'Your friend wants to be a Devil-worshipping drummer.'

He gave a sly grin. 'I told Mandeep all he needs to know to be a true rocker,' he said.

'All he needs?'

'Yes, Rindu,' he said. 'Every true rocker must learn to worship the Devil because Devil worship alone has made every great rock band great. Did you know that Robert Plant's son died at age four?'

'Yes,' I said. 'I heard about that recently, actually.'

'Do you know why?'

I burst out laughing. 'Let me guess,' I said. 'Sacrificed to the Devil?'

'Yaar, Rindu,' he said, breaking out into a broad grin, 'you know how it is, sometimes we have to wait for hours at ISBT for the bus to Doon. You have to do something to amuse yourself. Your floormate seemed very keen to learn all about rock.'

'And so, Devil?'

'And so, Devil.'

I decided at some point to be a drummer. Maybe I too wanted to be taken seriously as a rocker. Perhaps I felt I hadn't heard as much rock as the others, I didn't know enough. Maybe I thought that the best way to appreciate rock music was from within, but I felt I could not sing and it would take years before I could play the guitar well enough. The half-made guitarist could aspire only to be a bassist in a band, and bassists were not in short supply.

Most of the people who played an instrument at IIT had learned how to play in school. By the time they reached college they were already proficient musicians. They would generally improve tremendously by the time they graduated, but people would still say things like: 'At the Fresher's Events, man, this guy just blew us all away.'

Those of us who started playing something after reaching IIT were seen as pretenders. It was as if the time between the first day we had come to IIT and the day we revealed that we had started playing the drums was tainted by this aspiration we had secretly nurtured. It made the musicians think they were better than us and everyone else think we were trying to be better than them.

And so the most important question was: 'How come you started playing the drums, Rindu?' I had anticipated this long before I actually took a pair of drumsticks in my hands. The answer I came up with was: 'Generally.' It turned out to be effective in more ways than one; it was too bland to be gossip and it made me feel more like a dilettante, someone who 'generally' took up new and different things to challenge himself, and less an upstart who at heart thought he wasn't cool enough.

'Rindu, heard you're drumming nowadays?'

'Hmm.'

'How come?'

'Generally.'

'Generally meaning?'

'Meaning nothing, just generally.'

I was in the music room a few days after my first lesson. A stickwork pattern my teacher had showed me was proving extremely tricky. Try as I might I wasn't able to reproduce the sound he had shown me. Played really slowly it seemed to work but as I speeded it up it fell apart, sounding laboured and confused. And when I tried to incorporate it as a roll inside a four by four beat I just couldn't understand when to launch into it and, even if I did start the roll, I didn't know how to return. I had been working on this for about an hour, sitting there in the music room on my own, when the door opened and Rocksurd walked in.

'Rindu? What are you … when did you start drumming?'

There were several times, before and after that moment, when I looked right into Rocksurd, through the window that was his face. There was the time when he had failed three classes and was dangerously close to being thrown out of IIT, there was the time when he rode into the hostel to announce that our hostel's candidate had won the election for general secretary, there was the time he told me of his first sexual encounter. But the expression I remembered when I had forgotten all the others was the one I saw that day in the music room. It was an expression we saw often at IIT, especially after an exam when two friends stood discussing the paper, one who had done well, one who hadn't: bemusement mixed with jealousy, a sense of betrayal and hurt, a premonition of impending defeat. We rarely acknowledged that expression and we never discussed it, but we all knew what it meant.

'Oh, I just started taking some classes.'

'Classes?' he said. 'With whom?'

'Fonseca.' I knew that Rocksurd had taken a few classes with him as well.

'You have a lot of money,' said Rocksurd.

'I just thought I'd take six or seven classes. Just learn a few things.'

He came up to the drumset, walked around to the side where I was sitting. I could see he was looking at my posture, how I held my sticks, where I kept the hi-hat.

'That guy is just interested in money,' he said.

'Who?'

'Fonseca. You can tell as soon as you reach his house. He's despo for money.'

'Ya, I guess so,' I said.

'I told him, teach me a few songs. Just fifteen songs, that's all, and let me go. But he has to tell you the flam, the paradiddle, all that shit. One hour you sit there, learn two things, pay a hundred bucks.'

'That's true,' I said, feeling that I had wronged Rocksurd somehow, that I could make it up by agreeing with him.

'Show me what you can do,' he said.

I pulled the snare drum a little closer, adjusted the hi-hat, moved up in my chair and positioned my arms to start playing a four by four. This was an exam I had to make sure I didn't do very well in. Starting the beat slowly, I played it for eight bars and then hit the crash cymbal.

'Can you play it faster?' he asked.

Playing a little quicker this time, I started again. Four bars, crash, four bars, crash. He was about to say something when I started the beat yet again, still faster. Three bars, simple roll on the snare, crash.

'Nice,' he said.

I got up and gave him the sticks. Moving the snare drum back a little, he lowered the hi-hat, and tilted the toms slightly towards himself. He rolled: from the snare through the mounted toms to the floor tom and finally into the crash. Again and again, faster and faster till it began sounding ragged and disconnected. Eventually he stopped, striking up a four beat at a much faster tempo than I had. He rolled around the toms and crashed every four bars, raising the tempo a little each time. Finally he gave a frenzied roll which lasted for two bars and crashed with a flourish, getting up as he crashed the way the drummers at rock shows sometimes did at the end of a song.

'Nice,' I said.

He handed me the sticks. 'So what else can you do?'

'That's all I have learned so far,' I said.

'That's good, man,' he said, putting his arm around my shoulders. 'You and I can be the drummers of Kumaon Hostel. Maybe we can form a two drummer band, like the Allman Brothers.'

'Band?' I said. 'Fuck, I am a long way from being able to play in a band. All I know is four by four and that too just barely.'

'Come on, Rindu. Rock drumming is just improvisation, man. Once you know the four by four, everything else you can just make up.'

'You just want to get on stage,' I said. And immediately I could see I had said the wrong thing.

'Oh, and you just want to drum for fun, hain? Fucking bullshit! You think you'll displace Titu as Kartik's drummer just because you and Kartik are such good friends. We'll see.'

In the second semester of our first year Kartik had formed a band, they had even performed at Stu Week for an audience of IITians. Kartik had complained to us a couple of times about Titu's drumming. 'He's slowing us down, man. I wish we had a proper drummer. He's a nice guy and all that, and he's senior so I can't say anything, but really, he's the weak link.' I suddenly realized that Rocksurd knew about this and he knew that I knew. That explained why he had taken up drumming and, to him at least, that was my reason as well.

'No, Mandeep,' I said. 'That isn't my trip at all. Really. Kartik's a really good guitarist and the other guys are pretty good too. It'll take at least a year or two before I am anywhere near as good as Titu is now and by that time he'll be much better. Anyway, I am not interested in replacing Titu.'

We walked out of the music room in silence. His scooter was parked outside. He gave me a ride back to the hostel.

'So, have you paid your mess bill?' I said. The semester was starting in a few days. Our third year at IIT was about to begin.

'No,' he said. 'Monday.'

'Same here,' I said. 'Have you moved your stuff in or are you going home?' His father had been transferred to Delhi from Dehra Doon the year before.

'I have to get my helmet,' he said. 'It's in the mess.'

As we were about to part ways in the hostel reception he turned. 'Hey, Rindu,' he said, putting his hand out.

I put my hand in his. He clasped my hand in a handshake, then pulled it up into an inward clasp till our elbows were touching. 'Drummers, brothers,' he said, looking straight at me.

'Drummers, brothers,' I mumbled, feeling stupid.

4

Asian Paints Woman

I WAS NOT AT HOME THE DAY BHAVNA DIED. I WAS AT IIT.

The morning's classes done, I returned to the hostel for lunch. It was a Friday, just one more session to go and I'd be on my way home I was thinking as I walked into the common room, ruminating on my post-lunch saunf. The TV was playing Hindi film songs, people were sitting on the sofas reading the newspaper. The carrom board was occupied, so I stood back and watched the game in progress.

'Oye Rindu! Don't you live in Mayur Vihar?' It was one of the guys on the sofas.

'Ya, why?'

'Did you know a girl called Bhavna? There's a news item about a Bhavna from Mayur Vihar.'

'I know a Bhavna.'

'Her boyfriend killed her.'

'What?'

'It's right here in the *Times of India*,' he said, getting up off the sofa.

'What fucking nonsense! There must be a hundred Bhavnas in Mayur Vihar,' I said.

The news was not about Mayur Vihar's other ninety-nine Bhavnas. It was about the one I knew, the one I had known. That moment in the common room would come back to me in vivid detail many times: the music from the TV's scratchy speakers, the sun streaming through the windows, the growl of our large desert cooler, the cool-wet smell of the air being blown through its straw pads, the newspaper open in my hands.

'Rindu? Did you know her?'

I handed him the newspaper and walked out of the common room. Tears welled up in my eyes. The public phone we had in the hostel was out of order as usual so I went into the east wing and called for Bhats.

'Bhats! Bhats behnchod, where are you?'

If you look west from C block's roof, or D block's roof, you can see the eastern skyline of Delhi. From Okhla in the south to the ITO power station in the north, with Nehru Place, Humayun's Tomb, India Gate and Connaught Place in between. In the evenings when there is a sports meet or a rock show or a cricket match or a mass wedding, the floodlights of Nehru Stadium blaze a dust-refracted yellow. The Lotus Temple and India Gate are always alight.

Ring Road, across the river, is a garland of sodium orange. Nizamuddin Bridge is a coughing, smoke-billowing stream of headlights, ebbing and flowing. But the lights I liked best were the ones on the pontoon bridge they constructed between the second nala bridge crossing and Sarai Kale Khan. The one they stopped using a few years into its short life. The approach road, cutting through the fields to the river, was a string of lonely beacons at night, deepening the darkness rather than alleviating it. And the lamps of the bridge itself, bobbing up and down in the gentle swell of the river were soothing and hypnotic. Often enough someone would throw something off the pontoon bridge and the thread of reflected lamps in the water would quiver and tremble, threaten to break almost, before the ripples passed.

The other side, facing east, is not as spectacular. The gnarled streets of leftover villages, dumpy yellow DDA boxes arranged in neat and not-so-neat rows, a school, some temples, and behind all this, marking the boundary between Phase 1 and Phase 2, a row of tall trees: Sanjay Van. Near it lies Sanjay Lake, a sewage and hyacinth lake which, together with the small oblong tree-lined park that is Sanjay Van, are dedicated to the memory of the man whose idea it was to clean Delhi up and deposit its human garbage east of the river.

There are only two days of the year when it makes sense to look east off the roof rather than west.

One of those days is Independence Day when in the evening the entire sky fills with kites. Every rooftop – DDA, village or society – fills with people holding kite strings, tugging, winding, unwinding. Dogfights proliferate. Swooping and cutting, bending away from a pursuer, cleverly entangling an opponent – pieces of paper mounted on two sticks come alive in a viciously elegant display of aerodynamic savagery. The vanquished float down to earth where bands of children run in pursuit, alarming motorists, falling off roofs. Up on C block roof it isn't possible to make out cries of victory or groans of defeat. All you can hear is a general buzz of excitement, a loud buzz, floating over all of Phase 1, and probably Phase 2 as well, although it is hard to tell through the trees.

But the noise of this stylish and anarchic battle does not compare with the noise of the other day when people climb the roofs and look east.

That other day is Diwali.

*

Bobby arrived at my house with a tika on his forehead and a fresh red thread around his right wrist. The din outside was increasing as the light faded.

'Come, come, Bobby,' my mother said.

'Happy Diwali, Aunty,' he said. 'Uncle, Happy Diwali. Where's Didi?'

'Come, eat something sweet,' said my mother, buzzing around the table putting some barfi and sondesh on a plate.

'Happy Diwali,' said my father, wearing the slightly embarrassed smile that usually appeared when he was forced to lower his newspaper and return some sort of greeting.

'She's taking a bath,' I said, answering Bobby's question.

'Do you have any patakas?' asked Bobby.

'Very few,' I said.

'Jijaji bought a whole lot but I told him, I am not interested in all this. I am going to meet Arindam.'

I nodded. Family patakas were meant for later at night. A few would be set off in the course of the evening but the bulk would be saved. The evening was reserved for going to people's houses and eating sweets, and then waiting at home for people to come and eat your sweets. It was only after this was done that the proceedings turned wholeheartedly pyrotechnic.

'So, what's the plan?' I asked Bobby once we were outside.

'Let's go to Abhilasha's house.'

'Really?' I said, stopping in my tracks. 'Are you sure?' I knew that Bobby and Abhilasha were getting on well, it was Abhilasha's mother I was scared of.

'It's Diwali, yaar. What can her mother say?'

I could hear my heart beating as we stood outside Abhilasha's door. Bobby's finger was hovering over the bell.

'Ring it,' I said.

'I'm scared,' he said.

'It's Diwali, yaar. What can her mother say?' I said in a mocking voice.

'Forget it,' he said, stepping away from the door. 'Let's go.'

'Fucking darpok!' I went up and rang the bell.

Abhilasha's sister opened the door. She saw me first, looked at me quizzically, then saw Bobby cowering behind me and broke into a smile. 'Come in, come in,' she said.

'Happy Diwali!'

'Happy Diwali! Abhi, your friends have come.'

When Abhilasha emerged from the prayer room, platter laden with diyas in hand, wearing a heavy red silk sari, it was like a life insurance ad, an Asian Paints hoarding come to life. She was just a girl playing at being a woman for an evening, I knew this even in that moment. But she made me feel like a man.

Bobby seemed equally impressed. It was a long time before he could croak out a Happy Diwali.

Much to our surprise, when Bobby hesitatingly asked Abhilasha's mother if we could take her to the roof to see the fireworks over the city she agreed. Mainly, I guessed, because on Diwali the roofs lost their shady reputation and became a place for the Society to congregate.

We walked in a strange formation, the two of them exchanging polite conversation while I, a step behind them, pretended to be entirely absent. The lift journey up to the seventh floor was wordless and awkward. I thought hard but couldn't come up with a way of making myself invisible in that small metal box. All three of us looked at the panel, its light lingering interminably on each number.

The whole Society wasn't on A block roof when we reached there but a large part of it seemed to be. On closer inspection it turned out to be Bhavna with a bunch of intermediates, the people who were not old enough to identify with the uncles and aunties but certainly not young enough to hang out with the school–college crowd.

Mayur Vihar was ablaze with light. Every house had decorated itself with at least one line of candles, some had electric lighting as well. Streamers of light rose in the distant sky, over Phase 2, Patparganj, Laxmi Nagar, NOIDA, and ended in star-bursts whose sound reached us a fraction of a second later. Down on the streets, on the corners and in the parks we could see small knots of people illuminated by the charkhis and anars and small bombs they were setting off. On all the other roofs in the Society, and on the roofs of tall buildings in other societies, people stood, like we stood here, watching this grand spectacle.

I found that Bobby and Abhilasha had broken away from me and were standing to one side, away from the crowd, looking south over the ledge.

Bhavna came up to me. 'Hi Arindam. Happy Diwali.'

'Happy Diwali.'

She was wearing a sari as well and looking lovely. She motioned at Bobby and Abhilasha with her eyes and smiled at me. I grinned back and gave her a thumbs up sign.

We both turned to look at them. I could see Bobby's hand on the ledge inching its way towards Abhilasha's hand. He touched her fingers with his index finger. She didn't move. He slowly moved her fingers up, insinuating his hand under hers. Her fingers settled onto his palm. He picked her hand off the ledge and slipped his palm into hers. Neither of them turned their heads.

Suddenly a rocket fizzed up onto the roof and landed on top of the water tank. There was a brief moment of panic, Bobby and Abhilasha turned, their hands disengaging in the process. I stepped backwards as well, hitting my ankle on a water pipe. The rocket exploded with a pop rather than a bang. Everyone heaved a sigh of relief.

I noticed that Bhavna was clutching my arm. Slowly her grip loosened. As she removed her hand her fingers brushed my forearm lightly. My skin tingled at her touch.

The Society's Diwali always culminated with the lighting of a long ladi. The small ladis, fifteen or twenty oblong red crackers tied in a line, were numerous. The braver kids would hold them in their hand, light the end, wait for just the right amount of time and then throw them up, the point being to make sure the explosions happened in the air. The slightly longer ladis, hundred or two hundred crackers, were rarer. They had to be lit on the road, they were too bulky to handle.

The way you compared your stash of crackers with another kid's was to tell him the size of the longest ladi you had bought and ask him his. A few hundred was impressive but quoting a figure in the thousands earned you true respect. Everyone else brought their crackers to where you were and waited for you to light your longest ladi.

Long ladis were expensive. In our Society, mainly populated by retirees and salaried people, there was one regular winner of the ladi sweepstakes. He was a stocky man who wore a white pyjama kurta. I saw him only at Diwali. At around eleven thirty he would arrive at the eastern gate of the Society with his son holding a huge box. Immediately people would begin to gather. Outside the gate, the jhuggi children would crowd to get a look in at the proceedings. The son would open the box. A murmur would run through the crowd. 'One lakh,' someone would say. 'Two lakhs.' I never got close enough to read the label on that box.

The laying of the Society's longest ladi was a ritual to be undertaken with due gravity. The son would unfold his ladi a bit at a time and the crowd would move slowly along with him, past C block, past the recreation room, past our covered parking space till finally the end came to rest just where the tank began. Each landmark was greeted with sounds of approval.

The stocky man would hold his son's hand as it moved gingerly to the engorged end of the charge. Some people would clap. There would be an initial fizzing as the powder caught and the lit end began moving toward the first of the crackers. Then the explosions would begin. The crowd would drift back the way it had just come, following the trail of paper the ladi left in its wake, the annual excitement at the sheer number of crackers in the ladi taking easy hold once again. The children would be shouting and cheering, the adults would be smiling in undisguised glee, people my age would be trying to appear unconcerned but would walk along nonetheless. Finally we would be back at the gate, finally the chattering serpent would fall silent.

A roar would go up from the crowd, then peter out into applause. People would disperse as quickly as they had appeared. Diwali was over.

Six weeks after that Diwali on A block's roof I returned to the Society having finished my first semester at IIT. I slept fitfully the first few nights, dreaming one fevered dream after another:

An hour before the exam Pratap comes to my room with a problem. He is sure it's going to be in the exam. We sit down. It seems easy but I can't work it out. The nib spirals uncontrollably. Meaningless squiggles fill the page. Page after page flies off the notebook. It's time for the exam. I still haven't solved the problem. Pratap has disappeared. It's time to put on my shoes and start walking to the Institute. I am still wondering what to do. This is pure panic, heavy, acidic panic. I know this problem is going to be in the exam. I am at the Institute. The paper lands on my desk. It's the first problem. Ten marks out of forty. Ten per cent of my grade...

The first night this happened I actually sat up in bed, reached over to a piece of paper lying on my table, picked up a pencil and wrote down the solution. It had been easy. I had been right. Then slowly the realization had seeped into my sleepy mind that this was my room at home, not the hostel. That could only mean one thing: the exams were over. Over!

A week after coming home I finally picked up the phone to call Bobby. He came over, parking his scooter, as always, in the visitors' parking near the gate. It was my turn to talk and I nattered on about how difficult the exams had been and how I was sure I had done really poorly. He appeared a little distracted.

'Something wrong, Bobby?' I asked finally.

'There's been a panga with Abhi.'

'What panga? Did someone say something?' I asked.

'Winky,' he said.

'Winky? What about Winky?'

'He told her some nonsense. She's not talking to me.'

'Where did Winky meet Abhilasha? What nonsense did he tell her?'

Bhavna had thrown a Society party while I was away at the hostel. Bobby had convinced Abhilasha to attend, she had never been to one. Winky had been there. He had been very drunk and had said something to Abhilasha. Some 'nonsense'. Try as I might I could not get the details of this nonsense out of Bobby. Whatever Winky had said had upset Abhilasha a lot and she had been avoiding Bobby. In fact she had stopped coming down in the evenings for the last three weeks.

I assumed at first that this was just another panga, it would pass. But weekend followed weekend and Abhilasha stayed away from Bobby. He remained optimistic that she would come around but it began to appear increasingly unlikely. I often wondered what Winky could have said to her that had led to this long standoff. Asking Bobby was out of the question, it was clear he would not say more than he had said already.

'Hi Arindam! How come you aren't in the hostel?'

'I thought I'd stay at home on Sunday as well.'

'Morning class bunk?'

'Bunk!'

We walked a bit in silence then suddenly a thought struck me. 'Bhavna,' I said, 'you know that Abhilasha is not talking to Bobby?'

She turned to look at me. 'Yes, why?'

'Do you know what Winky said to Abhilasha at that party?'

It was as if I had slapped her.

'No, I don't,' she stuttered.

'Because,' I continued. 'I know he said something but Bobby won't tell me what. And you were there, right? It was your party. So, I thought you might know.'

We had reached the gate of the Society. She hailed a rickshaw.

'Aren't you going to take a bus to college?' I asked.

'It's better to take it from the Pocket 1 stop,' she said, her face averted from mine. 'It's less crowded there.'

When she had settled into the rickshaw she turned to me. Her smile was back.

'Bye Arindam. See you next weekend.'

Kanti Mallick picks up a bottle of talcum powder and shakes out a healthy quantity of the white stuff onto his palm. He applies it liberally to his neck and armpits. Brushing down the fringe of hair that sits wreath-like on his scalp, he puts on his tweed coat and, with a final look in the mirror, heads out of his house. It is the second day of Durga Puja and Kantida is going down to the pandal for lunch.

He emerges from A block into the autumn forenoon and heads for the front lawns. Naren Chatterjee, my father, spots him too late to change direction.

'Naren!' he calls. 'Good morning.'

'Kantida,' says my father. 'How are you?'

'Fine, fine. Did you see my article in this week's *Sunday* magazine? You know that when I was in Calcutta my columns on football used to appear regularly in the *Anand Bazaar Patrika*? Although nowadays I am really very busy, I thought that I should share my views on the state of Indian football. You see, I am an experienced commentator on these matters. Chunni Goswami is a good friend of mine, I used to play with him in college.'

'Yes, yes, Kantida,' says Naren Chaterjee who is well aware of the longstanding association between Kanti Mallick and Chunni Goswami.

'In fact, in 1952, I once scored such a goal that Chunni said that I was a much better player than him. You have a natural feel for the game, Kanti, he said.'

'It is Indian football's loss, Kantida, that you decided to give up the game and concentrate on your career.'

'Yes, I am a family man you see,' says Kantida.

'So, you are going to eat bhog,' says my father, determined to steer the conversation away from the tragic history of Indian football.

'I am going to see the idols and pray. I could not come last evening because I was busy, you see. What is for lunch, by the way?'

That Kantida is always busy is another well-known part of Society lore. Naren Chatterjee smiles. 'Puri and vegetables, with rasagullas for dessert,' he says.

'Hmm, so we will eat well today, eh Naren?'

'Yes, Kantida.'

They reach the pandal. Onjoli is underway. The priest stands in the centre, near the idols, chanting a word at a time. People stand with flowers cupped in their hands repeating what he says. The prayer is in Sanskrit spoken with a Bangla accent. When the word is a somewhat difficult one the chorus of repetitions is muted. But when a simple article or recognizable word comes, the gathering shows its devotion with a full-throated chant. At the end of the verse they throw their handful of flowers at the idol. Some of these land on the priest and the white-sari-red-border aunties who are assisting him.

'Are you going to join the onjoli, Kantida?'

'No, no. I have eaten a bit in the morning. The doctor does not allow me to remain hungry for too long. When I was in college I could go two days without eating and play two games of football everyday. In fact, once Chunni said to me, Kanti you are not a man, you are a camel, you are the ship of the desert.'

Before this monologue gets the opportunity to develop into *The Collected Sayings of Chunni Goswami*, I interrupt them. 'Hi Papa! Nomoshkar Kanti Uncle. Are you giving onjoli today?'

'No, no. I have eaten a bit in the morning. The doctor does not ...'

'Umm, Kanti Uncle,' I say. 'I think the second round of onjoli is about to start.'

'Your son is a brilliant boy, Naren. Brilliant. Just the other day I was telling Mr Ghosh from D block. Naren Chatterjee's boy, I said, brilliant. He is doing Computer in IIT Delhi. Very intelligent,' says Mr Mallick.

My father does not say anything, he just nods and smiles his embarrassed smile.

'He will not stay,' says Kanti Mallick.

'What do you mean, Kantida?'

'When I was playing football, Naren, I got an offer to play for a nationally reputed side. I don't want to say which one. It was a good offer, they would give me a job and I would not have to do much except play football and put in an appearance in the office two or three times a week. But it was not in Calcutta. I thought about it a lot. Playing football had always been my dream but Calcutta was my home. My mother did not want me to leave home and I knew that my wife, she was just a girl then, would miss Calcutta a lot. I asked Chunni. He said to me, Kanti, do what your heart tells you to do. That was when I decided that I had to stay. I got another job with a company which had no football team but was willing to post me to Calcutta. I still played football when I could, in my locality and for small teams here and there, but I gave up my dream of being a professional football player because I knew that I had to stay.'

Mr Mallick has a faraway look in his eyes. He is looking at the table near the podium but he is seeing a sepia past in a faraway city.

'But, Kantida, what does that have to do with Arindam?'

'He is not one to stay, Naren. All these intelligent boys go away to America and England and Germany. They dream of being the world's best in whatever they do. When Chunni told me to follow my heart he probably meant that I should follow my dreams. But in the end my heart wanted to stay in Calcutta with my parents.'

'But then how come you settled down in Delhi finally, Kantida?'

'A few years after I started working they posted me to Delhi. Thirty years later I was still here when I retired and there was no one left to go back to in Calcutta. But never in those thirty years did I protest or ask for a posting back to Calcutta. That was something Chunni taught me: a good player never questions the coach.'

Bobby appeared, as expected, on shoptomi evening. It had been almost a year since Bhavna's party, and weeks since I'd last seen him. He had started working with his jijaji and that was keeping him busy. But I knew that he would come to Durga Puja at least once on shoptomi. It was almost certain that Abhilasha would attend at least this first evening of the Puja. It was the event of the year. The whole Society came down to the pandal – a site of flirtation and genuflection, a forum for matchmaking and feasting, an arena for hidden talent and exhibitionism – on this one day.

My nervous glances towards the gate were finally rewarded with the sight of Bobby's white LML entering the Society. Seeing me waiting for him at the pandal entrance his step quickened. 'Is she here?' he asked.

'She must be getting ready,' I said.

We looked around for a place to sit.

'Good evening ladies and gentlemen. The Puja Committee welcomes you to this year's celebration of Durga Puja. As you know, our Puja provides a showcase for talented children, and their talented parents.'

A polite titter ran through the crowd.

'The first event this evening is the kids' dance competition. This is open to children of ages four to eleven. We have six teams registered. If any other team would like to participate please give your names to Mrs Das.' The announcer indicated a lady in her late forties who, on cue, flourished a largish note pad in which, she seemed to imply, she would write down the names of tardy registrants. There was scattered applause for Mrs Das.

'And now, the first team,' said the announcer, his voice rising appropriately. 'From A block, Rinku, Sonu and Nikita.'

There was some clapping and much cheering. Three children came on to the stage. They positioned themselves hesitantly, the two boys on either side and the girl with her back to the audience in the middle. Music began to blare from the speakers.

Squeals of delight rent the air as the dance began. The little Raveena Tandon cavorted convincingly around the two underprepared little Akshay Kumars. I tapped my feet along with the music. Bobby put two fingers into his mouth and let out a loud whistle. When it was over everyone clapped. Three proud mothers went up to the stage to hug their children while three proud fathers crouched and knelt behind three autofocus cameras.

'Let's go up to the roof,' said Bobby.

We walked into A block and took the lift up to the seventh floor. It wasn't a roof we went to regularly. Last Diwali had been one of the few times we had gone up there. On shoptomi we went there because it overlooked the pandal.

'I want to show you something,' said Bobby once we had taken up our position on the ledge which looked down on the lawn. He reached into his pocket and brought out a hip flask.

'What's that?' I asked, knowing fully well what it was.

'It's a hip flask. A friend gave it to me. His uncle brought it from abroad. I told him, let me keep it for a while.'

He opened it, sniffed the cap, and handed it to me: 'It's whiskey. I know you don't drink but smell it anyway.'

I knew what whiskey smelled like. My father had a collection of different kinds of alcohol, a collection culled from the duty free shops of the several airports he had visited on official trips, bought with dollars saved from meagre daily allowances.

'Hmmm,' I said, returning the cap to him. And then, catching me unawares, he took a quick swig from the flask before capping it.

'What do you think, Arindam? Do you think she will come back to me?' asked Bobby, his elbows on the ledge, his eyes fixed on the pandal below.

For years after that Bobby would return to the Society every Durga Puja. Even after I had left for Baltimore, he kept coming for the Puja. I would talk to my mother the weekend after and she would tell me where the idols had been bought from and what they looked like, what the menu was for each day, what plays or musical programmes had been put up, which uncle made a fool of himself and so on. Then finally, when she had exhausted all she had to say, she would tell me that Bobby had come on shoptomi and was asking about me. Or at least my first few years in Baltimore she told me so. At some point he must have stopped coming. Or maybe she forgot to mention it and I forgot to ask her.

I didn't know what to tell Bobby, up there, above A block. In my world, boys like him never married girls like her. At most they whistled at them on the street and got slapped for their efforts. But I didn't want to tell him I thought so. I kept quiet and we kept looking down at the pandal, shining like a paper lantern on the lawn far below. As we stood there the evening arti began, and the pandal began pulsing with a slow repetition of the familiar Durga Puja beat.

By the time we returned to the pandal the arti was nearing its end. Conch shells were being sounded. Finally, a climax of noise and smoke and devotion later, people began to disperse, some heading out of the pandal returning home, others lingering to socialize and chat and wait for the night's entertainment to begin.

Just as people began to drift out Abhilasha appeared near the stage with her sister. I saw her spot Bobby. She turned without a word and left the pandal.

More than a year was to pass before Bobby actually got to talk to Abhilasha again. In this year news came that she had a boyfriend at the University, a gelled-hair, metal-rimmed spectacle wearer with whom she was often seen sitting under a particular tree.

Bobby came to the Society several times after Puja as well. He wanted to talk to Abhilasha. But she didn't want to talk and that made it impossible to have a conversation in the Society. It was difficult to accost her, there were only two or three points suitable for an ambush and the Society's girls knew them better than anyone else. Besides, even if Bobby managed to waylay her, there would be no privacy amidst the constant traffic of aunties and children and servants.

The opportunity, when it finally came, came in the most unlikely of places: Pragati Maidan. The vast complex of exhibition halls between Lutyens' Delhi and the river had been the site of an annual pilgrimage for my family when I was in school. Every year on the fourteenth of November, Nehru's birthday, the India International Trade Fair would start. For the next fifteen days the whole city would descend on Pragati Maidan and spend an entire day going from pavilion to pavilion, fiddling with crafts from the north-east, gawking at motorcycles from Japan, buying big bags of tart digestives from Uttar Pradesh. People ate and watched street plays and collected bags full of brochures on *The State of Soviet Industry.* It was the biggest mela in the city and every year, like everyone else, we would visit it on a well-chosen day. 'Saturday and Sunday are just too crowded. The first few days half the stalls aren't even set up. You can't go in the last three days, everyone is frantic to see the fair and besides most of the stuff has been sold.' We would park far away and walk to one of the grand gates of Pragati Maidan, encountering street vendors with all kinds of wares on the way. Two or three hours later everyone would be exhausted. Most of the pavilions would have been left unvisited, nothing useful or interesting would have been bought, a ride on the little train which ran inside Pragati Maidan would not have been taken yet again. But we would have all enjoyed ourselves and the walk back to the car – it felt twice as long as the walk from it – would be an animated one, interrupted only by excursions into a sweet sticky web of candy floss.

Although Pragati Maidan's Gate 1 lay on a major road into the centre of Delhi from East Delhi and we passed it almost every day, our visits to the trade fair became rare after we moved to Mayur Vihar. It was no longer a fascinating panorama of the world for my family. Television filled that function now. The trade fair was reduced to a fortnight-long traffic jam.

The first semester exams at IIT were always scheduled a week or two after the trade fair ended. Despite this a few people did go to see it. Most often they were guys from outside Delhi, the Dilliwallahs would just dismiss the whole business: 'I've seen it hundreds of times. The same thing, tractors and tanks.' Late in the evening the returning trade-fair-goers would trickle into the common room and the conversation would divide itself into two major topics: the cars and motorcycles at the Japan pavilion and the sexy female attendants at various stalls.

More than a year after the Puja at which Bobby drank whiskey neat from a hip flask, Abhilasha got a job at the trade fair. I came to know a month later when I returned to the Society after the exams.

I answered the door to find Bobby outside it.

'I talked to Abhilasha,' he said, even before I could open the screen door.

'Let's go down,' I said.

We went instead to D block's roof. Bobby lit a cigarette.

'She was working at a stall in hall six,' he said. 'She was looking really good.'

'Was she wearing a short skirt?'

'No, no, Arindam. All the girls at her stall were wearing saris with the same pattern. Like air hostesses.'

'How did you know she was there?' I asked.

'My friend at DU told me. The guy who told me about the boyfriend.'

'What happened?'

'I went there, straight to her stall. She saw me coming, left the stall and started walking away. I immediately went around the other way. When she saw me we were too close for her to run. There was such a crowd, where would she go? I told her, do you want friendship with me?' He stopped at this point and turned away. The sun was setting across the river. The end of his cigarette was glowing in the dull evening light.

'You just said it? What did she say?'

'She said no.'

'That's it? That's all? No?'

'Yes.'

My first year in college was also the first year I went on the nobomi night tour of Delhi's big Durga Pujas. My parents never took the tour, nor did they ever go with the immersion party on doshomi, and so I had never been either. But some aunty or the other would inevitably come by the house the next day and rave about the pandals they had seen and the crowds and the lights and the idols, and I would inevitably resolve not to miss out next year.

The bus came around nine thirty, just as the last stage show was coming to an end. Word ran through the pandal. The girls and aunties immediately disappeared into the apartment blocks. Some of the men stood up as if to go to the bus and then sat down again. It would be at least an hour before the caravan hit the road.

Loitering around the pandal on my own – Bobby had eventually given up hope that Abhilasha would come down – I felt a tap on my shoulder. 'Hi Arindam, long time no see.'

Ghontu Sanyal was exactly my age. Bobby and he used to share cigarettes some times: 'He smokes like a charasi, takes really long drags.' Whenever I met Ghontu, his large frame always appeared slightly hunched over to me, like he was about to take a very long drag on a joint. He had once fractured his shoulder playing football in the Society. I hadn't been there but Bobby repeated the story often: 'Just think Arindam, not his shin or his ankle or his knee. His shoulder!'

He crushed the hand I offered and returned it to me. 'Coming on the bus this year?' he asked.

'Yes,' I said although I hadn't asked my mother yet.

'Some of the chicks at these pandals are really cute, yaar. It'll be a lot of fun.'

The older people took their places at the front of the bus. Bhavna, her brother and their gang sat at the back. I knew these people and they knew me, but only because I had played football or cricket with some of the guys, and I had politely nodded my head at some of the girls' mothers as they walked their rounds of the Society. There was no space for me in the conversation that bounced and swirled around the back of the bus, it was too densely populated by familiarities I shared only partially. So I sat with Ghontu in one corner.

'Have you heard Gravy Train?' Ghontu said, as the bus rolled away from the Society gate. 'They are fundoo, man. Their guitarist, Christy, is a good friend of mine. What feel he has!'

'Yes, they played at the IIT fest.'

'Fuck man, Rendezvous is a great fest. I got so drunk at the rock show, I don't remember how I got home.'

I was struggling to keep up my end of the conversation when an impromptu antakshari broke out amongst the others.

'Shit man,' whispered Ghontu. 'Antakshari! These people are such locals!'

But I wasn't listening to Ghontu any more. I was watching Bhavna sing. What would it be like to have a girlfriend in the Society, I was thinking; to meet on the walkways and look out over the cricket games being played downstairs, sit quietly on the scooters parked in the dark corner behind C block, exchange glances across the Puja pandal.

The antakshari continued as the bus crossed the river and headed towards North Delhi where the oldest Pujas were. I watched the players sing and flirt and touch and laugh. Almost all these relationships would dissolve, replaced by marriages my mother would report to me on the phone. The girls would go away to Allahabad or America, returning occasionally, wearing saris, children in tow. The guys would remain in the Society, turn older and fatter, their moustaches would grow thicker. I'd run into them at the children's park where they would be watching over their little daughters: 'We used to laugh at the others earlier, now it's our turn,' they would say and wink. But despite all the hindsight whenever I thought back on that night in the bus I would always feel as if I missed out on something important.

The pandals were awash with people like us, groups of Bengalis from all over Delhi. We had to jostle our way through them to get to the idols. Our bus driver had to fight with their bus drivers for a place to park. The decorations at these old and rich Pujas were splendidly ostentatious compared to the ones we had at the Society. Their idols were much bigger, their trappings much more gorgeous, their girls much prettier.

At each pandal we would get about twenty minutes to see the sights. Then the person who had 'taken responsibility' would gather the flock and take us, responsibly, back to the bus. The expedition continued through the night, wending its way across the city. The antaksharis grew less boisterous, Ghontu's conversation began to flag, the stops grew shorter, till finally we reached our last destination: Chittaranjan Park.

My mother would always tell me how we could have had a plot in CR Park if my father had had the papers that proved that we were East Pakistan Displaced Persons. But he hadn't, so I didn't grow up in a place where shops displayed their names in Bangla. Whenever I went there I felt lost. I couldn't read the Bangla script well, the conjoined letters got the better of me, so being in CR Park was almost like being in a foreign country. It was more frustrating though, because if I hadn't known the script at all I wouldn't have felt compelled to read.

We walked down the street from where the bus was parked. I read off the names on the houses: Ghosh, Das, Sen, Mukherjee, Bhowmik, Dhar, Choudhury, Ganguly, Bhattacharjee.

'So many fucking Bongs!' said Ghontu Sanyal.

We laughed all the way to the pandal.

The main tent was supposed to be a replica of the Victoria Memorial in Calcutta. The idols were paper sculptures rather than clay and straw. I walked through quickly, it was too late at night to be awestruck. Outside the pandal I saw Bhavna standing by herself.

'Hi! Where are the others?' I asked.

'Hi, Arindam!' she said, smiling at me. 'They've gone to get ice cream.'

I didn't know what exactly to say. She was looking at me expectantly, waiting for me to continue. Nervousness clutched the inside of my stomach.

'Nice pandal,' I said. 'Really big.'

She looked up and nodded. 'Huge,' she said.

'Really huge.'

'Are you okay?' she asked.

'Just a little sleepy,' I said.

Out of the corner of my eye I detected a large form lumbering towards us. I turned towards it in relief.

'Damn!' said Ghontu. 'The fucking idols are made of fucking paper!'

Then he noticed Bhavna. 'Oh! Sorry,' he mumbled. She muffled a laugh and, spotting the others coming out of the refreshments tent, walked past a deflated Ghontu without replying.

The eastern sky was light by the time we reached Mayur Vihar. The bus had been silent on this last leg of the trip. Ghontu had nodded off. When the bus finally came to a halt outside the Society and I got up to leave I saw Bhavna two seats ahead, her head against the window, strands of saliva hanging out of her mouth, dazed and half awake.

I felt grateful that I would be back at IIT in a day's time.

I jumped a traffic light and took two wrong turns on the way home that evening. Eventually, when I reached the Society, I found it charged with an uneasy silence. There were no footballers on the front lawn, no young mothers sitting with their children on the stage, no little girls cycling circles around the Society, no one lounging on the water tank. I parked my scooter and went up. When I reached the door I could hear voices in the living room, but when I opened it a sudden hush fell over the three aunties who were sitting there.

It wasn't as if people didn't die in the Society. Every few months I would hear that some uncle or some aunty had passed away. Sometimes in the evenings, I would be walking in the Society and it would strike me that I hadn't seen one particular face down there for a long time. I would ask my mother about it. Most of the time she would tell me that the aunty in question had gone off to America to spend four months with her pregnant daughter. But there were other times when she would tell me that person had passed away a few months ago. Somehow the news had not made it to the weekend updates I got when I came back from the hostel.

The Society too would take the departure in its stride. The aunties would go to the flat where the body lay and commiserate with the family. The managing committee would put up an obituary notice on the board opposite the lift in each block. People would tell affectionate stories about the dead person, set in progressively earlier years as they tried to establish who had known him the longest.

In Bhavna's case this didn't happen. My mother did tell me about how her car had broken down just outside the Society's gate the week before and Bhavna had helped her push it to the parking spot, but that was all I heard.

'She was such a sweet girl. So quiet and so helpful.'

Perhaps the conversations did go on but I was not part of them because I was not close enough to any of the aunties or uncles or their children. Perhaps it was because I was away from the Society or perhaps it was because I was to be shielded from the illicit nature of the circumstances in which it all happened.

Maybe it was because I couldn't be part of the Society's collective mourning that I felt Bhavna's death was different from all other Society deaths. For years after it happened I couldn't look at her parents without remembering her, couldn't laugh at her brother's jokes for fear of offending her memory, couldn't take the lift in her block without thinking of the hundreds of times she must have gone up and down in it.

I was home from Baltimore one summer and had been taking a nap in my room, when Bhavna's mother and another lady who had moved away from the Society came to visit my mother.

My mother was sitting in the living room with the two aunties when I staggered out drowsily. 'Do you remember her?' she said pointing to the visitor. 'She's Pooja's mother.'

I did remember Pooja and I did remember to nod and smile politely but it was the look on Bhavna's mother's face that woke me. On the surface lay a sullen acceptance of the fact that Pooja's mother still had a daughter and she didn't. But in her eyes was a dull anger that made me wish I had not come out into the living room at all.

Bobby and I walked all the way to the NOIDA road, crossing the bridge where I used to wait for the school bus, then the road itself, till we were on the embankment. He was silent all the way there. I couldn't think of anything to say either. His face was impassive, his expression guardedly quizzical, like it used to be when I tutored him in maths. We walked some way and then sat on the edge of the embankment facing west towards the rest of the city.

'Why did he do it, Bobby?' I asked tentatively.

'I don't know,' he said. 'Winky was crazy.'

'Was he in trouble at college? Had he been suspended? What was he doing in Delhi at this time of the year?'

'Winky was crazy,' he repeated.

'Was he always like this? Did he do anything like this when he was in the Society?'

He looked at me and shrugged his shoulders.

We sat in silence. The sun had almost set. A grimy greyness coloured the horizon, making it look like the collar of a dirty shirt. Across the river, on Ring Road, headlights twinkled like a string of Diwali lights.

'If the neighbours had heard her shouts earlier, maybe it wouldn't have been so bad,' I said.

'She wasn't shouting, Arindam,' he said quietly in Hindi. 'She was screaming.'

The horror of that distinction ran through my body. I put my arm on his shoulder. His body was convulsed with silent sobs. He moved away, straightened up and turned towards me.

'You moved into the Society in 1990, right?' he asked.

'Yes, but ...'

'You had wood-work going on in your house for the three years before that, right?'

'What has that got to do ...?'

'You had a Sikh contractor, right?'

'Yes,' I said. 'Surinder Singh.'

'We made good friends with his labour. We would give them half a bottle from time to time. In return they would let us use a room in your house.'

'Use a room?' I said. 'For what? Which room?'

'Your room,' he said. 'The one which is now your room. Winky, Bhavna and I would go there.'

'To do what?'

'To have fun,' he said. 'We would have fun there. Bhavna's brother knew about that place. He would go there too sometimes with Winky's sister.'

Shock and disbelief burst like a balloon in my head. My mouth ran dry.

'That's why Abhilasha isn't talking to me. Winky got drunk at that party and told her about those days in that room.'

He stood up and turned towards the road. I tried to stand but couldn't.

'Forget it, Arindam,' he said. 'Winky was crazy, Winky is dead. It's too bad he took Bhavna with him. Forget about it.'

He never mentioned Bhavna again.

I couldn't get to sleep that night. Lying in bed, looking around my room, I felt like someone else was there with me, hiding in some corner or behind the door. I went out into the drawing room and tried to watch TV, it was too late to wake any one else up. The chowkidar passed by from time to time, tapping his stick on the road and blowing his whistle.

My whole body was aching. I went back to bed and lay down. I tried to sleep. But whenever I closed my eyes I saw Winky and Bhavna standing next to my bed. He would be stroking her thigh with one hand, palming her breast with the other, nuzzling her neck. Her body would tense, arch a little. Her eyeballs would roll up into her lids with pleasure. And, beyond her eyelashes, framed in the door would be Bobby, tears pouring down his cheeks, his face contorted with grief. I woke next morning to find my pillow was soaking wet and salty.

Bhavna must have left college after her morning classes. She would have crossed two streets and waited for a bus at the same stop I used to wait at when I came to Lodi Estate for IIT Study Circle classes. Any bus would take her to Khan Market from here, just one stop away. She would have got on from the front and just stood by the door. The conductor wouldn't have asked her for a ticket, he would have known that everyone getting on at this stop went to college here. Asking any one of them to buy a ticket was to invite trouble.

Khan Market would have not been particularly busy when she passed it, mainly peopled by fruit vendors and rich housewives out for some afternoon shopping. Bhavna would have walked right past and turned into the gateway that led into Rabindra Nagar. Despite the heat there might have been a small after-school rubber ball cricket game in progress on the green patch. The cricketers would have seen her walk by and would have nudged each other. One of them might have let out a low whistle, another would have shouted out Winky's house number and made an obscene gesture. She would have ignored them, but her step would have quickened.

Winky should not have been in Delhi at the time. Maybe he had been suspended from college for rowdiness, maybe he had just decided he didn't want to be there anymore. She must have spent an hour there before the neighbours heard noises coming from the house. They had knocked on the door, then banged on it but it hadn't opened. Finally they had called the police.

When the police broke the front door down they found Bhavna's body lying near it. Her head had been smashed in with a dumb-bell.

Winky lay next to her. He was clutching his stomach. There was a pool of vomit near him, and a can of Baygon. He died in the hospital later that day.

Had they argued? Had they fought? Had he proposed something she wasn't willing to do? Had she wanted to break up with him? Had she suggested he go back to college?

All these were questions the police couldn't answer. But they did find a half empty bottle of whiskey in his room. And a trail of blood that led from his bed to the front door of his house.

5

Hey Joe

TITU RAISED HIS ARMS IN THE AIR. HE CLICKED HIS STICKS together.

'A one, two, three, four.' His fleshy face screwed into a grimace as he brought the right stick down on the hi-hat, his spectacles wobbled with the effort of striking the snare with the other one. The outer skin of the bass drum throbbed rhythmically as the beat took off.

Guitars screeched in confusion. The count had been much faster than the beat. Only the bassist, a frizzy-haired guy from Nilgiri hostel, seemed unconcerned, plucking his strings with a mellow enthusiasm. It was his first time on stage and his preparation for it had probably involved smoking some substance or the other.

The rhythm guitarist, Gogi, looked worried. He and Titu were classmates, and friends. Kartik, on the other hand, was neither Titu's classmate nor his friend. He looked furious.

The vocalist had been holding his mike with both hands like he was about to kiss it. Axl Rose couldn't have struck a better pose. But now he was looking back at the pandemonium behind him, one leg frozen in front of the other, and the mike still on the stand, clutched between his palms.

'Play it faster, behnchod,' I could see Kartik saying. At KLS after the show I would recount this incident as my contribution to the post-show dissection, adding that Pete Townshend would often shout 'Play it faster, you cunt,' at Keith Moon.

The beat lurched forward and then slowed again, then almost broke down into a racket before picking up again at its original pace. The guitarists adjusted. Kartik took his annoyance to a corner of the stage.

The vocalist turned back towards the audience. His face took on an intense expression, his head bent into the mike, his eyes half closed, looking down. 'Keep your eyes on the road,' he growled, 'your hands upon the wheel.'

A cheer went up. 'Yea Gobar,' a few people shouted. Gobar made a fist in the air with his right hand in response.

'I'm goin' to the roadhouse,' he continued. 'Gonna have a real,' then a pause, a toss of his hair, 'good taaaaaaeeeeeem.' His voice cracked near the end. The experiment, crossing Robert Plant with Jim Morrison, hadn't been a total success. But Gobar didn't care. The bass was pumping behind him, the drums were rolling and crashing and the guitars were wailing. All of us who stood below the stage could see clearly that as far as Gobar was concerned, he had died and gone to heaven.

It was our second year. This was Stu Week, IIT Delhi's internal fest, three days of interhostel competitions in the middle of the second semester. The culmination of Stu Week was a rock concert by the newly formed IIT rock band. It was their first show, barely three weeks after I first got to know they existed.

I felt I should have known earlier. After all, my closest friend at IIT, Kartik, had formed the band. He had mentioned he was thinking about it a couple of times, but it was from Rocksurd that I first heard of the crystallization of the project.

'Rindu, man, a band right here at IIT. Isn't it great?'

'Really?' I said.

'Shit, Rindu, your own roomie starts a band and you don't know about it?'

'Oh yes,' I said. 'Yes, Kartik's band.'

I had no idea this was going on. Kartik explained it to me later: it was halfway through the second year and his position as the overall Institute topper of our year was secure. It was time to branch out.

Kartik's friendships were clearly compartmentalized. His friends from school, his friends from the department, his friends from the world of rock and his friends in the hostel were kept separate. It was not as if he went out of his way to keep these different groups apart, it was just that he never actively encouraged any interaction between them. There might have been a hierarchy in his head, I often conjectured. His friends from school were not smart enough to meet his IIT friends, his friends from the hostel were not cool enough to meet his rocker friends. If he did actually think so, he never let on. But he rarely mentioned Bagga and his other friends from school to me and later when he left the IIT band to play for an established Delhi band he never introduced us to the band members or the women who hung around with them.

Most of Kartik's first band was one batch senior to us. Kartik and the bassist were the two guys from our year. But it was clear even in this first show that although Gobar was the showboating front man and some of the really difficult guitar solos were handled by the reticent Gogi, who actually turned away from the audience while playing them, it was essentially Kartik's band.

The show ended with cymbals crashing, guitars feeding back and Gobar screaming theatrically. Behind Titu I could see Rocksurd sitting on the floor. Other drummers always sat behind the drumset. In a few months time I was to join those ranks, but at that time I stood in the audience watching Rocksurd wave his arms as he crashed with non-existent sticks on imaginary cymbals, matching Titu stroke for stroke.

'Thank you, thank you,' said Gobar, in the airy way he and I had often seen on MTV. It sounded more like: then-gyoo, then-gyoo. 'We are Instigate. You guys have been great.' And then, cocking his head to one side: 'Hey, that rhymes.'

It was prime time at KLS when I reached there, 11 p.m. A big circle in the centre was the crowd from the Stu Week rock show. I broke into the circle and recited the line I had been rehearsing in my head on the way over. 'Wow, Gobar really lived up to his name today!'

Johri was standing directly opposite me. A mischievous delight lit up his face. 'He's standing next to you, Rindu. Why don't you tell him yourself?'

Gobar had been well hidden, standing right next to where I had entered the circle. He bristled at this unexpected insult. We all sniped at each other, gossiped about each other and slandered each other. But we did it behind each other's backs. This was an unusual situation and, without the benefit of some time to think about it, he put together an awkward response. Perhaps to the others it was an anticlimax, it wasn't able to trump my line. But the challenge he posed in that line stung me, shamed me, and made it impossible for me to look him in the eye even months later when it was clear that he had forgotten all about it.

'If you think it's that easy, Rindu,' he said, 'why don't you get up there and do it yourself?'

*

In the mornings, on his way to class, Kartik would come barging into my room. Shutting my half-open eyes and turning away wouldn't help. He would sit next to me, 'Rindu, come on, don't you have a class?' I would mumble something about ten more minutes. 'Rindu, you lazy ass!' he would say and hug me as I lay in bed. I would curse and try and shrug him off, but the fact was that I enjoyed that morning greeting, that physical gesture of friendship. It would last a moment and then he'd be off. 'Okay, okay, I have to go to class now.'

The main reason Kartik and I became such good friends was that we had very similar backgrounds and fundamentally different temperaments. Perhaps if my CGPA had been closer to his or if I were in his department, things would have been different. If I had been a guitarist he might have seen me as competition. But somehow the races we were running were different. While he was pushing hard to stay ahead of the pack, to be the best at whatever he did, I was jogging within sight of the rest of the field, trying to ensure that my academic performance didn't slip too much while I did all the things I could with the wonderful freedom the hostel afforded. In IIT, where your grade point average defined who you were, he was a dassi, a ten-pointer, I was a satti, a seven-pointer.

Our relationship deepened with time. We had been assigned the same hostel by chance, but it was by design that we took rooms next to each other. All four years we were almost roommates, separated by just one wall. As time passed I became his confidant. He would come to my room and worry aloud about how the guy in Electrical who was his closest competitor for the President's Gold Medal, the prize for the highest CGPA in a graduating class, might be gaining on him. He would complain about how his band was not gelling as a unit, or, later when he changed its composition, he would excitedly tell me about how he felt they were now ready to compete with other bands in Delhi.

He would talk about his parents and tell stories from his childhood. 'You know, when I was small I wanted to be a taxi-driver. I really liked their yellow-black look. I went to my mother and told her: Mummy, I want to be a taxi-driver. She said: Very good. Now go and study because to become a taxi-driver you need to study hard.'

His family was from Rajasthan, they were brahmins. They were, he told me, very respected in their community. His sister's marriage to a wealthy doctor settled in the US had been a major social coup for their family. It was important, he would often say, that his brother and he did very well in life because that would further raise his parents' prestige in the community. I didn't quite understand this side of him. My own extended family was spread all over the world and didn't seem to have any particular affiliation. And while I recognized that the manner in which I made my way in the world would be discussed in the Society, I never thought it was a matter of life and death the way it seemed to be for Kartik.

He would often talk about how his father was the first PhD in their community, the first man from his village to become a college professor. But his children were to take it even further. Kartik's sister had married extremely well and her husband was a highly paid doctor in the US. His brother was studying in the US. He had almost won the President's Gold Medal in his time and was now studying business at Wharton. Over the years, as one conversation layered on another, I realized that Kartik's project was to demonstrate success on a much larger scale than his father or his elder siblings; his project was to show them and the community how high one man could rise.

The singlemindedness of his pursuit became clear to me one day in our third year. It was a time when I was beginning to wonder what I was going to do after IIT. The options were well defined. Either I was to get into a management school or I was to go abroad to study or I was to take the civil services exam. It was a crossroads where, to my mind, the first arrow pointed to money, the second to the pursuit of knowledge, and the third to power. Although my mother was keen on the third option, I didn't want to go into the civil services because I didn't want my entire life to have been determined by competitive exams. I had succeeded in several difficult ones and perhaps that was why the success which lay at the end of an examination seemed like an empty one to me.

Slowly I was also beginning to bend away from the first option, beginning to convince myself that running after money was something dirty, something below me. By the end of the second year I had begun consciously brainwashing myself that I wanted to do something better than making a lot of money. By the time the third year had come along I was convinced. It was around this time, one evening, that Kartik and I went for a walk.

'I am going to apply to business school next year,' he said, as we walked out of the campus through the back gate.

'You want to do an MBA?' I said. 'There's no funding for that in the US.'

'Not an MBA,' he said. 'I am going to apply for a PhD. Just the top schools, Wharton, Stanford, MIT, Sloan, Kellogg.'

'A PhD?' I said. 'In management? Like your brother?'

'Ya,' he said.

'But if you want to do research, why not do engineering research?'

'Rindu,' he said, 'the top people in any company are always management people, not engineering people. Besides, the only technology area which has big money in it is Computer Science, and that's not my area.'

'But you chose not to get into it because you thought it would be easier to get a schol in Chemical Engineering,' I protested.

'I took Chemical because it would be easier to be the Insti topper in Chemical,' he said. 'There's no future in Chemical.'

'I am thinking of doing research in Computer Science, probably theory,' I said hesitantly, not sure whether I wanted to admit this to anyone else yet.

'Rindu!' he laughed. 'You are a satti! Remember?'

'I am almost up to eight now.'

'Oh Rindu,' he said, patting me on the back. 'Research is for naukkis and dassis. And even that is stupid, there's no money in it unless you start a company or something.'

I was quiet. Stuffing my hands in my pockets I lengthened my stride. Inside me a sentence was struggling to come to the surface. I fought it for a few seconds, then released it.

'Money isn't everything.'

He turned his head towards me. I felt his gaze on me, and kept my eyes consciously on the road in front of me. 'There's only one clear measure of success, Rindu,' he said, finally, his voice hardening with certitude: 'Money.' He paused for a second, waiting for this to sink in. Then, in a softer tone, he went on: 'The more money you have, the more successful you are. That's the only way to keep score.'

My stomach contracted at this statement. I felt something like anxiety grip my head, as if I had something I wanted to say but wasn't able to find the words.

'What about friends?' I said, eventually.

'What about friends?'

'Isn't that a way to keep score? How many friends you have?'

'If you have money,' Kartik said, 'everyone is your friend.'

We had walked up Aurobindo Marg, past Adhchini Village and were walking along the eastern wall of IIT campus. At one point there was a small diamond-shaped compound cut into the wall in which stood a government-style whitewashed building. The board outside proclaimed the building as an office of the International Airports Authority of India.

'What is this place?' Kartik said.

'It's the place where they give the planes coming to Indira Gandhi Airport an alignment signal. That's why all the landing flights fly over the campus. They line up here as they descend.'

'Really?' said Kartik.

With his hand he described an aeroplane coming into land. 'Whoooo', he whistled as the hand-plane descended on an imaginary airstrip, the pitch of his whistle lowering as the plane lost height and speed. Finally his plane landed, and then, even before it came to a halt, it picked up speed again and took off from the same imaginary airstrip, ascending at an unbelievably steep angle into the night sky.

Titu's tenure as head drummer of IIT was to be a brief one.

In one of the other hostels, we got to hear one day, there was a fresher from the south, an Anglo-Indian, who had been playing the drums since he was ten. The guys from his hostel claimed he was major. We took this with a pinch of salt; during the ragging period everyone tried to make out as if the freshers in their hostel were the most talented. But even so I decided to go to the music competition for freshers.

The competition was held in the large common room of Shivalik, one of the two postgraduate men's hostels. By the time we reached it was already packed to bursting. Bhats and I fought our way across to where our hostel's contingent sat. They were surprised to see us. Normally, freshers were chaperoned by second year-ites. Third year guys might come to a fresher's event if it was in their own hostel or if it involved something they themselves were good at, like a senior quizzer might go to the freshers' quiz, but it was rare for third year people to just show up at an event they weren't involved in. The second year guys hid their puzzlement by greeting us more effusively than normal. Or maybe they were asserting their new-found place in the hostel. It had, after all, been just one year since we had brought them to events like this one.

'So, Lallu,' Bhats said to the fresher from our hostel, 'what do you do?'

'I am going to sing, sir.'

Bhats half-patted half-slapped his cheek. 'Sing, beta? What are you going to sing?'

'Hotel California, sir.'

'Hotel C? You? Sing Hotel C?' Bhats laughed. 'Good yaar, very good.'

The second year guys sniggered. The fresher's face had the usual apologetic fresher's expression on it, mixed with a bit of nervousness. Bhats was about to say something when the buzz that had been going around the room rose to a crescendo. The girls were here.

The senior girl came in first. She was in her second year. The swagger in her step was a little exaggerated, as if to show the frightened young ones that there was nothing to be afraid of, or at least to show them that she was not afraid of anything. She went up to the Music Club Secretary, exchanged a few words with him and laughed loudly. Then her wards came in.

They walked with their heads down, their necks bent. They took short, quick steps and quickly reached the four chairs that had been vacated in the front for them. I remember thinking that they looked impossibly young although they could not have been more than two or three years younger than me. Looking at their plain, scared faces I wondered how many guys in the room were falling in love with one or the other of them right that instant.

Eventually the competition started. The participants came on one at a time and sang, or played an instrument, cheered loudly by their hostel's contingent. Some of them were naturally shy, some were natural performers, some were discovering where exactly they lay in between those extremes. Whenever someone struck a pose or took a note higher than required or, in one particular girl's case, made eye contact with the audience, the room cheered and whistled. It grew hotter and hotter as one participant was replaced by the next, but not one person showed any signs of leaving.

'Now we have Darrell Sebastian from Karakoram,' the music secy announced. 'He's going to play the drums.'

In the months to come, like all the drummers at IIT, I was to learn to treat Darrell almost on par with a professor. It was only in the few seconds, from when his name was announced and he stepped out of the crowd of guys from Kara to when he picked up his sticks, that I was able to see him as a fresher, as unsure and scared as the three hundred others who had joined IIT along with him that year. Once he started playing it all changed. He became Darrell.

With most of the other competitors there was the implicit understanding that they were bathroom singers who had signed up for the Western music competition because they felt they should show 'enthu'. Some of them were good, some of them played the guitar or the keyboards competently. But no one expected genuine talent to show up at the freshers' events. When it did, like it did that night, they didn't know what to do. Whistling along with an intricate drum solo was not only difficult, it was inappropriate. Running up to Darrell and patting him on the back might throw him off his stride. Dancing in front of the drumset would prevent people from watching him play. There didn't seem to be any way to interact with this performance. And so they listened in silence. And watched as his hands danced over the drumset creating moments of sound which were in turn arousing and soothing, delicate and muscular.

Darrell blew me away that day in Shivalik's common room.

I sought out Kartik when I got back to the hostel. He was in his room fiddling with his guitar.

'Kartik, you won't believe what I heard!'

He didn't look up, he kept picking at the strings. 'What?' he said after a while.

'This guy, Darrell, a fuchcha from Kara. He's the most fucking awesome drummer I have ever heard.'

'I know,' he said.

'What?'

'Yes. I've kicked Titu out. Darrell is Instigate's new drummer.'

During the winter holidays that year I went from the Society to the Institute one Saturday. I was working for Professor Kanitkar along with Sheikhu and Neeraj and I was supposed to meet them outside the department. They were late and after a while I got bored and decided to go and check if they were in the hostel. On holidays the door to block VI, where my department was, was locked, so I had parked outside block V. I crossed over to block V on the first- floor walkway and was about to climb down the stairs when I saw someone sitting on the stairs of the ground floor. It was a big guy wearing a blue sweater waving his arms. It was Titu. He was playing an imaginary drumset. He seemed to be in the middle of a roll. He pounded the imaginary toms, his foot pumping the imaginary bass pedal. Finally he came down crashing hard with both hands on what seemed to be a forest of imaginary cymbals. Then he got up and threw his imaginary sticks, one by one, deep into the imaginary audience.

Sometimes I would just beat the bass drum one hundred times in sets of four, to improve my control on it. Other times I would try playing a beat with only my left hand. It was weaker than my right and needed strengthening. But these little exercises were not enough. I needed to play along with a guitarist. I wanted to be a musician.

Kartik agreed after some pleading. We went to the music room once a fortnight. I tried hard not to lose the count but still had to take 'Yaar, the drummer is supposed to give the beat, not follow it' from time to time. He taught me how to mark the end of a chord sequence with a crash. 'Listen for it, Rindu. Just hear me once then you'll know when the chords are about to repeat. Crash just when I start the new sequence.' It was hard at first to figure out where the changes had to happen. I would just count to sixteen in my head and then crash. Once I started getting the hang of it I would add a little roll at the end. But this would confuse me sometimes and I wouldn't know where to return. I would stop playing and sit there with my arms by my side waiting for him to look up so that I could ask him to stop as well.

I was heading out to one of these sessions one evening when I ran into Johri near the music room.

'What's up, Rindu?'

'Nothing, yaar. Just hanging around.'

'I heard your left hand is weak?' he said, grinning broadly.

Johri was the leader of a squadron of eagle-eyed hunters who pounced on the tiniest scrap of conceit or bigheadedness. When I first heard the word 'hubris' I immediately realized that it exactly described the quality that Johri and his ilk looked for. Once they found it they attacked it with lethal doses of ridicule. To be at the receiving end of this ridicule you needed a rhino's skin or an equally thick protective layer of incomprehension. I tried to remain on the good side of these people, preferring to be part of the crowd whose grating laughter was supposed to grind the offender into the mud. Thinking aloud about my left hand had put me squarely in the firing line. There was only one remedy; I started attacking myself.

'Oh ya,' I said, 'I'm a cool drummer, you see. Total rocker.'

Johri laughed. I heaved a sigh of relief. 'Good yaar,' he said, putting his arm around me. As he did so my sticks hit him in the arm, I had put them in my pant pocket and tucked them under my T-shirt.

'Off to strengthen your left hand?' he asked.

I just grinned in reply.

'Going to play alone? Or is Kartik coming as well?' he persisted.

I shouldn't have been surprised that Johri knew about the jam sessions with Kartik. At IIT nothing was a secret. Especially from people like Johri who made it their business to know everything that went on. Every piece of information, however trivial it might seem at first glance, had value. Even if it wasn't useful in itself, it could be bartered in the gossip market for something you wanted. I hid my surprise. The least I could do was deny him the satisfaction of knowing that he had caught me out.

'Yes, Kartik's coming too,' I said casually. 'In about an hour. I just thought I'd practise a little before he got there.'

'Trying to impress him with the stuff you are learning from Fonseca, haan? It's no use, Rindu. The fuchcha is too good. There's no way you are going to replace him in Instigate.'

I protested immediately and excessively. If there was one thing I didn't want it was for Johri to go around telling people that I wanted to, or had wanted to, get into Instigate.

'I'm just a beginner, man,' I said. 'Total beginner. No way I will get on stage for many years. Not even in a Hindi Music Night. Kartik's just teaching me the basics of playing along.'

He considered this and accepted it. And then, unexpectedly, he said: 'I'll come along with you.'

We went to the music room where he fiddled around with the decrepit old bass guitar. Just this once, Kartik decided to come on time.

'Are you a bassist, Johri?' he asked.

'When I last heard, there was no shortage of bassists in IIT Delhi,' said Johri putting the guitar down. 'I don't want to add to their nunber.' We all laughed. Bassists were an easy target.

'So, Kartik, I've heard you guys are entering the rock prelims this year,' Johri said.

Kartik was plugging his guitar into the amp. He just grunted a yes.

'You think this new guy, this Darrell, is a good enough drummer?' asked Johri. 'You want to take him on stage in Rendezvous. Bands from all over the country will be there.'

'I know what happens at the rock prelims, Johri,' Kartik said, strapping his guitar on. 'I think we're ready. We might not make it to the finals but I think we'll put up a good show. And Darrell is a really good drummer. You should hear him play, he totally fills up the sound. He keeps doing small things here and there which make the song sound so much better.'

'What does he do that Rocksurd can't?' asked Johri. I was taken aback. I had expected him to say Titu.

'Rocksurd is no drummer,' said Kartik beginning to play scales.

'Come on, Rindu,' said Johri. 'What's wrong with Rocksurd's drumming? Tell us, you're a drummer as well.'

Even as I started speaking I knew I should just say nothing or, at most, say that his drumming was fine. Instead I said: 'He's limited, yaar. He just knows a couple of beats and a couple of rolls. He can't improvise and he can't pick up a beat just by listening to it.'

Johri looked across at Kartik to see what his reaction was. Kartik hadn't even heard, he was fiddling with the amp's knobs. Johri looked back at me. A smile played around the corner of his lips. 'Chal Rindu,' he said. 'I'll let you guys get on with your jamming. I'll go and get some chai at KL.'

I struck up a beat slowly as he left the room, feeling scared of I knew not what.

'Hey Bhats! I know that guy!'

Bhats raised his chin off his chest slowly. His eyelids lifted a fraction. 'Guy? What guy?'

'The guitarist, chutiye, the guy on stage.'

The rock prelims had been going on for five hours. This was the sixteenth or seventeenth band to play. The Convo was heavy with the smoke of contraband cigarettes. The odours of vomit, alcohol and marijuana circulated sluggishly around the huge room. For the true rocker, however, at this time of the day, on this weekend of the year, this was the only place to be. It was four thirty in the morning and I was on the verge of leaving for the hostel when a trio headed by a short guy in a black hat came onto stage.

'That guy,' said Bhats. 'Pandit?'

'His name is Pandit?'

'You know the guy,' snorted Bhats. 'But you don't know his name? Good, yaar, Rindu.'

'Abbé, he's from Mayur Vihar.'

'Oh no,' groaned Bhats, his head slumping onto his shoulder. 'Not that fucking Mayur Vihar again.'

I had often seen Pandit around, but had not known his name for a long time. He was quite unmistakeable – short, with curly hair and light eyes. He walked in the strange way that small people often do, bobbing up and down on the balls of his feet. Sometimes he wore a wide-rimmed black hat. Later, when we became friends, I plucked up the courage one day to ask him about it.

'It's a strange story, yaar. It was August, maybe two or three years ago when one day I heard that Stevie Ray Vaughan had died. Shit man, I was so depressed. All day I sat at home, told my parents I am not feeling well. I thought I'd play some of his tunes, to honour his memory sort of, but the guitar felt like it weighed a ton. In the evening finally I got up and decided I'll go and get some stuff from NOIDA, but for some reason I found myself walking towards the Pocket 1 bus terminus. I don't know what it was, yaar, but something was telling me, go to the terminus. When I came out on the road I found that the Thursday bazaar was on. It was really crowded, man, all sabji shops and shit. I just walked through till I reached the bus stop. I was wondering what to do when my eye fell on this hat. It was lying in one corner of a pavementwallah's plastic sheet. I went straight to him and asked how much for the hat. Hat? he said. What hat? This one, I said. He looked at it like he had never seen it before and then quickly he said – these guys are clever, man – quickly, he said, fifty rupees. I have twenty, I said. He took it. When I touched the hat it was like I had touched a live wire, man. I was almost knocked unconscious. Immediately I put it on and ran home. That night I played Stevie's songs all night, I played solos I hadn't even heard before. Fuck man, it's like that whole Dalai Lama thing, you know, when they look for a child and all at once the guy dies? It was like Stevie's soul had come looking for a body to possess.'

Bobby and I had seen him walking by the Society once.

'Do you see that guy there?' Bobby had asked, pointing at Pandit. 'Don't take pangas with him.'

For Bobby, I had learnt by this time, the world, or at least the world of men, was divided into the people you could and could not take pangas with.

'Why?' I had asked.

'He lives in Pocket 4. Goes to Bhagat Singh. He plays the guitar very well. If you mess with him you have to answer to the Bhagat Singh boys.'

The chain of reasoning, having taken in a weak link or two, had ended with a convincing argument. The mythical Bhagat Singh boys were titans who ruled the streets of the University, hockey sticks in hand. I had not pressed the matter.

And now here was Pandit at IIT, playing the guitar very well indeed.

The song finished. There was scattered applause. I wanted to cheer but my mouth tasted stale.

Pandit came to the mike and, reaching up slightly, said in a soft lisping voice: 'The next song is a self-composition entitled, The Night Calls Me.'

He stepped back, closed his eyes. His head bent forward towards the stem of his guitar. He struck the first notes of the intro. His bassist and drummer were silent; the entire Convocation Hall was silent. The sounds of his guitar sprang lightly from the massive speakers. You could feel the audience waking up as the music began to fill the air, their variously intoxicated minds quickening to the clarity of Pandit's song.

Before they'd decided to keep the roof terraces of the Society buildings locked, there had been this one day when I was alone, up above D block. It was dusk, the last flush of dusk. Orange had become pink. I was slowly turning my head, like a camera panning, from north to south. The tint was draining out of the sky as my eye scanned the horizon, uneven with landmarks. And then, there was the Bahai temple, the stone Lotus, its white petals glowing in an aura of pink stucco.

I felt pure joy, a mellow sensation coursing up my body. It was like a feather caressing my calves, my thighs, my arms, moving to my torso, playing with my chest and dragging lightly up my neck to my face. I felt the beauty of that scene tingle in my face.

With my eyes closed in the Convocation Hall, with the sounds of Pandit's guitar in my ears, I remembered that evening alone on the D block roof. I remembered how I had looked away for a fraction of a second and when I looked back, there was only grey. The last of the crimson had leaked away.

There was a moment of stunned silence when the song finished. And then an eruption of applause. I beat my numb palms together again and again till they turned a stinging red.

No one in the Society ever complained when I bought a drumset and played on it two hours every Saturday and Sunday, when I was back from the hostel. A few months after it arrived I was able to convince Kartik to bring his guitar and amplifier over when he came to my place on occasional weekend trips to Mayur Vihar. It was on one of those trips that I finally met Pandit.

We had jammed for about an hour. Afterwards we went down for a stroll. It was evening. The small children were out on their bicycles, the slightly bigger ones played cricket on the lawns, the even bigger ones lounged on the water tank. The evening walkers strode purposefully on their daily rounds.

Kartik and I strolled around for a bit and then went and sat on the stone bench behind C block. After a while Pandit and two other guys came around the corner. Kartik knew Pandit slightly, they had met at a rock show. When Pandit saw Kartik he came up to us.

'Are you the guy who plays the drums?' asked Kaustabh, one of the two guys with Pandit.

'Yes,' I said.

'See,' he said turning to the third chap. 'I told you the guy with the Led Zeppelin T-shirt must be going to where the drums were.'

It turned out that Kaustabh played the guitar too. Pandit was like a guru to him. We talked for a while. Before we parted I asked Kaustabh and Pandit to come and jam at my place some time. 'I have a drumset at home.'

Months passed before they actually took up my invitation. Months in which I would see Kaustabh or Pandit or both on the street and start a desultory conversation with them which would end about five minutes later with me emphatically saying that we must jam together soon. This happened so many times that when they actually rang my doorbell, guitars and amps and all, I was surprised.

They set up the amps in my room. Kaustabh had just bought a new guitar. It was a Gibson. His brother had brought it from the US, and it looked just like the ones I had seen in the posters that Kartik used to have up on his hostel room wall. He said that the sound was really good and when he played it for me I agreed, although it sounded just like any other guitar to me. I asked Pandit what he thought of it. He nodded his head vigorously. 'It's good,' he said. He nodded his head a little more.

Kaustabh started playing a riff and I started hammering out a beat to go with it. Pandit was sitting behind me on the bed. From time to time he would get up and pace the cramped room. He peeked into the little bathroom that we had converted into a store. Then he came back and sat on the bed again. I kept drumming. Kaustabh started soloing. The steadiness of the riff had been giving me time so now I had to concentrate much harder. I closed my eyes and kept the beat going, really scared that I would make a fool of myself. Finally Kaustabh's solo reached a crescendo. I gave a drum roll and returned to the beat at the exact moment when Kaustabh returned to the main riff. Pleased with myself, I looked back over my shoulder to get Pandit's approval.

He had a syringe planted in his elbow and was slowly pushing the plunger in.

The shock of that moment would cut through my memory like a knife whenever I thought about it later. Here we were, just a flimsy wooden door, not even bolted, away from my parents, in my house. My mother could walk in at any minute, any minute now, with three cups of tea on a tray.

Kaustabh had not noticed. Kaustabh was lost to this world. His eyes were closed, his body arched over his guitar. In this moment, when I was falling down a long black tunnel, he was soaring over a huge stadium full of adoring fans. I closed my eyes tight, gritted my teeth and just kept grinding the beat out.

When we finished I saw Pandit standing near me. I cast a nervous glance back to see if he had left any telltale marks. He hadn't.

'Can I go in here?' he asked, pointing at the storeroom. His voice was steady. I looked at his eyes. I expected them to be glazed over or glinting with intoxication, that's how drug addicts are supposed to look after getting their fix, I thought. But he was looking at me evenly.

'If you want to use the bathroom, you can go to the other one. This one is boarded up.'

'No, I just want to stand in there.'

Kaustabh started playing again. Through the ajar storeroom door I could see Pandit standing facing the frosted glass window, his hands fisted on either side of him, like Tarzan about to break out into a wild cry. But his body was not tense. It stood there, small and compact, filled with an unnatural ease.

After about five minutes he came out and tapped Kaustabh on the shoulder. Kaustabh looked over at him. He gestured that Kaustabh should stop playing. Kaustabh stopped. Pandit reached out wordlessly and took the guitar from Kaustabh. He slung the strap over his shoulder and ran the pick across the strings.'My time has come.'

A few years later, on a trip home from Baltimore one summer, I met Kaustabh and asked him how Pandit was.

He shrugged his shoulders. 'He was some guitarist though, wasn't he?' I said, trying to fill the awkwardness with a platitude.

'Those musical ideas,' said Kaustabh, brightening up. 'They were beautiful. He would be playing something and then he would just touch a note and you would think, shit, this is how it should be. Whatever else happens, those ideas will never go.'

That day in my room, I saw those ideas, I saw the beauty, the wisdom, the transcendence of those ideas. I saw them from two feet away. For all Pandit knew, though, I might have been in Pitampura.

We played for some time and then they started packing up their stuff. A book lying on my desk caught Pandit's eye. It was a book on computer networking for Unix. He picked it up and started flipping the pages.

'This is a good book,' he said, his head beginning to nod again.

Later Kaustabh told me that Pandit had begun attending Aptech. His parents were sending him there. Everyone said that there were good jobs in software. And they were right.

I was least expecting the phone call when it came. It was near the end of the summer after my third year. It had been a long summer, riding to NOIDA every day, working all day in a company for my 'industrial training', eating lunch in a canteen where people wore pants instead of jeans, shirts instead of T-shirts and worried about their wives and families instead of classes and grades.

It was during this brief trailer of what I could expect life after college to be, that my last chance at rockstardom presented itself.

'Hello, can I talk to Arindam?' lisped a soft voice on the phone one evening.

'Yes,' I said.

There was a silence at the other end.

'I am speaking,' I said.

'Hi Arindam, yaar, I didn't recognize you.'

It was Pandit.

'Pandit, how are you? Long time, yaar,' I said, surprising myself with my effusiveness.

'Arindam, yaar, I am forming a band,' he said straight away. 'I want you to be my drummer.'

'You're forming a band?'

'Yes, yaar. Do you think you can play the drums for me?'

Did I think I could play the drums for Pandit? Of course, I did. I was elated. I made an effort to contain my excitement.

'Umm, ya. Sure.'

'Great, man. Buy Extreme's new album. We're going to play some songs off that.'

'Okay. Who else is in the band?'

'I'll tell you later. When we practise. Okay, I have to go now, have to get back to work.'

'You got a job?'

They were late.

It was eleven thirty and my band was yet to arrive. The rock prelims would start in half an hour. I had been here, standing outside the Seminar Hall, for the last hour. They had closed the doors of the main building now, only participants were being allowed in. But neither Pandit nor Kaustabh were among the trickle of humanity that made its way in past the sturdy check-dam of Rendezvous security.

The Convo hadn't been opened yet so everyone waited here, outside the Sem Hall. They had been accumulating slowly, rockers from all over the country. Guitar cases and cymbal bags and rucksacks lay all around. People stood around in knots of three or four or five. The nucleus of each group was a band. Around this nucleus revolved a hanger-on, who, if asked, would most likely identify himself as the band manager. A few of the bands had girls with them, girls with large nose-studs, dirty hair and tight blouses.

My hands were thrumming with nervousness. I walked up and down, from the public phone to the lifts and back. It struck me that of all the people in the lobby I was the person most familiar with it. I had climbed these stairs for innumerable lectures, taken the lifts up to the canteen every day for three years, and yet I was the person who was most ill at ease right now.

Kartik must have slipped in when I wasn't looking. He stood talking to Ganju at the far end of the hall. I made my way across.

'Hi Kartik,' I said. 'All set for the prelims?'

Kartik and Ganju turned to look at me. I noticed that Ganju did in fact have eyeliner on. I had seen him at many rock shows, he fronted a heavy metal band called Ministry. 'Ministry Means Metal Man' was the legend scrawled across a skull and crossbones background on his T-shirt. He was a tall guy with long curly hair that he tied back with a rubberband. He wore a dirty red jacket, jeans torn at the knees and large black boots. And, it was clear at this distance, he had black eyeliner on.

'Hmmm,' said Kartik and turned back to Ganju. 'So, what are you guys playing tonight?'

'Some Slayer, maybe a little Megadeth, you know, man. The hard stuff. What we usually play.'

'Lot of good bands from the north-east tonight,' Kartik said. 'And those guys from Bangalore are here as well. It'll be hard to qualify.'

'Listen man, it isn't about winning or any of that shit. Just do your thing, play your music, you know. That's all I care about,' said Ganju with a toss of his ponytail. And then, looking at me, 'Isn't that right, drummer guy?'

I realized that I was clutching my sticks very tightly to my chest. I loosened my grip on them and started stuffing them into my pocket as I nodded my agreement.

'You on tonight?' he asked.

'Ummm. Ya. Yes.'

'What's your band called?'

'Ice Fire.'

'Nice name,' he said. 'Who's your guitarist?'

'There's this guy called Pandit …' I began.

He snorted with laughter.

'Oh, so you are Pandit's new band, haan? I heard he had something going this year as well. Who else?'

'Kaustabh,' I said. 'Playing the bass.'

The name meant nothing to him. He continued to contemplate the fact that he had accidentally run into one third of Pandit's new band.

'Good guy that Pandit, he's a really good guitarist. If he just kept off the, you know,' he said pushing an imaginary hypodermic syringe into his forearm.

'Ya,' I said, drawing a little confidence from the fact that Kartik seemed to have disappeared into the crowd. 'But there are a lot of really good musicians here. I hope we don't make fools of ourselves.'

'Listen, drummer guy,' he said, putting his arm around my shoulders. 'That Pandit of yours, he's the real musician.

The rest of these people, they aren't musicians. Just a bunch of long hair and attitude.' Having said this, he took off his rubberband and threw it to one side, ran his hands through his hair a few times and turned to go.

'We're on after Instigate,' I told his receding back. 'Kartik's band.'

He raised his hand without turning. 'Good luck, drummer guy.'

A commotion at the door made me turn. It was Johri and Rocksurd lugging three large round boxes and a huge sports kit. Johri was the coordinator for the rock show.

'Hey Rinds,' Johri puffed. 'Drumkit's here finally. Come and help us set up the fucker.'

'Chutiye,' said Rocksurd. 'Rindu is a par-tee-cee-pant.'

'Okay, all right,' said Johri. 'Can't ask Rindu.'

'Fuck you, guys,' I said. 'Give me a box.'

Johri put on his serious face. 'No, Rindu, it's the rules. No participants inside the Convo before the event starts.' Then he grinned. 'But you can carry the shit till the door of the Convo.'

He handed me two boxes. My sticks slipped out of my hands as I tried to take them from him. Rocksurd picked them up and threw them into the kit bag.

'Hey!' I said. 'Those are my sticks.'

'I know, yaar,' said Rocksurd. 'Take them when you need them. Why do you cry so much for everything?'

'Don't you cry tonight,' sang Johri.

'I still love you bay-bee,' said Rocksurd.

'Don't you cry tonight,' they sang in tandem. 'Don't you cry-yaiy, don't you ever cry-yaiy, don't you ever cry-yaiy tonight.'

'Fucking choots,' I said, dragging the boxes behind me as they laughed their way up the stairs.

As I turned to head down to the ground floor after dropping the boxes off at the door I thought I saw Kaustabh near the other door of the Convo. Walking out into the corridor I saw Kaustabh and Pandit head towards the toilet near the Academic Section. I called out but they didn't seem to hear so I walked around and followed them in.

'Who is it?' said Kaustabh, turning with a start, his hands behind his back. 'Oh, Arindam, come, come. We were just, you know –' he brought his right hand in front. There was a lit joint in it. 'Want some?' he asked.

'You guys carry on,' I said, feeling my voice quiver a little. 'I'll just wait outside.'

I walked up and down the corridor, looking at the closed doors of the Acad Section's offices, wondering at how easily a creeping sinisterness had suffused this familiar space, how entirely it had been deserted by its comforting associations: identity cards, attestations, grade sheets, rude clerks.

Pandit came out first. He walked right by me, heading towards the Convo. Kaustabh emerged next. He smiled when he saw the look on my face and patted me on the back.

'Ready?'

I was ready to give up by the time we had our third, and last, practice before the rock prelims.

'No, no, yaar. Not like that. Play it like this.' Pandit waved his hands in the air, right hand holding the time, left hand hitting the snare. 'It's snare then bass on the half, empty and then bass again.'

'I'm trying,' I said. I had been trying for the last two hours.

'I'm the guitarist, yaar, you're the drummer. If I have to tell you all this, it's no use. Tell me, Kaustabh, what's the use?' said Pandit.

Kaustabh looked away.

'Okay, okay, yaar,' said Pandit. 'Let's try it again.'

In the two months between the time Pandit had called me and the rock prelims we had managed to get together only twice before this third practice. Pandit would call me and give me a time. 'Wednesday, yaar, three o'clock, your place.' I would miss my afternoon classes and drive all the way back to Mayur Vihar. Three would become four, four would become five. No one at Pandit's office at the TV company seemed to have heard of him and they didn't know where to find him. Kaustabh's mother would tell me that he had gone to Ghaziabad to meet his cousin or he hadn't returned from college or something. Then, a week later I would get another call from Pandit.

I finally worked up the courage to complain.

'Sorry, yaar, I just forget. I am working at BiTV nowadays, it's hard to get out of there. Next time I'll be there. Definitely.'

We had managed to get together for two dismal rehearsals in which we somehow dragged ourselves through our song list. And this third rehearsal was turning out to be no better.

'Listen, Pandit,' said Kaustabh finally. 'Let's do Hey, Joe a few times. Let's at least get that one right. The rest we'll manage.'

Pandit seemed puzzled more than anything else at Kaustabh's forcefulness. He nodded and bent his head over his guitar.

'Let's do it a little slower,' said Kaustabh looking at me. 'It'll be easier that way. Follow the bass, closely.'

Hey Joe was the song I had wanted to play since I had started drumming. My first drum teacher had played it for me when I had gone for my very first lesson. 'It's like one long drum solo going on in the background,' he'd said. 'All improvised.' I had played that one song on my stereo again and again, trying to drum along with it till even my mother recognized it. But this was the first time I would be playing it with live musicians. And this time I would be the only drummer; I wouldn't have a muffled Mitch Mitchell backing me up off a worn out Jimi Hendrix tape.

Pandit struck up the intro. I sat with my sticks poised over the snare. He played the riff twice and I came down with full force just as Kaustabh struck the bass. It sounded just right.

I crashed to end the intro and settled into the beat, still a little scared but allowing myself to enjoy the deliberate syncopated pace, allowing myself to groove with the muscular, laidback bass line.

'Hey Joe,' whispered Pandit, barely audible over the instruments. 'Where you goin' with that gun in your hand?'

This was my cue. I shut my eyes and began hammering the toms. It was a long roll, energetic and complicated in the orginal, a little easier but still quite involved in my version. I felt each furrow in my brow as I concentrated, my right hand leading my left from one tom to the next. It had not been more than three seconds since I had leapt out of the security of the beat, but it seemed like a lifetime later that my right stick crashed into the cymbal. The bass line picked up from the start. Pandit launched into a second Hey Joe. I had returned on time, I had executed the roll to perfection.

The arch of my back tightened, my arms and feet seemed to explode with energy. From that first roll to the end of the song was the one time in my life when anything seemed possible, when everything I did seemed exactly right, totally in sync; the one time in my life when I was not a bespectacled Bengali computer scientist sitting in a small room in Mayur Vihar, but Mitch Mitchell himself, the master of the drumset, the king of percussion, sitting on a raised platform above Jimi Hendrix in front of an audience of thousands at Woodstock, creating sounds that would blow the world away.

'That was great,' Kaustabh said. 'If we do this there, we're sureshots for the final.'

'Total sureshots,' I said, twirling my right stick between my fingers.

Pandit was quietly putting his guitar into the case. 'Chal yaar,' he said. 'I'll see you at IIT on Friday.'

'What did you think, Pandit? Wasn't that a good version of Hey Joe?'

He sniffed and nodded. I thought he was agreeing but it was just his head shaking like it sometimes did. 'It was okay,' he said.

'The next band on stage is Ice Fire from Delhi.'

There was a smattering of applause. From the back a lone voice, Bhats, yelled, 'Yea Rindu.' I went up to the drumkit. Darrell was getting up, Instigate had been on before us.

'That was great, Darrell,' I said. 'I think you guys will get through.'

'Really, man? You think so?' he said, a big smile spreading across his face.

'Of course.'

'Good luck, Rindu. You'll do great,' he said. 'Be a little careful of the small cymbal here, I think it's a little loose.'

My first time on a real drummer's stool, I sat gingerly and pulled the snare a little closer. I placed my sticks on it, I had finally retrieved them from Rocksurd: 'Thanks, Rindu, I used them to test the sound of the drumkit. Forgot to get my own sticks from the hostel.' The stool was a little low so I adjusted its height, revelling in the knowledge that there was no need to put cushions on it to raise myself. I fiddled with the cymbals, readjusted the gap between the hi-hats, then played a desultory roll and looked up.

Kartik was plugging Pandit's guitar into the effects board. I could see Kartik explain how the board worked. He was pointing at the pedals and saying something. Pandit was nodding. I didn't understand why Pandit was using Kartik's board. For our practice sessions he had brought his own little distortion pedal, very much like what most guitarists in Delhi used.

'Ice Fire, you have twenty minutes starting now,' Johri said.

The Convo stage was not new to me. Every semester I came here to register. There had been quizzes in which I had sat on this stage, both as an organizer and a participant, both as a winner and a loser. Everything was just as it always had been, the dirty orange carpet, the sluggish ceiling fans at the side, the ugly square tables and broken chairs, but they all appeared strange tonight, like they didn't belong here, like they were objects in a dream, transplanted from their natural habitat by a fevered mind. Mahatma Gandhi's face was there as well, larger than life, toothlessly grinning on the back wall, but he seemed to be laughing tonight at a joke I had not been invited to share. And the lights that always seemed gloomy at the thought of yet another semester on the mornings of registration, those same lights burned like the sun.

Much as I tried later I couldn't remember which song we played first. It must have been Pandit's self-composition, The Night Calls Me, the song which had first drawn me to his music, and it must have gone off really well because it was a beautiful song, but those first four or five minutes we spent on stage never returned to my memory no matter how hard I tried. And after what transpired that evening I wasn't able to ask anyone later.

For our second song the judges asked us to play Metallica's Master of Puppets. Whatever our first song had been, it hadn't required distortion but this song had distorted guitars all through. Pandit pressed down one of the pedals and struck the first chord. It came out totally clean. He played the chord again. There wasn't a trace of distortion, it sounded like an acoustic. Pandit pushed down another pedal and struck the chord again. There was a little reverb this time but again no distortion. Some people started hooting, others started clapping. Pandit pressed down the third pedal and struck the chord yet again. Nothing. He looked around. Kartik was nowhere to be found. I turned to Rocksurd and Darrell. They were sitting behind me.

'Where's Kartik?'

Rocksurd shrugged his shoulders. 'I'll look for him,' Darrell said.

'Arindam, just play,' Kaustabh said.

A steady clapping had broken out in the crowd, one guy was whistling tunelessly along with the applause. Pandit was helplessly staring at the electronic display on the effects board.

'Come on, Pandit,' Kaustabh hissed. 'Let's just play, we have to play.'

'No,' said Pandit, gathering himself. He stepped up to the mike. 'Sorry,' he said. 'We have some technical problems. We are going to play Hey Joe instead.'

Kaustabh walked across the stage to Pandit. 'Listen Pandit, if we don't play the judges' choice we will be disqualified.'

Pandit didn't answer. He turned away and struck the first notes of Hey Joe.

'Fucking shit,' said Kaustabh, and stepped back to his own mike.

I tapped my sticks together along with the intro, trying to work myself into the time. The left stick shifted a little in my hand but I didn't think much of it. Just sweat, I thought and quickly wiped my hand against my pants. I played the opening roll and settled into the beat. Pandit began the vocals.

'Harder,' a voice behind me said. I played the first roll and turned to look. It was Rocksurd. 'The snare,' he said. 'You need to hit it harder, isn't loud enough.'

I nodded an okay and turned.

The second line was near its end. Launching into the second roll, I hit the snare, right left, right left ... And then as I struck the first tom with my left stick there was a cracking sound, the sound of wood tearing and I saw the tip and the first few inches just disappear. I looked around, like a batsman who doesn't know where the ball went after hitting him, and then I looked back at the stick.

It wasn't a stick anymore, it was a stump.

Later I was told, many many times by each person who had been there, that the tip of my left stick described a long smooth arc into the audience landing right on someone's face.

The auditorium erupted with applause. Laughter and clapping and Kaustabh's bass all merged into each other as I sat there staring at the half stick, as I thought of the thirty rupees I had somehow managed to collect to buy this pair, my only pair of sticks, the care with which I had tested the weight balance in that shop in Connaught Place. I could feel the tears in my eyes as I looked at that useless piece of wood sitting there in my hand, mocking me, like everyone else in the hall was.

*

I skipped the last two days of Rendezvous. For the only time in four years I missed the rock show, going home Saturday and staying there till Monday morning, returning to the hostel to pick up my books and heading out directly for class. I ate lunch in the staff canteen and in the evening I spent time in one of the labs in the department. But by seven I was really hungry and I had to return to the hostel for dinner.

Disregarding the calls of 'drummer and a half' and 'Hey Joe' I headed to the mess. I filled my plate and decided to go and sit next to Maiti. He was a fifth year BTech who hadn't been able to complete his degree in four years, a 'backlogger'. He had been very active in hostel politics, one of the causes of the backlog, but now that his batchmates were no longer around he was a mellow, slightly melancholic, elder statesman. He walked through the hostel slowly, nodding at people with the gravity that befitted a person of his advanced age, twenty-two, and experience. No one wanted to be Maiti, but everyone was comforted by the sight of him sitting on the steps leading into the hostel, smoking or standing at the back of the common room wrapped in his shawl, watching the world go by with a sad but indulgent expression on his face.

I put my plate next to his and sat down.

'Too bad about the other night,' he said.

'Hmmm,' I said.

'This kind of thing happens,' he continued. 'When I was in my first year, there used to be this guy called Khullar. He was the best volleyball player in all the IITs. There was this one time in an Inter IIT, I think it was in Kharagpur, or was it in Kanpur ...'

'It was Kanpur,' I said. Like everyone else in the hostel I had heard all the Khullar stories there were to hear, some of them several times.

'Yes, yes,' he said. 'It was Kanpur. He went up to spike the ball and his shorts went down. And do you know what?'

'What?' I asked, fully aware of the answer.

'He wasn't wearing any underwear! Fuck man, with all the girls sitting there and all.'

He was trying to comfort me the only way he knew, by bringing out the story from his stock that seemed to be best suited for the task. The story itself was mediocre, I hadn't found it funny even the first time I had heard it, but I felt touched that Maiti wanted to comfort me rather than make fun of me.

'Shit man!' I said. 'That must have been embarrassing.'

'Fucking embarrassing, man, his dick swinging like a pendulum in front of an audience of three hundred people.' Maiti broke out into loud chuckles; he had given up actually laughing on entering the fifth year.

'Hey, Rindu!' a voice called from across the mess. It was Rocksurd. 'Wait,' he said. 'Coming.'

I wanted to leave but at the same time I realized I had to face the ridicule head on, the only way to deal with it was to participate in it.

'Total chutiya cut in the prelims, man,' I said when Rocksurd came and sat down at the table opposite me. He had a broad smile on his face. 'Do you know why?' he asked.

'Why?' I said. 'Why what?'

'Why your stick broke on stage? Why you got fucked in mid-song?'

'Why my stick broke?' I was confused. 'What do you mean *why* my stick broke? It was a stick, it broke. It happens.'

He laughed out. 'Yes, it does,' he said. 'It does happen. Especially if you saw through it a little with a knife beforehand.'

'What? What the fuck are you talking about?'

'You know very well what I am talking about, Rindu,' he said evenly, the laughter falling out of his voice. 'So I am a limited drummer, is it? I just know a couple of beats and a couple of rolls. I can't improvise and I can't pick up a beat just by listening to it.'

'I never said that,' I said.

'It's useless denying it, Rindu. All of IIT knows that it's because of you I couldn't become Instigate's drummer. You convinced Kartik not to take me, to take Darrell instead.'

The first thought that went through my mind was that Darrell was a much better drummer than Rocksurd. But even in that state of shock I realized that this simple fact would not get through to him. Sitting there in the mess, the logic of his revenge unfolded clearly in front of me. It left me sick to my stomach.

'I have always thought,' he was saying, 'if you want to fuck a guy, don't do it directly, do it with his own help. So I took your sticks and put a notch in the left one. I knew you would be too nervous to notice. That's why I was telling you to hit the snare harder. It was the last song.'

Back in my room as I examined the stick I saw that the stump did have a smooth cut about two millimetres deep at the point where the stick had snapped. I hadn't thought much of it when I had seen it at first, but now I realized that this was where the knife had done its work. The disbelief – and visceral fear – I felt at that moment stayed with me for a long time.

Sitting there across the table from Rocksurd I didn't know what to say. I couldn't ask him why, when or how; he had already told me. I couldn't ask for an apology, he clearly didn't think he owed me one. I couldn't beat him up, I didn't know how. I even thought of apologizing to him for what he thought I had done to him, but that would be admitting to a crime I hadn't committed.

'One Kumaon guy doing this to another Kumaon guy. It's shameful.' This was Maiti. 'In our time this would never have happened. The whole hostel would have come together to beat up the guy who did such a thing.'

His voice had a mournful rather than accusatory tone. For a second both Rocksurd and I thought that he was going to make good his threat but Maiti kept sitting there, breaking off brittle triangles of roti, dipping them in oily sabji and putting them into his mouth. Fratricide, his faraway expression seemed to say, was inevitable in this dark age. He looked like a powerless blind Dhritrashtra, alone in his palace, far from Kurukshetra, forced to listen to a blow by blow account of man killing man.

Kartik was drunk when he returned to the hostel that night.

'Hey Rindu!' he said, kicking his way into my room. 'What's up, dost? How are you?'

'Okay,' I said, not looking up from the book I was reading.

He came up to my bed and sat next to me. He put his arm around my shoulder. 'Come on, Rindu, tell me what's up?' he said, grinning broadly.

'Well,' I began, wondering how to explain what Rocksurd had told me. 'I was talking to Rocksurd and ...'

'You know what the judges said about Instigate?' he cut in. 'They said we were among the top three bands to not qualify. The top three, Rindu! Later this guy from Hindu College came and asked me if we want to perform in their college fest. Do you know how much they are paying? Ten thousand bucks! We can get a new bass with that, the college bass is a piece of junk.'

'Where had you disappeared to Kartik?' I asked him.

'Me?' he said. 'I was in Karakoram, just hanging out over there drinking some daaru.'

'Not just now,' I said. 'That night.'

'Which night?'

'At the rock prelims,' I said. 'Where were you while we were playing?'

'I don't know, must have been outside or something.'

'Why didn't the effects work?' I asked. 'There was no distortion.'

He started laughing. 'I heard about that,' he said. 'Master of Puppets with no distortion. That's funny.'

'Why didn't the effects work?' I persisted. 'I've heard you get distortion out of them before. I've heard it for hours and hours.'

'Come on, Rindu,' he said, patting me on the back like he was telling a child why he couldn't get more chocolate. 'I explained the whole thing to Pandit. Press the red button and then punch zero four six on the keypad. That's it, the left pedal will give you fundoo distortion.'

'You know what kind of guy he is, why didn't you just set it for him?'

He looked at me. I could see him realize that I was angry. He took his hand off my back. His eyes narrowed. 'It isn't my business,' he said, 'to take care of every charasi guitarist in Delhi. Where was his own distortion?'

Later Kaustabh was to tell me that Pandit's distortion, the one we had used in practice, had disappeared mysteriously a few days before the prelims. Pandit had said he'd lost it.

'I don't know,' I said. 'But you could have just set it up for him, it would have taken you five seconds to do it. It was our judges' choice song, Master of Puppets.'

'Big deal, yaar,' he said. 'Pandit's guitaring career has always been like this, one fuck-up after the other. He's changed bands at least ten times.'

'Those other bands didn't have me in them,' I said, quietly.

'Oh, poor Rindu,' Kartik said, smiling again. 'Has your drumming career been nipped in the bud?'

For the first time in all the years we had spent together I felt like hitting him.

'Fuck you!' I said.

'Come on, Rindu, there will be other bands,' he said. Both he and I knew that there wouldn't.

'It isn't just about me,' I said. 'What about Pandit? You have your engineering career, your flight to the States, your future. What about Pandit's future? Music is all he has. He needs the college fest performances, the rock show prizes, much more than you do.'

'That Pandit is a useless fellow,' he said.

'He's a much better musician than you,' I blurted out, regretting the words even as I formed them. And then, like vomit pouring involuntarily out of the stomach once the first bit has been forced: 'You have to work for hours to copy one solo correctly, he produces music out of nothing. Pandit is an artist, a musician. You're nothing but a fucking fraud.'

Kartik stood up and went to the door. I thought he was going to leave. Instead he shut it and turned around. 'Listen, Rindu,' he said. 'I am glad that bastard Pandit got fucked. He thinks he's such a great rocker, doesn't he? Well, he's nothing now. Nothing. He's just a fucked-up drug addict who borrows money and sells other people's things to feed his habit. And let me tell you, I knew he wouldn't be able to get distortion out of that box, he was too high. I didn't set it up for him on purpose, I disappeared on purpose. Let him make a fool of himself! Great rocker that he is, he doesn't need distortion to make him great. Let his huge talent carry him through.' He paused to take a breath, then he opened the door: 'Success is all about hard work, Rindu,' he said. 'It's all about busting your ass to get where you want to go. People like your good friend Pandit don't realize this.'

Even if there had been a response to this, I was too tired to come up with it.

'I am going down to the bus stop,' Kartik said. 'Come.'

I looked at him standing there framed in the doorway, neon light glinting off his spectacles, the night yellow with reflected streetlights behind him. My body felt weary, heavy.

'Okay,' I said, getting up and putting on my slippers. 'Let's go.'

A year and a half after I had left for Baltimore, I returned to Delhi for the first time. Three days into the trip I met Kaustabh in the Society.

'Arindam! When did you get here?'

I told him. He followed it up with the inevitable: 'When are you leaving?'

Kaustabh told me about how Pandit had been caught on the roof of one of the Society's buildings. In its next meeting the managing committee had decided that the roofs were to be kept locked at all times and only opened for maintainence work. Pandit had been to California. His sister lived there. The idea had been that he would go there and find a job.

'What about his job with BiTV?' I asked.

'There had never been any job in BiTV,' Kaustabh said. 'Some of his rocker friends worked there. They had told him, as a joke, that they would get him a job there. He would go there every day and they would keep telling him that they would talk to their bosses soon and get him the job. Behind his back they all laughed at him.'

'What happened in the US?' I asked.

'He came back in fifteen days. No one knows why.'

'That's strange,' I said. 'Is he around? I should meet him.'

'In case you do, Arindam,' he said, breaking into a smile, 'I told him that you saw him across the street in America but he disappeared before you could stop him.'

A few days later I ran into Pandit at the Society gate.

'Yaar, Arindam, why didn't you stop me, yaar? Kaustabh said you saw me across the road in America and you called out to me but I didn't hear you.'

I didn't say anything. Instead I asked him how his trip to the US had been.

'Yaar, Arindam, America is good for a holiday, but home is home. I didn't like it there, I decided to come back. But I had a really good trip. I had stocked up on a lot of stuff, because I thought it would be difficult to get it there. But then I was in the airport and I thought I might never come back to India so I got senti-like and decided to take one last hit, one last high in India, you understand, and I went to the bathroom and, you know ... I was really afraid that they'll catch me but nothing happened. I went to the lounge but the people there were all boring, chutiya types. So I went to the bar. I saw this guy sitting there. He was a big American guy, wearing a Stetson and all. And he had a guitar case with him. I thought, boss, this is my type of guy. So I went and sat next to him, ordered a drink. I asked him do you play, so he looked at me. I don't know why but he started talking to me. He was like some kind of professor or something. And he knows Prince, he has some connection in Prince's band, you know, the New Power Generation. So I told him I also play. And we talked about music and all. He showed me his guitar. It was a Fender, a really good one. In India, man, we only get those Calcutta Fenders, totally shitty sound. His guitar was something, yaar. A real Fender. On the flight I said that we should sit together and I told that woman, but he was in first class so she couldn't put me next to him. Too bad, but I met him at the airport on the other end. Those air-hostesses are so stupid, man. It was a totally non-smoking flight, even the bathrooms have smoke detectors. But I just lit one up under my blanket and took a quick puff. She came and sniffed around. I just lay there with my eyes closed, pretended to be asleep. But this guy, he was really great, yaar, he gave me his number and said, you want to meet Prince, you want to jam with the New Power Generation? You call me, okay? he said. So, I went and then one or two days just sat quiet with my sister and brother-in-law, then I called this fellow and I said, do you remember me and he said, of course. He had come to India to meet his spiritual guru. All these rockers, man, they all have spiritual gurus in India. So, then I went and I jammed with the New Power Generation. That Barbarella, she is a great guitarist. We jammed and we jammed. She showed me some cool riffs. I also showed some of my stuff. For one hour we jammed.'

'Wow, Pandit,' I cut in. 'You jammed with the New Power Generation! That's really great. Did you meet Prince?'

'Yeah. I didn't jam with him but I met him. That guy is really on his own trip man.'

'Why did you come back, Pandit?'

'Yaar, it was really difficult to get stuff there. And my sister wanted me to get a job, and my brother-in-law was very strict. And, yaar, home is home after all, isn't it? I stayed for fifteen days and then I told them, I'm going back. Although the New Power Generation guys had said come back whenever you want, but I thought, forget it, man. There, in the US, everyone is a good guitarist. They start playing when they are children, man. So many of them. It's difficult for someone like me to make it there. I was ready to struggle, man, I can do it. But my brother-in-law wanted me to get a job. So I told them I am going home. This place is fine for a holiday but home is home...'

He paused to catch his breath. Then he went on.

'But Arindam, yaar, Kaustabh told me that you saw me across the street. If you had stopped me my plans might have changed, man. It could have been different. Why didn't you stop me, man?'

I didn't have the heart to tell him that I lived on the East Coast. I had never been on any side of any street in California.

'I called to you, Pandit. But you didn't hear me,' I said.

Surfing the Internet once I came across a listing of the members of the New Power Generation. There was a Barbarella. Tommy Barbarella. From what I gathered, he was a man. And he played the keyboards.

6

Bandhu

PRATAP GRABBED HOLD OF ME BY THE WAIST AND TURNED ME around. 'Let's go to Sassi,' he said, putting his head into my back and propelling me out of the hostel door.

It was lunchtime, near the end of my first year at IIT. I had just returned from a long chemistry lab. 'Behnchod!' I shouted. 'Let go of me!'

I said the last part in English. He stopped, then straightened and looked at me quizzically. 'Abbé, did you mind that?' he said in Hindi, using the word 'mind'.

I couldn't say I hadn't because I wouldn't have spoken in English if I hadn't. It was too early in my stay at IIT to be able to articulate spontaneous anger in Hindi. Swearing in Hindi was not a problem, I could do it as well as anyone else, but it would be some time before I could argue or rage in that language.

'Sorry, yaar,' I said, putting my arm around Pratap. His arm snaked around my waist and his hand went into my left pocket, another one of those things it was taking me time to get used to, and we set off towards Sassi's dhaba.

Pratap's full name was Pratap Singh Thakur. Anyone else with that name would have spent his four years at IIT being called PST. But there was something about Pratap which seemed to preclude this possibility. It wasn't his superb physique, or his indomitable athleticism or even his easygoing nature. It might have been the subliminal sexual charge that adhered to him – the supreme ease with which he seemed to inhabit his body – that made it impossible to diminish him in any way. Pratap could do things that other people wouldn't think of doing. But, more than that, he could make people do things they wouldn't normally dream of doing. JP, his roommate in the first year, once said that there wasn't a single guy in the hostel whose penis Pratap hadn't seen. He was probably right.

Pratap had come in to IIT under the Scheduled Tribe quota. His name had sounded unequivocally upper caste to me but I had thought it better not to point that out when we were introduced. I heard somewhere that lower caste people sometimes did that, take on upper caste names, to hide their original caste. While we were together at IIT, I never brought it up, simply believing the rumour that had floated by me in the course of an otherwise forgotten conversation.

The pavement outside Sassi's stall was lined with people from our hostel. The hostel's kitchen was clearly having an off day, as it often did. We ducked under the canvas awning. A large black clunker of a phone instrument sat there amongst dirty glass jars containing biscuits of uncertain vintage. Inside stood Sassi – no one I knew had ever directly asked him if that was indeed his own name – frying an omelette on one flat pan and a thick paratha on the other. He turned his head slightly towards us.

'One anda paratha,' I said.

'One butter paratha and one anda paratha,' said Pratap.

Sassi nodded slightly and turned back to his frying. A small boy, one of the many Chotus in Sassi's employ, pushed past me and went in. He picked up a stainless steel glass and dipped it into a large pot. When it emerged, the glass had a whitish liquid in it. On top of it floated jagged little icebergs. 'Oh yes,' said Pratap, pointing at the pot. 'One shikanji.'

We took our places by the side of the road on the whitewashed blocks of concrete lining the verge. Early afternoon traffic rolled down Outer Ring Road and came to a halt in front of us at the Africa Avenue junction. Occasionally the crossing would get so crowded that a scooterwallah would ask us to remove our feet so he could squeeze by a car. We obliged without rancour. Our parathas and eggs and butter and tea and shikanji came and were consumed. The plates were collected by a Chotu who dutifully dunked them in an aluminium bucket of scummy water.

Forty-five minutes later the others began to leave for their one o'clock classes. Pratap and I both had a free slot from one to two so we stayed. TK, also from my hostel and in my department, appeared at the cigarette stall, just a box with a man sitting behind it, for his post-lunch fix of gutka. We waved him over.

'This guy is really good,' he said, sitting down next to me. We waited for an elaboration of this statement as he threw his head back, opened his mouth wide and poured the contents of the small sachet in. We sat in silence as he masticated, then tucked the chewed up gutka against his cheek.

'Which guy?' I asked, unable to take the suspense any longer.

'Thishpaanvaava.'

'This paanwallah?'

'Yeff.'

'Why?'

He gave me an annoyed look. I could see his tongue moving inside his mouth, stirring through the paste of saliva and gutka. Finally, after a few vigorous rictal exertions, he turned away from us and spat a stream of liquid into the gutter between the asphalt and the concrete. A small cloud of dust flew up at the impact.

'He gives me all the new brands of gutka to try. Today he gave me this one, it's called Power Gutka,' he said, holding up the sachet. Then suddenly he thought of something and pumped both his fists into the air in the manner of the cartoon He-Man and yelled out in a loud voice: 'By the power of Greyskull! I have the power.'

TK was laughing at this joke much after Pratap and I had stopped. 'TK,' I said, finally. 'Shut up. I need to talk to you guys about something.'

'So talk na,' he said. 'I'm listening.'

'I am thinking of standing for class convenor,' I said.

They both looked puzzled. The hostel elections, all the excitement of door-to-door campaigning and sleepless nights of feverish speculation, had finished a month ago. It seemed a little late for me to be wanting to stand for a post.

'What's class convenor?' asked Pratap.

'It's actually short for Class Committee Convenor. It's the guy who calls a meeting of the class committee in which two representatives from every tutorial group discuss their problems with all their professors. Each department has to have a class convenor.'

'But why do you want to be class monitor?' TK asked.

It wasn't a post with a budget, so it wasn't money I was interested in. The job itself was a hassle, running after professors to set up meeting times. But there was the attraction of being the person my classmates would come to if they had any academic issues. It was the idea of representing them to the department, to the Institute, which had caught my imagination. But I went with my prepared answer instead.

'See, the thing is that the Academic Interaction Council General Secretary is elected by class convenors so if our hostel gets a lot of convenors elected then one of our guys can be AIC G-Sec. That will mean our hostel organizes Tryst next year.'

'Cool, Rindu,' said TK slapping me on the back. 'Good idea.'

'But I need your help. You have to convince guys from other hostels to vote for me.'

TK jumped onto his feet. His fist rent the air. 'Vote for Rindu! If you want to save the nation, Rindu is the only solution! Rindu struggle on for truth, we are by your side!' Then suddenly, in the same loud voice: 'Oh fuck, look at the girl!'

We turned to see a school bus drawing up to the intersection. The girl TK was talking about sat at the window just behind the rear door. She had long straight hair, sharp features and bright black eyes. I realized with a shock that the bus was from my old school. The girl looked familiar as well, but only vaguely. Two semesters at IIT had more or less filed the sharp edge off my memories of school.

TK put his fingers into his mouth and let out a piercing whistle. I turned away disconcerted, hoping she hadn't recognized me. This was a scene I had seen many times, three guys standing by the street ogling a girl sitting in a school bus. The difference was that the other times I had been sitting inside the bus looking out.

'Look, look, Rindu,' said TK. 'She's sexy.'

I turned back to see that the girl, far from being daunted by the situation was looking straight back at us. But it wasn't the spindly pimply TK she was looking at, nor was it my plump bespectacled figure she was staring at. She was looking straight at Pratap.

'She's looking at you, Pratap,' sang TK, gleefully. 'She's giving you line.'

The girl's right hand came into view at the window. She curled in all her fingers except one. She thrust her middle finger upwards, then put it in her mouth.

'Behnchod!' said Pratap.

The signal changed and the bus carried away the sound of her derisive laughter with it.

Pratap gave his crotch an absent rub and readjusted his sitting position.

TK let out a loud breath. 'I'm going to get a cigarette. More school buses must be coming. Let me put on a little style.'

'Fuck man,' I said to Pratap. 'That chick was something.'

He shook it off. 'Forget it, yaar,' he said. 'What were you saying about that class monitor thing?'

'Convenor,' I said. 'Nothing, I just need your help. Tell people to vote for me, just that kind of stuff.'

I could see he was thinking hard about the matter. Suddenly a thought occurred to him. He made as if to speak, then stopped. An embarrassed look came over his face. He turned as if searching for something. I saw his eyes fix on TK standing at the cigarette stall. His eyes flickered towards me for a split second then went back to TK. When he spoke his voice was low, but he sounded more abashed than conspiratorial: 'Don't worry about the SC ST vote,' he said. 'I'll get you that.'

It was a late April afternoon in my last year at IIT. In two weeks' time I would have to move out of the hostel for the final time. I went from one floor to the other, one wing to the next. I grazed the wall with my hand as I walked, gently exfoliating its whitewashed skin.

It was almost four thirty when I finally found myself down near the carrom room. It was empty. I turned to see if there was anyone in sight. Through the concrete screen wall that ran from the door of the common room to the stairwell I saw Meena entering the hostel. 'Meena,' I bellowed. 'Meeeeeen*aaaa*!'

He came into the courtyard looking puzzled.

'Carrom, Meena?' I shouted.

'Not now, yaar,' he said, walking up to me.

'One last time, Meena,' I said, the senti angle had been working well in these last days.

He grimaced, then shrugged his shoulders. I ran into the carrom room, started getting the coins out of the pockets and sprinkling powder on the board. He came and sat across from me, putting down the spiral-bound book he was carrying.

I had met Girdhari Lal Meena outside the carrom room the day after the ragging period ended in my first year. Freshers weren't allowed in for the first three weeks. It was only after the elaborate rituals of Freshers' Night were completed that we were free to be full members of the hostel with access to the common room and the carrom room.

There had been four seniors playing carrom my first time in there. I stood and waited for their game to finish. When the last coin was pocketed, they simply reset the board and continued playing as if I didn't exist. When that board finished and they began to get the coins out of the pockets, I spoke up hesitantly. 'Can I play?'

'Where's your partner?'

'Partner?'

They laughed. One of them took the break and the game started again.

'What partner?' I asked.

'It's the rule,' one of them said. 'If you have a partner, the two of you are entitled to play. If you don't, you have no rights. These are the carrom room rules.'

The carrom room rules were not written down anywhere but everyone in the hostel learned them sooner or later. In all my time in the hostel I never saw anyone fighting to jump the queue. They tried to slime and prevaricate to get to play – that was second nature to most of us at IIT – but if they were caught at it they withdrew gracefully and took their place in line.

I walked out of the room, walking straight into Girdhari Lal Meena.

He was a short guy with the sort of complexion TV announcements for missing persons would call wheatish. He always wore a synthetic short-sleeved shirt, never T-shirts, on brown pants, never jeans. His hair was always oiled and combed down flat across his head. I thought about Meena years later, when, studying in the US, I was the one dressed unlike everyone else, forced to decide whether I wanted to change my dress, or get my hair cropped and gelled, or whether I bore some kind of loyalty to the style I had adopted as the accepted uniform of college Delhi. Meena too must have had to make a similar decision.

He spoke little. His face reflected an inner calm, admixed, in the early days, with a certain quizzicality. With time the curiosity passed. His expression now seemed to say, like Ghalib, that the world was a children's toy to his eyes. In Delhi, far from his village, subdivision and district, he watched indulgently as this skit of urban life was played morning and night.

There were times, though, when his mask would drop. It would happen if we had beaten some of the hostel's established carrom gods or if we came back from being many coins down and won the game. But most often it would happen when he attempted a shot that required great precision of judgement and execution, and pulled it off. He would look up at me, for a second or two, and he would smile a gloriously mischievous smile.

Most teams formed at the carrom room were temporary ones. You found someone in the common room or the mess and you dragged him along with you. But some teams lasted. Those people searched out their favourite partners and only played with them. If the other guy left for some reason, his partner would play on for a while but his form would wane till he too would quit and spend the rest of his free time lounging in the common room. It was like in cricket when after a long partnership one batsman would get out, the other would often follow. 'A loss of concentration' would be the curt diagnosis. To elaborate any further would be to admit that that man was missing his partner.

Meena and I became a longstanding team. As soon as I finished lunch I would find him and we would go to the carrom room. After dinner he would come and get me. We spent hours in the carrom room every single day through our first semester, except on the weekends when I went home. I knew his strengths, he knew my preferences. We rarely talked while we played, a nod or look was generally enough to convey whatever was required. He never stopped me from taking a risky or difficult shot, I think we both realized that the delight of pulling off a piece of skill was much more valuable than winning a game. And it was perhaps because winning wasn't important that we won so often.

I knew Meena was in IIT on the Scheduled Tribe quota. I had learned in my short stay at IIT that his surname was a caste name associated with people who were eligible for reservations. But this was not something he and I talked about.

At IIT it seemed, like in the carrom room, the accepted rule was it wasn't who you were but what you could do that mattered. This rule was not just unwritten, it was unspoken as well. But sometimes it was not observed very closely. There had been a time during the ragging when three seniors had been interrogating me in one of their rooms.

'Does your sister have a boyfriend?'

'Yes, sir.'

'Does the boyfriend fuck your sister?'

'I don't know, sir.'

'What if he comes and says, I am going to fuck your sister?'

It was a standard line of questioning. At the point where your sister was being fucked you were supposed to break down and cry. I decided to go a different way.

'It's up to her, sir.'

They were shocked, and amused.

'You must be a shadda,' one of them said casually. 'They're the only ones who are so shameless.'

Through that first year of hectic carrom playing, Meena and I spent many hours together every day without mentioning caste. I sometimes thought about it on my own, feeling like I was doing something progressive and laudable by spending so much time with a person whose shadow my ancestors would have avoided. It was much later that I realized that I was the only one who called him Meena. Pratap and the others always called him Girdhari.

My carrom addiction petered out after the first year. And with it the time I spent with Meena came to an end. We still played together occasionally but no more than once or twice a semester. I had moved on to other things: drumming, debating, quizzing. I met him sometimes in the mess but there wasn't much to say. But two weeks away from our last day in the hostel, almost by magic, he appeared just when I was remembering our time together in the first year.

I set the coins for him to break, knocked the striker against the far side of the board a couple of times and passed it to him. He set it down and took strike. The afternoon sun was streaming through the window. It hit the cellophane cover of the spiral-bound thing he had been carrying and shone into my eyes. Picking it up, I turned it around. The title said 'Bandhu Batch of 1996'.

'Is this your department yearbook?' I asked. I knew the hostel yearbook wasn't done yet.

He looked at it then looked up at me. 'No,' he said.

I flipped open the book. It was like any of the other yearbooks produced at IIT, not much more than a set of photocopied pages spiral bound between cardboard covers. Every page had a photo and write-up. I turned the pages one by one. There were people from different departments, different hostels. There were a couple of girls as well. I knew most of them, they were all from my year.

'This is our SC ST yearbook,' he said evenly.

'The Bandhu Batch of 96,' I said, more to myself than to him. It was a phrase I had never heard before: bandhu batch.

'That's what we call it.'

Pratap was in there. Meena was in there. Guys I had done pracs with, and chatted with for hours in the mess, and studied with, and copied homework from, and shown exams to, and been ragged with, and joked and laughed with, were in there. Surprise gave way to a heavy feeling of sadness. An image of a tubelit hostel room full of all these people flitted through my head. I had always identified them in the ways IIT had taught me: this guy was from Nilgiri hostel, that guy was a five-pointer, the other fellow was from Chemical, such and such girl was, well, a girl. And here was evidence of this secret society they had formed, to which I wasn't invited, that no one had told me about.

'Rindu,' said Meena. 'Rindu, it's your turn.'

I took the striker in my hand and looked down at the coins on the board. For a moment my mind went totally blank.

'Which one am I?' I asked. 'Black or white?'

I spotted Maiti talking to Raman near the door of the mess. JP was standing with them.

Raman, the guy standing for AIC G-Sec from our hostel, was in his third year. He had formed a core group to ensure that the convenor elections were well managed. The higher the number of convenors elected from our hostel, the less he would have to bargain with other hostels. Maiti had eagerly settled into the role of kingmaker. My class, first year Computer Science, was part of his brief. He was the one who had told me about the whole convenor thing.

Maiti was a Bengali from Kanpur. He failed his classes with unfailing regularity, rode a three hundred CC monster of a Yezdi and chewed paan in an inexplicably anglicized way. He was physically large, and he moved through the hostel deliberately, commanding respect from his peers, evoking fear in his juniors.

To my astonishment I found him standing outside my door one day. 'Do you want to be class convenor?' he had said brusquely in English.

Maiti hadn't ragged me much but he must have known that I was considered to be an 'Inglis Boy'. I had battled this charge resolutely, swearing continuously in Hindi and saying 'behnchod' with three different regional inflections. This was not enough. The challenge had been posed in the form of a tattered old book of smutty Mast Ram stories. I translated a whole page, making mistakes, hesitating. It was good enough. I would remain an Inglis Boy, but an acceptable one, much like Maiti who usually spoke Hindi but was obviously very fluent in English. Maiti was the sort of guy I could become in time. Perhaps this was why he had singled me out.

Maiti and Raman finished talking. JP trailing behind him, Maiti walked into the mess and started scanning the tables looking for someone. His eye settled on me. He strode across to where I sat.

'Finished?' he asked.

'Yes,' I said.

As I washed my hands I wondered why JP was with him. JP was my classmate, one of the toppers of my class after the first semester. He was acknowledged by all to be extremely intelligent and was arrogant in a feudal sort of way, graciously haughty. Unlike most other freshers he wore shirts with elaborate floral patterns and carried himself in a stylish, effeminate manner. He was from Jaipur.

Chewing on a mouthful of saunf I made my way outside the hostel. Maiti was sitting on a scooter. JP stood beside him, looking pensive. 'Abhishek wants to stand for convenor,' Maiti said. Abhishek was JP's given name.

'Oh.'

We stood in silence for a while. I looked at JP. He was looking down. I could feel Maiti's eyes on me.

'Well?' said Maiti finally.

Since Maiti had explained what the class convenor did, I had increasingly become interested in getting the job. Arguing with the head of the department for some extremely righteous cause, maybe even leading my class in a mass bunk to protest some unfairness done to one of us, had become a recurring daydream. I would get up and declare: 'What happens to the one, happens to us all!' And I would storm out of the room.

Everyone would follow. The cruel professor would be left standing in an empty classroom.

'I told Abhishek that you wanted to stand. And you have already started campaigning,' Maiti said. 'But ...'

He paused after the but. I looked up. He looked at me unflinchingly. 'Abhishek has a much better CGPA than you. He's a better candidate.'

That was the conventional wisdom about class convenor candidates, toppers were supposed to be better suited. Professors listened to them. A seven-pointer like me had no credibility.

'What has CGPA got to do with?' I found myself saying. The conversation so far had been conducted in Hindi. But in that moment, when I could see my small ambition slipping away, I involuntarily switched to English. 'I can articulate their problems better than anyone else can.'

My heart was racing. I was transported back to school, standing up on the podium debating euthanasia or whether America should rule the world, in front of an audience of two hundred. This was an audience of just two, but this time it really mattered. 'I understand the way the system works, I understand the pressures both students and professors are under, I can do this job better than anyone else.'

Maiti gave me a sympathetic look, like an executioner might give a condemned man. 'Arindam,' he said, 'the AIC G-Secship must come to Kumaon. That's our aim. We have to put up the guy who is most likely to get elected.'

Anger surged through me. Why did JP deserve to get this job? He didn't know anything about what it meant. I was the guy who made friends with guys from all hostels and passed funny notes around class while JP sucked up the lecture and cracked his exams. He had a nine-point CG and sat in the front benches while I was a seven-pointer sitting in the last row with all the down-and-outs. I couldn't let him get away with this.

'Okay, so it's decided then,' said Maiti, getting off the scooter.

'One sec,' I said.

'What?'

'All the SC ST guys will vote for me.'

Maiti halted in mid-stride. JP's head swivelled towards me in surprise.

'Are you sure?' Maiti asked.

'Yes,' I said. 'I hang out with them in class. I know them all very well. All of them, from all hostels.'

'Abhishek?' said Maiti.

'They're all friends,' JP said weakly. He looked beaten.

'I think,' said Maiti, slowly, turning to address JP, 'we'll let Arindam stand for election this time. What do you think, Abhishek?'

7

Three Bistable Partitions

NIZAMUDDIN BRIDGE WAS JAMMED THE DAY THEY DECLARED THE IIT result, a truck had overturned. Cars were backed up almost till the NOIDA crossing. We drove into the jam and waited. I must have had the window rolled down because it was June, but later, whenever I thought about that trip from Mayur Vihar to IIT, I would always think of myself sitting inside a sealed box of a car, looking out over the fields between Mayur Vihar and the river like I was seeing them for the first time. Those tomato fields, that stud farm, those lines of eucalyptus, these scattered clumps of sugarcane had always soothed with their familiarity, they would do so again in the future. But on that journey they lay outside the car, burning listlessly in the afternoon sun while I shivered inside. We spent half an hour stuck on the bridge, three times as long as it normally took in crossing the river.

I didn't think of all the effort I had put in, studying for the exam, or of all the bus rides to coaching classes, or of all the hours spent discussing problems with classmates and friends; all of that didn't seem like something I had done in anticipation of this day. Studying for the entrance exam had been my life for the last two years, the only way I had known how to live my life for those two years. In the car, on the way to the culmination of my entire school life, I didn't think of the past or the future. I thought only of the tightness in the pit of my stomach.

The dirty stucco of IIT shone dully in the sun the first time I saw it the strange parabola of the Convocation Hall and the large rectangular block of the main building juxtaposed looked like a massive oceanliner about to hit an iceberg. My mother parked some way from what I was to later learn was called the wind tunnel, the passageway through the main building where the results had been put up.

There were a lot of people there, almost all boys, almost all my age. From the car I could see them, in groups, yelling, backslapping, crying. There were a few girls around, chaperoned by aunties and uncles, looking lost and afraid.

'I'll take a look and be back,' I told my mother.

'Should I come with you?' she asked.

'That's okay.'

Fishing the piece of paper with my roll number on it out of my pocket as I went, I approached the huddle of eager bodies. I knew the number by heart, I had since the day it had come to me in the mail, but I took the piece of paper out anyway. Entering the crowd, I slowly moved forward till I could make out the small type that filled the sheets of paper up on the wall. This moment would flit through my memory like a dream again and again for years to come: the press of people on either side, felt not seen; the concrete column; the sheets of paper pasted crudely on it; the neat rows of printed numerals. I didn't put my finger to the paper, I didn't have to scan the pages for my number. My eyes just focused and my roll number was there. I looked past it. There were four digits inside parentheses. The first two were zeros, then there was a six and finally a two.

Many people asked me, in the days that followed, in the years I spent at IIT, even after, how I felt at that moment, at the moment when I realized that I had made the top hundred, when I realized that of the two hundred thousand of my peers from around the country who had taken that exam only sixty-one had scored higher. I never told them that the first thought that ran through my mind was: there's been a mistake.

I stepped out of the crush. I saw Rohit there, a friend from school. He was grinning from ear to ear. 'I've done it, Chatterjee. I've made it. Four forty-seven. Just go and check once, will you? I can't believe I have actually cracked it.'

I went back with his roll number in hand and checked. It was there. 'It's there. Four forty-seven.'

He hugged me and, still grinning, walked away. Then turned back and asked: 'And you?'

'Sixty-two,' I said.

He froze for a second, then he put up both his hands in a double high-five motion. 'Fucking crack, man! Top hundred! You cracked it Chatterjee, you're a fucking god, man!'

I walked back to the car. My mother was standing outside it. She saw my face and said, 'It doesn't matter. You'll get in somewhere else.'

'No, Ma. I got in.'

'It doesn't matter if you got a bad rank,' she said.

'I came in sixty-second.'

She hugged me. We went back to the notice board, her arm wrapped tightly around my shoulder. I felt like crying.

On the way back to Mayur Vihar we stopped at a friend's place on the way. We wanted to call my father and give him the news.

'Hello, Papa,' I said as he picked up the phone.

'Congratulations,' he said, his voice taking on the slightly embarassed tone it did whenever a display of emotion was called for.

'How did you know?' I asked.

'One of the boys from your school called to congratulate you. He told me.'

Most of my friends ended up going to DU and studying Economics or Physics or History, while I went to IIT and did Computer Science. They spent their next three years travelling home in U-specials, chatting with each other in English, growing their hair long, acquiring girlfriends and making plans to study at Oxford or Cambridge, while I lived in the hostel and talked to my exclusively male friends in Hindi and got five-rupee haircuts at the campus barbershop.

In the four years I spent at IIT and even in the time after, I often thought I should have gone to DU instead, I should have stayed in a world I recognized, in a world which recognized me. But there was a part of me that knew even then that for people like me safe harbours were an illusion; you could stay but you would inevitably become the only one left behind, lonely and dissatisfied.

Sheikhu's hand shot up. No other followed it.

'Sir, delta is always upper-bounded by one over epsilon,' he said.

'Very good, very good,' said Professor Dhar. 'This boy is very clever, is it not?'

'Yes, sir,' came a voice from the other end of the lecture theatre. 'Very clever.' This was followed by a tunelessly sung line in Hindi: 'The picture Sheikhu draws, no one can fathom.'

A chorus took up the refrain: 'Shiekhu thinks and thinks and thinks.'

'What is this? Hey, you boys, why are you singing? This is a class, is it not?' spluttered a nonplussed Dhar.

When Rakesh Goel, now known as Sheikhu, was being ragged in the hostel, some senior, probably a new convert to the creed of the cryptic crossword, had decided that Shaker was a better name for him than Rakesh. This new name had stirred a memory in another senior's mind, the memory of an old television serial on Doordarshan. The lead character was a boy who lived in a village and was very interested in science and experimentation. This boy, Lekhu, had a social conscience as well as a scientific temper, using his ingenious contraptions to make life better for his fellow villagers. Whenever he was faced with a problem he would, as the theme song went, 'think and think and think' and then he would draw a picture which would depict the solution to the problem, a solution usually based on some simple scientific principle. He would show it to his parents who would not be able to 'fathom' it. At this point he would explain his idea and, I later imagined, a collective gasp of astonishment would escape all the twelve-year-old boys who sat in front of their televisions late on a Sunday morning, cheering him on.

To a lesser or greater degree all of us who went to IIT were Lekhus in our own small corner of the world, in our school or colony. But Rakesh had been known in Delhi, or, more precisely, the 'serious' kids of the public schools of Delhi had known that there was a fellow called Rakesh Goel who was very likely the most intelligent person in our batch of school-leaving graduates, at least on the engineering side of the Science stream. He had, of course, been selected for the Junior Science Talent Search scholarship and the more prestigious National Talent Search scholarship. He had made it to the final stage of the Indian National Maths Olympiad, the camp of thirty or so from which the team for the International Maths Olympiad was selected. He had been expected to get a very high rank in the IIT exam and he had delivered, getting the highest rank in the Delhi zone. The name Sheikhu, a combination of Lekhu and Shaker, came to him in a roundabout way but it was the right one. Sheikhu was Delhi's Lekhu.

He took Computer Science in Delhi. Computer Science was accepted as the top of the IIT food chain; if you could get it, you took it. That was why I had taken it. For someone as highly ranked as Sheikhu, opting for any other branch would have been unthinkable. He could have gone to Kanpur or Madras. Even Bombay was supposed to be better for Computer Science. But he chose Delhi for the same reason that I chose Delhi, I guessed later, because he lived there. In that first semester there was no doubt in my classmates' minds, or mine for that matter, that he would have impressed the smartest of the Kanpur people, or the Madras or Bombay guys, had he chosen to go there. He certainly dazzled us in the hardcore mathematical classes that we Computer Science people had to take.

I watched from the last bench as he fought front row battles over the arcana of analysis and functional programming. I was too sleepy from staying up night after night playing carrom, too concerned about all the homeworks I had to submit, too absorbed in the lovely sprawling views of the city that I had out of the windows of the lecture rooms high up in the main building, too excited at meeting people the like of whom I had never met before, to be able to compete with Sheikhu. I watched his fellow frontbenchers marvel at him and envy his quickness, and agreed vehemently when people said that Sheikhu was topper material. It was the first semester, the transcript was still a blank page, but everyone accepted that he was a frontrunner in the race to be the frontrunner of our class.

The grades when they came, in a tumble of elation or disappointment or just plain relief for most of us, must have been a shock for Sheikhu. He hadn't done bad by most standards, his cumulative grade point average was just less than eight on a scale of ten, but the competition in our class was much harder than in the others. His departmental rank was in the twenties in a class of forty-five. Just four months into IIT we had learned that those two numbers, your CG and your DR, defined who you were, they were branded onto you like the owner's marks were branded onto the cattle that often wandered into the campus from the hostel gate. Sheikhu had been a potential naukki, nine-pointer, but his grades made him a satti, seven-pointer. And in the Computer Science department a satti was not to be taken seriously academically; not by his classmates or people in other departments or even by his professors; not in his first year, not in his final year, not years later when he might have a job, a wife or even his own company. At least that's what it felt like then. I was a satti too, after the first semester.

I didn't know Sheikhu well at the time and later, when we became good friends, I never brought it up because I always felt it must have been a humbling experience for him. Because of my timidity, or oversensitivity, I didn't try to find out how he himself felt about it. But I did know how I felt about his situation. In the first few weeks of the second semester every now and then someone would mention his low DR in a hushed tone, like they were talking about a chief minister losing an assembly election. It always led to an awkward silence. There was a sobering sense that we all walked precariously close to the edge of a very high cliff of expectations: our friends', our family's, our own. We were all scared of falling off the cliff the way Sheikhu had fallen.

It could have been the end of Sheikhu's academic aspirations at IIT. He could have withdrawn into himself as some did, or into music or sports or alcohol like some others. He could have started reading all the newspapers and magazines that came to the common room in preparation for the civil services exam. He could have latched onto one of the two or three religious cults that operated on campus and disappeared from view, waking at four in the morning for a cold bath and prayer, sleeping at eight.

Sheikhu didn't go down any of these roads.

Some years after I graduated from IIT I ran into one of my classmates from school, Bose. He had gone to IIT Kanpur after school so we didn't have too many friends in common any more. I was struggling for conversation when I remembered that Bose had been selected for the Maths Olympiad camp along with Sheikhu. They had gone to TIFR in Bombay, where they had been coached intensively for a few weeks and then tested to determine which three people would represent India in the International Maths Olympiad.

'Do you remember a guy called Rakesh Goel from the Olympiad camp?'

'Rakesh Goel. Ya ya, he went to IIT D, right? Where is he now?'

'He's working in Bombay.'

'Ya, I remember him well,' said Bose. 'He was a sharp guy.'

'Yes, Sheikhu – we called him Sheikhu at D – is really intelligent,' I said.

'But at that camp, man, it was no use.'

'What do you mean, Bose?'

'See there was this one guy, Venkat, you know, the guy who was the topper in JEE, he just impressed all the profs totally. The prof would ask a question and before you can say anything Venkat will raise his hand, even if he has half an idea in his head. He wasn't very much smarter than the other people there, but once someone starts talking everyone else just relaxes, right, and then he would just work it out and the profs would think he was very smart. It was really difficult competing with him.'

'What does that have to do with Sheikhu?' I asked.

'Your Sheikhu was really determined to get the better of Venkat. He would try to contradict what Venkat said, he would try and answer before Venkat could get his hand up, he would waste his time in exams attempting the hardest problems first. You could tell that he wanted to show us that he was better than Venkat. I tell you, Arindam, it was simply not possible to be better than Venkat. I accepted this. I gave up. I decided, let me just have a good time, learn some new things. But not Rakesh. He just fought and fought and fought.'

Sridhar Kanitkar stood chalk in hand staring at the blackboard. He shook his head in irritation. A fine spray of sweat rose from his curly hair as it bounced on the nape of his neck. He stepped across to where he had kept his gym bag, the handle of a squash racket sticking out of one end. He took out a towel and wiped his neck, grimacing as he walked back to the board. He put the chalk to the board and wrote an equation, then he crossed it out and looked at it, his back to the class, his hairy muscular arms akimbo, his hands bunched into fists resting on his hips. Finally he tossed the piece of chalk into the gutter and stepped off the little platform in front of the board. 'I am not getting the big idea,' he said. 'Come back on Tuesday.'

A murmur ran through the class. It was more than the usual buzz of bottled-in conversations, the jostling and shutting of books that usually erupted once a class had been declared over. There was a frisson of excitement at the little performance we had just witnessed.

Ten minutes earlier, Kanitkar had walked into the room, five minutes late for class, wearing white shorts and a T-shirt. He was sweating profusely. It was the first time I had seen him, or any other professor at IIT, come into class after a game of squash. Our seniors had told us that this might happen. He would come into class straight from the courts. It had seemed unbelievably glamorous at the time. And now, here he was, shod in sneakers, his stocky but sinewy legs in full view. To his colleagues he must have seemed youthful and vigorous, but at that time, to me, he appeared very grown up, very much what a man should be.

If any other professor had said that he couldn't continue the class because he hadn't understood the material, he would have been a laughing-stock for the rest of his career. But Kanitkar was the man who had shown how to find a three bistable partition in general graph topologies.

'In general graphs, man, that's the big deal. It's obvious for planar graphs. But for general graphs nothing was known till 1983, when Kanitkar and Lovász gave an n squared time Algorithm.'

Three bistability was an old and legendary problem. I had heard about it in school although I didn't know at the time what it meant. When, in my second year, I had learned enough to understand what the problem was, I began to see the magnitude of Kanitkar's achievment. The proof for planar graphs was based on an observation of Euler, the inventor of graph theory, who had also given a construction that could be used to find a four bistable partition in a general graph.

The first time someone had pointed Kanitkar out to me I had visualized him chatting and laughing with the legendary Lovász whose strange East European name alone was enough to imply a massive reputation. I thought of the portrait of Euler I had seen, a smudged angular profile in a poorly produced copy of *Science Today*, and I saw a direct line of connection crossing two centuries between him and this very real man who seemed to fill the whitewashed corridors of the Computer Science department with his confidence.

Many of our other professors had PhDs from famous universities abroad, but Kanitkar was obviously the coolest of them all. He strode the halls, they slouched when they walked, even the younger ones. He played squash and went jogging, they went to Lucky restaurant for their afternoon tea, smoked cigarettes and chatted.

We instinctively grasped that Kanitkar was not hemmed in by India and by IIT the way his colleagues were. He was fair-complexioned and spoke with an American accent. He wore sweatshirts and Nike shoes but was also known to love Hindustani classical music. He had been lured to IIT with an offer of full professorship, the story went, otherwise he would never have left America.

It was in the first semester of our third year that we finally got to take a class with him. He taught Algorithms, acknowledged as the toughest of all the theory classes we were required to take. Although it was a gruelling regimen of lectures, three a week, and problem sets, not different from any of the other four credit classes we were taking, it seemed like we were sailing in a different boat here. Captained by the internationally renowned Kanitkar, we were exploring the ocean of big ideas.

And ideas mattered more than mere knowledge, of this we were fairly certain. There were classes in which learning by rote was the only challenge. Doing well in such a class was not considered a great achievement. In fact, there were people like Neeraj who made it a point to do badly in such classes. But to do well in classes that required conceptual clarity, a funda class, was what marked you as smart and led people to say that you had clear fundas. And if you could do well in a funda class without having studied much, then you were in a league of your own. And no class was as much of a funda class as Algorithms taught by Kanitkar.

There used to be two sets of minor exams every semester, partitioning it into three neat chunks of five weeks each. As the first minor approached in that first semester of the third year, I felt a growing anxiety about the Algorithms class. As usual I had missed a lecture or two and had lost the thread of what was being taught. I sat through the classes blankly, copied the homeworks, and just hoped that I would be able to get into the material when the exams came around. It was my fifth semester and I knew that it could go either way. I had almost never followed a course week by week, always waiting for the exams to come around before I got into it in earnest. Sometimes I crashed and burned, sometimes I did okay. Like most others, I kept my head above water.

But this was Algorithms. I liked what I understood of it. Sometimes when I followed along in class I could solve things in my head before Kanitkar had even written down the question completely. Once or twice I had even answered one of his questions before anyone else could raise his hand. But all this had only made me more anxious. Perhaps in those weeks before the first minor I had a premonition that this exam would change my life.

There's a day left to the minors. Just one day. The hostel is noisy. Every floor is humming with activity, everywhere people are scurrying around with books under their arms, anxiously scanning dense pages of photocopied notes.

I have put off studying till after dinner, putting it off is what I have been doing all day. My table is a mess, books lie buried under piles of corrected homeworks, under notices for hostel events I was supposed to publicize but didn't, under tutorial sheets. Some papers have fallen off the back of the table. My tapes are scattered on the table, their covers nowhere to be seen. There's a coat of dust on the tape recorder. Two books and some pairs of underpants are on the study chair; I haven't sat in it for days. I wipe the sweat off my brow, or if it is winter I roll up my sleeves, and set about putting the table in order. I have found out early enough in my stay at IIT that the times I clean up the table before the exams, I do well; the times I don't, I don't.

An hour later it's nine o'clock. My desk is in order, or I discover a torn back issue of a porn magazine – *Debonair* or *Fantasy* – under a pile of papers and put it to good use, or I pick up one of the tapes and realize that I haven't heard it for a long time and really want to, right at that moment. Either way, I am a little less tense now.

I am the only person from Computer Science, the only compguy, on my floor. I don't really hang out with them too often, the other compguys in my hostel. My friends are mainly from Delhi. We speak in Hindi because it isn't cool not to, but we think in English. After a year of living in randomly assigned rooms we have chosen to form our own corner on one of the floors assigned to us.

My hostel's compguys come from places like Jaipur and Meerut. They live on a different floor. For the next four days I am going to spend almost all of my waking hours with them. When I first met them the only person I could compare them with was Bobby. But by the time we graduate I am going to know them better than I will ever know anyone else, and they will also see sides of me that I am never going to want anyone else to see.

We don't compete amongst ourselves. It is accepted that JP, the name comes from the city he's from, is the smartest amongst us. He's the only compguy in my hostel who has a CGPA above nine. I'm next in line I like to think, I lie more than one whole grade point below JP. Along with me is Govind, his nickname Gobhi never really caught on although I thought it was clever when I coined it. Then come TK and Pratap. TK's nickname is an abbreviation of Tension Kumar, nothing to do with his real name, which I will often have trouble recalling in the future. Every batch in every hostel is supposed to have a Tension Kumar, it is a designation rather than a nickname. Our own TK entirely belies the name; it was given on the basis of appearance, by being least concerned about anything but gutka which he consumes in large quantities.

Finally there's Loda Kumar, his superciliousness has been rewarded with an abusive nickname. His low CGPA puts him unequivocally in the bottom third of the department, but Loda Kumar is also often known as The Compguy because of the oneliner he had delivered during the ragging period: 'It's not fair to rag us compguys,' he had declared simply, indicating his firm faith in the divinely ordained superiority of those of us who did well enough in the entrance exam to get Computer Science. It is commonly believed that the term 'compguy' was first used in this famous sentence.

They're all gathered in JP's room. JP is sitting on the bed and reading something. Govind is sitting on the floor looking at him expectantly. TK and Pratap are leaning over some notes placed on the table. Loda Kumar is not there. He acknowledges JP's paramountcy but prefers to study on his own. That's why he often makes mistakes the rest of us don't make. Occasionally he manages to do better than all of us.

Everybody looks up when I kick the door open. Everybody except JP. 'Finally found time to study for the minor,' he says.

There is one book, one set of photocopies of the notes, one set of previous years' papers taken out of the hostel library. A complex negotiation begins. The owners get to use them during the day. The others get night slots. The notes are unstapled, separated out into lectures and restapled for better distribution. JP produces a register from his bag. 'These are my notes,' he says. 'Do you want them?' We look at him for a second, then everyone laughs. JP is the cleverest guy we have met. He is also the laziest.

There's a lot to be read, a whole lot. I don't know any of this stuff. It can't just be read, it has to be digested. I have to be able to solve problems. I know when I have understood something, and when I haven't. We all do. Before the exam begins I can tell which topic I am going to get fucked in and which topic I will survive. I almost never know when I am going to do well, except in the Humanities classes which I do well in because my English, learned in one of Delhi's missionary schools, is better than most other people's.

I take my share of the loot to my room and struggle with it for a while. At eleven Bhats comes by.

'Chai,' he says.

'Fuck off, Bhats,' I say.

'Come on, Rindu. How much are you going to mug?'

The phrase is derived from 'mug up'. A few years later in graduate school in America many of us are going to have to face quizzical looks when we tell someone we spent the night 'mugging'.

'Fuck off, Bhats,' I say.

Bhats walks in. He potters around amongst my tapes. 'Can I take this Who's Next?' he says.

'Return my Led Zep four first.'

'Come on, Rindu. It'll just take ten minutes to get chai.'

An hour later I return to my room. The watery coffee at KL – I drank three cups of it – has made me sleepier than I was before we left. I look at the notes lying on the bed, I was reading the second page of the first lecture when I left. Kicking my door shut I pick them up again. It's no use. The symbols are dancing in front of my eyes. I find myself reading mechanically, reaching lecture five without having begun to understand what happened in lecture one. I shake myself awake, then decide I have to go and find someone to study with.

TK and Pratap are sitting on the floor in Pratap's room. Pratap asks me a question from what he's reading. I take his notes and look at them, quickly trying to figure out the answer to his question, talking as I go. He's looking blank. I try again from the beginning. It's becoming clearer to me as I go over it again. I stop, stand up with the notes, pace for a step or two. I get it. Pulling a chair I sit, take out my pencil and start making a diagram. I watch his face as I explain the problem to him. The explanation is filtering through. Whenever he falters, confusion comes back into his eyes. I keep at it till I feel he's understood it as well as possible. We pick out a problem. He solves it. I feel really good, I feel pumped for a night of study.

'Let's have a shagging contest,' says TK suddenly.

'What's the contest?' I ask.

'Whoever comes first wins.'

'Count me out.'

They wait for me to leave the room. I reflect on how sexual Pratap and TK are as I head towards Govind's room.

Pratap especially seems to radiate sex. Some people say Pratap has seen every hostel guy's dick. I think back to the time he and I were studying together sitting on his bed and I found him absently stroking my crotch. My bemusement began to turn into arousal. I shifted away and he went on reading his notes as if nothing had happened.

JP is sitting in Govind's room. They have just returned from Karakoram he tells me. There are new fundas to be given. I settle in as he backs up a little and starts explaining what he has learnt. At one point I ask him to explain the significance of a particular concept.

'Just assume it's like this,' he snaps. 'Do you think you're here to learn?'

We learn despite ourselves, the professors trick us into learning by making sure we won't do well in the exams if we don't. Later I am going to admire them for this.

'Rindu!' a voice echoes outside. 'Rindu, fucker, where are you?'

I poke my head out of Govind's window. It's TK standing in the courtyard below with Pratap. One hand is cupped. It does not appear to be empty.

'I won!' he shouts. 'I came first.' He dances a little jig.

The exam is at eleven the next morning. I sleep at three and wake at six thirty. The morning passes in frenzied reading, running to JP's room from time to time. At ten fifteen I return from the last visit. The next half hour is for carefully going over the things I think I know and desperately trying to cram in the things I don't. My mouth keeps running dry but I don't have the time to go to the water cooler.

Finally, at ten forty-five, I come out of my room and start looking for porn. It's a difficult job. The hostel is resounding with doors banging shut as everyone performs the last pre-exam ritual. Some say it relaxes them, some say they do better in exams if they shag before them, and then there are others who say they have no reason, they just like shagging.

I get a magazine from someone who had a nine o'clock exam and run back to my room. Slamming the door shut I settle quickly on my bed, hoping against hope that five minutes from now when I kick my scooter to go to the Institute I will be feeling calmer and more composed. It's never happened before but I am determined to keep trying.

The guy whose paper lay on top seemed to have a zero but it could have been an eight or a ten. His paper sat atop the white pile, a magnet for forty-five nervous eyes.

Finally Kanitkar put the chalk down.

'And now, the papers,' he said. Picking up the first one, he flicked through it. 'Horrible,' he said, shaking his head. 'You guys are absolutely useless.' He picked up the pile and dropped it with a heavy thud on the first desk. 'Does someone want to guess the class average?'

Our resident specialists in one-line answers to rhetorical questions decided to hold their peace.

'It's three. Three!'

A gasp went up.

'Out of thirty!'

The reminder was unnecessary but nonetheless met by a sharp intake of collective breath.

'Only five people have got more than one and a half. Only four have more than ten and only two have more than twenty.'

If this had been the news of a car accident or a terrorist attack, we were now at the stage where shock would have given way to wailing and breastbeating. But we thought of ourselves as men, so we resorted to a more dignified stunned silence instead. Also, each one of us probably hoped he was one of the two who had crossed twenty.

Kanitkar began to call the names one by one. One by one we hurried up to the front and then dragged our deflated selves back. The nine-pointers looked shocked, the eight-pointers defeated. The seven-pointers appeared resigned. The rest tried to grin at the hapless plight of the others. Been here several times, their faces tried to say, used to it. They convinced no one.

'Arindam Chatterjee,' said Kanitkar.

My stomach clutched at itself as I walked the aisle. Up near the front desk was Kanitkar's outstretched hand with my paper in it. He was looking at the pile. He must have read out the next name as I walked. I didn't hear it.

My hand snatched the paper from him. He looked up at me, his eyes seemed to be registering my face, separating it out from the crowd.

'Good,' he said curtly.

Good? I thought.

On top of my paper in large numerals was the number seventeen.

I headed to my seat in a daze. The third highest marks in the class were inscribed on my paper, I had beaten at least fifteen of the guys who were above me in the department rankings. A smile began creeping onto my face. I fought it back. It was more important, and harder, to be gracious in victory than in defeat. Struggling to keep my excitement from taking control of my right fist and pumping it in the air, I tried to look shocked. It was a neutral emotion. I felt shocked, that was definite. My face contorted into a grimace. The others must have thought I was about to cry.

I felt a hand on my left wrist. It was JP. It might have been that he had noticed the absence of the ironic self-deprecation with which I usually took bad marks or it might just have been idle curiosity. His eyebrows bounced questioningly. I turned the paper towards him.

His grip slackened. Unalloyed astonishment flashed onto his face. He looked up at me with a mixture of awe and nonrecognition. I turned my eyes away. His paper was lying on his desk, a big two inscribed on its front. He squeezed my wrist and then let it go. When I looked back at his face he was smiling with spontaneous selfless joy.

'What is wrong with you guys?' Kanitkar said once all the scripts had been handed back. 'Aren't you even ashamed of yourselves?'

On any other such occasion people would have been lining up to have their papers rechecked. They would have begged and pleaded for half a mark till the professor gave up in exasperation. But no one seemed to have the courage to go to Kanitkar. Encouraged by this he worked himself up into a righteous fury. 'You are supposed to be the cream of the nation. You miserable dolts. Your seniors were jumping at this point. Jumping with excitement!' He seemed to be about to leap off the platform himself.

'You don't deserve to be at IIT,' he thundered. 'You should all have gone to Roorkee. No, no, even Roorkee is too good for you. You should get your Computer Science from NIIT.'

The sound of cars passing on the road beyond the boundary wall heightened the silence as he stood there fuming. I couldn't look up at him and I could see that my classmates were also sitting with their necks bent, avoiding his accusing gaze.

'Tell me this,' he said. 'How many of you find this stuff really exciting? How many of you think you want to do research in Algorithms?'

I looked up to see two hands in the air. Sheikhu and Neeraj: they were the two guys who had got more than twenty.

And then, as if of its own volition, I found my own hand going up.

Years later I was still trying to figure out why I committed myself to such a risky ideal that day. Perhaps I had been biding my time through school and the first two years at IIT, floating in the direction I had been pushed. Maybe I had been seeking a passion, something to which I could give my heart and soul and suddenly I had found it.

Because it is there, Mallory had said. Why climb a mountain? Because it is there. In the person of Kanitkar I had seen what, to my mind, was the highest point I could hope to reach. Like any other summit it glinted hard in the sun sometimes and sometimes lay obscured by clouds, its presence in the sky throwing down a challenge to me, standing with my feet stuck to the ground.

And once I had raised my hand in response, there was no question of going back. In that class, with my precious Algorithms answer sheet sitting face up in front of me, I stood naked, my aspiration revealed, not just to the world but also to myself. If I reneged on this promise I might live down the ridicule of my peers but I would never be able to face myself again.

'Three people,' snorted Kanitkar. 'In a class of forty-five.'

But our show of hands had taken the wind out of his sails.

As we came out of the classroom, looking at each other's answer scripts and racking our brains over solutions, I saw that my classmates' mood had been lightened by Kanitkar's shouting. The desired effect was to humiliate us into becoming serious and sincere students, but I could feel the people around me had recovered from the horror of the exam results by easing into the familiar situation of being insulted by a professor. People were now trying to lighten the mood by telling each other that it was time to start studying for the NIIT entrance exam.

Loda Kumar, The Compguy, however was not amused. 'How could he say that we should go to NIIT?' he protested. 'We are IIT Delhi compguys after all.'

I feel my brow furrowing in concentration as I stare at the Dark Side of the Moon poster up on Sheikhu's wall. In my head I rearrange the mathematical terms. Straining to see the equation reforming itself, I focus harder and harder on the prism in the centre of the poster. The symbols dance in the space between me and the Dark Side of the Moon, palpable but invisible. I divide a few things, move one coefficient down to the other side, and suddenly it all makes sense.

'Sheikhu,' I say, turning towards the bed. 'Just take the small set contribution and divide it into three parts, and it works.'

Sheikhu's eyes are on me but he is looking through me. 'One sec,' he says. 'I'm thinking.'

The directness of this statement turns my cheeks red, the ease with which it is delivered stuns me. But this is just the first time. Algorithms research is mainly about collaboration, I am going to learn. It is often about sitting together for hours and thrashing ideas out, about introspecting and interacting in alternation. There are going to be many moments when I am going to crack the eggshell of someone's contemplation or have mine cracked in turn. But it is going to be a long long time before I get over my abashment at being asked to shut up, and an even longer time before I am going to be able to say the words 'one sec, I'm thinking' myself.

'Hmmm Rindu,' Sheikhu says finally. 'What were you saying?'

'I was thinking,' I begin, 'that we could …'

He isn't listening. Picking up my pen, he scribbles a few things in his notebook. Then he looks up.

'Look at this, Rindu,' he says. 'These small sets don't have to be counted together. We can just divide them into three parts.'

The expression on the page corresponds exactly to what I had said a few seconds ago. I look up at him in disbelief, but his face carries nothing more than an expectant look. He really hasn't heard a word of what I have been saying.

'But that's what I was … hmm, let me see,' I say, taking the notebook from him. I am not reading what is written on the page, I am counting to ten. 'Yes, this looks right.'

He stands up.

'I think we've cracked this one, Rindu,' he says, expansively including me in his we. 'We have something to tell Kanti tomorrow.'

Kanti is pronounced to rhyme with auntie, it's our name for Kanitkar. We are doing an independent study with him now, so we have the right to give him a nickname. The rest of the class will pick up on this nickname but the credit will stay with Sheikhu and me. It was my idea but the authorship will be collective.

'Hmmm,' I say and then, faking the tone of guarded excitement that will become the mainstay of those moments when a theorem is freshly proved: 'It seems okay. Let's see what he says.'

'I am going down for tea, do you want to come?' asks Sheikhu.

It's against the rules to drink tea in another hostel. Normally that doesn't stop people from doing it. Occasionally a vigilant mess committee member will spot the offender and threaten him with a fine. A minor furore will erupt in the mess, the chant of 'fine, fine' is a popular one. It helps enliven the dullness of evening tea. No fine will be levied, it's almost impossible to enforce these things across hostels. The only punishment is slight embarrassment. Most of us are too thick-skinned for it to register.

'No,' I say. 'I'll have tea at my hostel.'

We are about to part near the mess door when he turns to me. 'Oh, I forgot to tell you: I talked to Neeraj yesterday, he's going to join us in the independent study.'

It was Neeraj who taught me that friendship between two men can have all the ferocity of a love affair. Of the many things I was forced to realize in reflecting on the time I spent with him, perhaps the most sobering and terrifying was the understanding that the strongest and deepest bonds we form in our lives are with people who know how to hurt us in the most devastating ways. It would be years later, after repeatedly wounding and being wounded, after resisting and then ineluctably reconciling, after limping off the battlefield tired and older, that I would remember with some clarity the prehistory of that association with Neeraj that Sheikhu had inaugurated casually one evening in the third year outside Karakoram's mess.

It was in the second year that, late one evening, I found myself in the Computer Centre. I wasn't one of those who spent weeks on end in the CompC, preferring instead to hammer out my assignments in a day or two, or simply copying them from someone else. Normally, I would go to the CompC the day before the assignment was due. Entering the white-panelled basement, I would run my eyes down the rows of computers: there were the third year people looking all grave and serious; there were the first years hunched over their terminals, still overawed by this impressively large and entirely airconditioned space; and there were my own classmates with expressions of worry or fatigue or boredom on their faces. Some would sit in pairs – relationships forged in this always cool room would last long after the room itself was no more than a memory. These were friendships being cemented in the heat of battle, a deathly struggle with intransigent code that refused to compile or, when it compiled, wouldn't run, or when it ran, would do everything but what you wanted it to do.

Then there were the people who were wheedling and cajoling others into parting with their painstakingly written programs. Once they had obtained a program and verified that it worked, they would sit for an hour or two changing variable names, moving sections of code around, changing its indentation, to make sure the professor would not be able to tell that it was all copied. It was a craft, almost, this process of redigesting the code while ensuring it still ran. The most aesthetically minded practitioners of this craft would grumble as they worked:

'Is this any way to write a program? No indentation at all, can't tell where you enter the loop and where you leave it. No documentation of any kind, one week later he himself won't be able to tell what this fucking program does. And what kind of variable names are these, x, y, z? No information at all about what they represent. Total fucking nonsense, yaar. Next time I am going to write this program on my own.'

When the next time rolled around they would once again come in the day before the deadline and once again rant in this charming fashion, as they crafted a work of art out of what had earlier been a mere program.

But it was not the night before a major deadline that I met Neeraj in the CompC. Perhaps Kartik was busy playing the guitar, maybe Bhats had something due the next day,

Rocksurd might have gone to Johri's hostel to drink. I was on my own, it was late in the evening, it was quite likely that I was in the CompC on a whim or because I was out for a walk and having reached the Institute I decided to see if any of my compguy friends were at the CompC.

A large head poked out of a dirty aquamarine sweater in the far corner. It was Neeraj. I went up behind him quietly, quickly took in the contents of his screen, it was some Prolog stuff, then slapped his back in greeting.

It had been late in the first year that the legend of Neeraj had diffused out of his hostel and begun to spread through the Institute. The second minor answer scripts for Digital Electronics had been handed back. It was a large class, more than ninety people in it. The word had come floating around that one of the guys from Computer Science had used only one op-amp to solve the third question. Just one op-amp! My informant told me that it was half credit for four op-amps – I knew that already – full for three. Two was really difficult but could be done with some effort. No one in the world had ever done one before. The professor had called Neeraj to his room and had given him a choice: either Neeraj wrote a paper on this along with him, which they would publish in a journal, or he took twenty out of twenty on the exam. Why exactly both could not be done was something no one clarified.

Neeraj chose to take twenty out of twenty.

Later, when we became friends and I asked him about this incident, hinting that it was stupid for him to prefer marks in a small exam over a published paper, he told me: 'Yaar, I wasn't bothered about the marks. I just want my first paper to be something really big. The op-amp result would have been a very minor one.'

Neeraj had a large squarish head that could make people forget how small and thin his body was. His moustache was a wispy pencil line across his upper lip – he was one of the guys who had regrown it after the ragging period. When he laughed he laughed with his mouth open, showing the gap between his teeth, his body pulsating like the exhaust pipe of an idling truck. When he did not laugh, his eyes bore a look that seemed to say: 'You aren't really getting what I am saying, are you?'

'Why are you working on Prolog?' I asked, pulling up a chair next to his. 'Is there some Programming Languages assignment due?'

'No, just generally,' he said.

I looked up at the screen. It seemed he was writing small Prolog expressions, just putting it through its paces.

'Show me something,' I said.

He wrote a small expression, then pressed the enter key. Suddenly a thought struck me.

'Neeraj,' I said. 'Do you remember how in last week's PL lecture the prof talked about how integers can be represented as functions? Do you think they can be represented as logical expressions as well?'

'Let's find out,' he said, sitting up in his chair.

Later that semester Neeraj's reputation would explode out of the realm of student folklore into the world of faculty canteen chatter. He would come up with a proof for the notoriously difficult Reconstruction Conjecture. He would present his proof to a roomful of faculty members, including Kanitkar, who would take weeks to discover the flaw in his argument. He would have realized by then, or perhaps he already knew now, that making a minor mistake in attempting something hugely ambitious was worth much more than being entirely correct about something pedestrian. His proof would bring together logic and combinatorics in an impressively mature way, making it difficult for experts from either field to catch the error. It would be many years before I would realize that the night I met him in the CompC he must have been refining his understanding of logic programming as he worked towards that famously flawed proof.

That night in the CompC, with the future still a few months away, I sat with Neeraj in one corner, jumping through Prolog's hoops and making it jump through ours. We corrected and augmented and fiddled as we built one idea on the other. He typed and I watched as our small logical expressions became bigger, as one concept laid the foundation for the next. When I had long forgotten the details of what we had done that night I remembered the pure joy of seeing mathematics and logic interlock and unfold on that old monochromatic screen in the Computer Centre.

It was almost three in the morning when we walked out of the main building and headed for our hostels. The campus was bathed in the soft light of sodium vapour lamps. The parking lot looked forlorn and empty. Its concrete flooring, hidden by dense bunches of cycles in the day, glowed dimly in the orange night. Three or four cycles stood in one corner, their owners having decided to spend the night in the CompC. Walking past the sleeping trees we turned onto the long road that led to the hostels.

'How come your JEE rank was so low?' I asked Neeraj, immediately regretting the tactlessness of the remark.

When he answered it was clear that he had understood what I was really asking: 'If you are as intelligent as everyone claims you are, how come you didn't make the top hundred at JEE?'

'I didn't study chemistry,' he said simply.

'Meaning?'

'Meaning, I don't like chemistry. I find it boring. So I didn't study it at all. I just went and sat in the paper, did whatever I could and came away.'

I was astounded. Everyone knew that in JEE even ten marks could be the difference between Computer Science in Kanpur and Electrical in Bombay, or Mechanical in Kharagpur and Metallurgy in BHU. I hadn't particularly enjoyed chemistry myself, but I had studied it nonetheless because JEE was something much much bigger than me, something I respected. To not study chemistry would have been taken as a level of arrogance I could not even begin to approach.

But, I was to learn in time to come, in Neeraj's world, to be true to your passion meant to neglect what didn't interest you. It was important for him to repeatedly point out how he never studied for his Humanities classes – the ones I always aced – and got Ds in them, how he had excellent grades in all the department classes but still had a low CGPA because of his single-mindedness. He was ranked in the bottom ten of the class, a badge he wore with pride.

'NT might be DR one,' he once said to me, referring to our class topper, 'but people give me as much respect.'

My own position in the middle of the class was buoyed by my good grades in Humanities classes. I had no real passion for anything I studied, although some of it interested me and I was competent at all of it. When Neeraj proudly reported that he had got a zero in his Management Studies exam or that there was a good chance that he might flunk in Rural Development, I felt like a hypocrite.

But that night as we walked home, I kept my composure. Realizing he expected a shocked reaction, I kept quiet.

'Where did you go to school?' I asked.

He named a small public school in South Delhi. I had heard of it but didn't actually know anybody who went there.

'Is that a good school?' I asked.

'Yes, very good,' he said, missing the condescension in my question. 'I used to be in a government school earlier.

When I was in class eleven I went myself and got admitted.'

'Yourself?'

'Yes,' he said. 'My father said that the government school was fine. There was no need to go to a public school and pay a lot of money to study.'

'Really?'

'My family is like that. When I told them that I was going to IIT they were very disappointed. They don't know what IIT is, for them Delhi University is the big thing. Actually I wanted to study Physics in St Stephen's College. Do you know St Stephen's? But my English marks were too low so they didn't take me.'

Some of my friends who hadn't made it into IIT had gone to DU colleges. They had spent a year preparing for their second attempt at IIT. And here was this guy for whom IIT had been the fallback.

'What does you father do?' I asked.

'He runs a restaurant in INA Market,' he said.

I had been to INA Market several times, when I was younger my mother used to buy fish there. I didn't remember having seen anything that I could call a restaurant.

'What kind of restaurant?'

'Mainly South Indian food,' he said. 'Also samosas and other snacks.'

'Vadas,' I said, as an old memory stirred in my head.

'Yes, vadas as well.'

'Is it next to a spice shop run by a bald guy who sells ajinomoto?' I asked.

'Yes, yes,' he said. 'How do you know?'

'I think I've been there,' I said. 'Next time, I am going to ask for free food.'

'Of course, yaar. Whenever you want. Just tell them you're Neeraj's friend.'

We parted at the roundabout and I walked towards my hostel. But instead of going into the hostel, I went out through the gate and sat at the bus stop. In my head I tried to conjure up the several visits I had made to the dhaba that had suddenly revealed itself to be Neeraj's. An hour later, when the eastern sky began to lighten, my head was swimming with the fragrance of golden crisp vadas, but I still hadn't been able to recall a single face from across the counter of Neeraj's dhaba.

Neeraj drove up to my hostel in a battered Maruti van one afternoon near the end of the third year. Sheikhu was sitting in the passenger seat so I had to drag back the sliding door – it bore a deep metallic gash along its length – and get into the back. The stench of stale vegetables hit my nose, a smell like the Yamuna's water gave off. We might have been on a joyride, or it could have been that Neeraj had some work he needed to do and we were along because we had nothing better to do. Whatever it was, one heartstopping dash across the city later we found ourselves out of breath and thirsty near Ashram crossing.

'My house is close by,' Neeraj said. 'Let's go there.'

His house turned out to be a second-floor flat in a yellow-grey DDA colony nestled behind a large construction site in a crowded locality. We climbed up the stairs to where an iron grille hung from a single hinge. The door behind it had a gaping hole instead of a lock.

The inside of Neeraj's house was covered in soot. Singed pieces of wood lay in a small pile in one corner, the remnants of what must have been furniture. Inside the kitchen some plates, a stainless steel glass and a black kadhai lay in a pool of scummy water. As my eyes adjusted to the darkness of the living room – we had just come in from a blazing summer afternoon – I saw an earthen pot standing against a wall.

I looked around for a place to sit. There wasn't one.

'There was a fire,' said Neeraj, walking across to the pot. Dipping the steel mug into the pot, he hit bottom. 'It's empty,' he said. 'Let's go in.'

I turned to follow him and came face to face with a short man dressed in dhoti-kurta. His long white beard poured down the sides of his face. In the middle of his head sat the shining oval of a bald patch. His face, set in a hostile frown, bore an unmistakeable resemblance to Neeraj's. What I was to remember of him more than anything else were his eyes. They were filled with hate without seeing what they hated.

'My father,' said Neeraj, and then, turning to him: 'These are my friends, Arindam and Rakesh.'

I folded my hands, formed my lips into a smile and nodded. Not a muscle on his face moved. Past his shoulder I saw a little girl sitting in another blackened room. She seemed no more than twelve or thirteen. The dress she wore, a light green tunic over a white blouse, looked like a government school uniform, like the ones worn by the girls who clambered onto DTC buses in loud, giggly hordes. But, unlike the dark-skinned smiling faces of those schoolgirls, this one's face bore an expression which, not sad, not frowning, was one of surpassing emptiness. Skeins of light danced from the TV, across the grey-black gloom, to her glassy eyes and bounced off them on their way out of the door.

'Here,' said Neeraj.

I turned to find him standing inside what looked like a bathroom. A tap encrusted with some kind of white residue hung off the end of a length of slim metal tubing over a sink. I turned towards it.

'No, here,' said Neeraj.

It was a decrepit washing machine. Neeraj reached behind it and undid a tube. Water trickled out of it, wetting the front of my jeans. 'Sorry,' he said. 'There's always a little left.' Lifting the tube he tried to bring it to my mouth. 'You'll have to bend.'

I stood there, bent over in that dilapidated bathroom with my hands cupped. He turned on a tap and the water flowed out of the tube, the glugging sounds from my throat breaking the silence. I stood there, like the weary traveller of so many folk tales, with my hands cupped as the plastic-flavoured water flowed out of the machine into my body.

Straightening, I saw that Neeraj's father was looking out of the window, his back turned towards us. Seeing us emerge from the bathroom, the girl got up off the floor and walked to the door of the TV room. In the daylight the skin on her thin face looked patchy. Her arms looked brittle, dangling aimlessly by her bony body.

I turned towards her, expecting to be introduced. By the time Neeraj emerged from the bathroom, his father had shuffled to his feet, the girl had shot him a quick look, then turned, gone back in and disappeared from view.

Sheikhu stood in the living room awaiting our return. The random patterns of black behind him made the room look like a Buddhist cave, half-burnt by invaders in a hurry. He was looking at a heap of twisted plastic and mangled electronic components.

'One of our VCRs,' said Neeraj. 'We used to have four.'

On our way back to the hostel Neeraj spoke unprompted: 'All he does is drink and fight with my brothers. They aren't any better. Whatever they can lay their hands on, they steal. You've seen our dhaba, Rindu. It's such a good location. We could easily make two lakhs every month. We make less than forty thousand. And even from that they steal. Everything goes on booze. It's all because of booze, it destroys people. It destroys everything.'

He didn't use the colloquial 'daaru' for booze, he used the word 'sharaab' like a disapproving wife in a movie or a voiceover in a public service advertisement.

I thought about my own father's carefully assembled collection of whiskeys and vodkas and rums and gins, with the odd Kahlua or Irish Cream or Creme de Menthe thrown in. I thought about the way he delighted in the different shapes and colours of the bottles, arranged and rearranged them to his satisfaction in the little cupboard which served as his bar. I thought about his careful evening ritual, hot water if it was called for, ice if it was required, soda if it was needed, the right amount of lime or salt, the exactly measured amount of each ingredient. It seemed a far cry from Neeraj's world where people seemed to blow up large amounts of money on nameless sharaabs which they drank till they were uncontrollably drunk.

'Who was that girl?' I asked.

'My niece,' said Neeraj.

I balked at the crisp brevity of his anwer. Turning to see what Sheikhu was doing, sitting quietly in the back, I saw he had stuck his head out of the window. His hair blew back slightly in the van's slipstream. He looked like a runner who had just finished a long race.

Kanitkar's hand flew across the sheet of paper. He drew line after line, connecting point to point. The sun glinted off the paper, it was late on a clear winter morning. We sat in the corridor outside his office, or rather he sat and we stood around watching him. People strolled by: lab assistants and office staff, some M.Techs, a professor or two. Seeing Kanitkar sitting on the bench in the corridor, unlike most people who took research meetings inside their offices, the students would stiffen slightly and quicken their gait, the staff would put on blasé but servile expressions as they ambled by, and the professors would look either irritated or indulgent as they passed.

The days Sheikhu and I were alone with Kanitkar we would sit for an hour or so. Kanitkar and Sheikhu would talk. I would interrupt them occasionally. If meetings were in the afternoon I would find my eyes growing heavy with sleep. At times I would feel my head jerk back and I would realize that I had fallen asleep. Guiltily, I would look up at Sheikhu and Kanitkar. They would pretend not to notice.

In the years to come I was to find out that there were often times when people nodded off in the course of a long meeting. I was to learn that everyone else noticed immediately and most people did not think it was a terrible crime. But there in Kanitkar's office, I battled with sleep as if my life depended on it. Even when I was wide awake I would sometimes entirely lose the thread of the discussion and I would struggle to regain it. I didn't feel confident enough to ask them to bring me up to speed and they never stopped to ask if I was following along. It was my first foray into the professional world. And I fought to maintain my foothold in it.

Sheikhu managed to keep the conversation up, this I did notice. But somehow things weren't getting done. We would discuss various approaches, Sheikhu would come up with different ideas. But nothing seemed to work out. 'If it's publishable, you'll get an A,' Kanitkar had said. 'Otherwise an A minus.' But publishability seemed really far away.

On the other hand, the days Neeraj came to our meetings, there was always the feeling that something was about to happen, some longstanding open question was about to be resolved, some classical result was about to be improved significantly. 'Yaar,' Neeraj was to tell me, 'there's no point in doing incremental research. You can't get the Turing Award by making small improvements to existing results. You have to attempt something big.'

From a small dhaba in INA Market to the Turing Award, it was ambition on an unbelievably audacious scale. On reflection, I realized that Neeraj's aspiration was like a gas which expanded to fill whatever space it occupied. And when it filled the space entirely, it discovered the way out into a larger space. From the government school he was in, the public school must have been the furthest he could see. From there, Delhi University would have been the highest point he could hope to reach. And now, having conquered IIT, he could look beyond it, past best paper awards and grants and endowed chairs all the way to the Turing Award. I wondered what he would do once he got the Turing Award, where would he go then?

The days Neeraj came to our meetings we would see his persona get larger and larger. He always came with a proof in hand, normally of some difficult theorem. Inevitably the proof would be wrong but it would take all our time to show this. That day, when Kanitkar drew on the sheet of paper, Neeraj claimed to have done something unsurpassably brazen: he had improved Kanitkar's famous three bistability result.

'What do you guys think?' Kanitkar had asked us after Neeraj told him the Algorithm. 'Does it work?'

I had mumbled something to the effect that I hadn't been able to find any mistake in it. Sheikhu had gone further: 'My intuition is that it's correct,' he had said. 'Because it's based on four bistability and that is a new approach.'

By the time Kanitkar finished drawing, there were almost fifty vertices in the graph and something like one hundred edges. He put his pen down and, with a flourish, handed me the sheet of paper. 'Run it on this.'

I took out a pen and started executing the Algorithm on the graph he had drawn. Sheikhu and Neeraj craned their necks as I worked. Kanitkar didn't. He turned his back to us and looked over the balcony down at the green below.

When the largest partition reached size sixteen – it took me ten minutes to get to that point – the Algorithm failed.

'Sir,' I said, 'there's a problem at sixteen.'

Kanitkar turned. He was smiling. 'So it's based on four bistability, is it?' he said, looking at Sheikhu.

I felt Sheikhu's embarrassment clutch at my own stomach. Neeraj had a faraway look on his face, he was already trying to find a way around the problem Kanitkar's example presented.

'When we first came up with the Algorithm for three bistability,' said Kanitkar, 'we spent a year just looking for counter-examples.'

The sun shone on Kanitkar's face like a spotlight. Whenever I remembered him in the future I would see him like this: out in the corridor of block VI with shadowy figures floating past in the background, his stature having grown inexplicably, the clean winter light throwing his craggy face into painfully sharp relief, a warrior facing the vanquished. 'Fundas, guys,' he exclaimed, breaking into a chuckle. 'Fundas!'

I sat on the grass and watched the guys trying to climb the common room wall. Jatty-Jat, the amateur mountaineer, was the instigator as always. He had scrambled up the brick wall in less than a minute, his long wiry frame crouching and straightening as he went from handhold to handhold. Years later I would visit him in Seattle and, driving me from the airport, he would point out Mount Rainier towering over the landscape and casually say: 'I climbed that in jeans a week after I moved here.'

Those who followed Jatty-Jat up the common room wall did not seem to share his easy control over flat vertical surfaces. They floundered and slipped and scratched their elbows. I sat on the grass and sniggered.

'Fat fucker, if you think it's so easy why don't you try to do it yourself?'

The appearance of two female figures in the distance, who seemed to be heading towards the hostel, injected urgency into the scramble up the wall. Jatty-Jat himself decided to repeat his demonstration. I turned to observe the oncoming female formation.

Both the girls were dressed in salwar kameez. The colours were earth dyes, soft tans and yellows. I was trying to look at them without making it obvious that I was looking, when one of them hailed me.

'Arindam Chatterjee?'

'Aparna Iswaran?'

'Hi, Arindam, how are you?' she said in an excited voice.

'What a surprise!' I said, getting to my feet. 'I haven't seen you since school. How are you?'

Out of the corner of my eye I could see that the climbing activity had slowed. The sentiment that floated unsaid towards me was quite clear: 'We climb the wall and the girls talk to him. It isn't fair.'

'This is my friend Neeta,' said Aparna.

'Hi,' I said, looking past Neeta's left shoulder. I was not used to making eye contact with girls I did not know.

'So what are you doing here?' I asked Aparna in an unnecessarily hearty tone.

'There's a SPICMACAY concert in Kumaon hostel tonight? That's this one, isn't it?'

'Oh yes, there's the SPICMACAY thing tonight. Yes, this is Kumaon.'

'Which hostel are you in?'

'Ummm, Kumaon.'

'So the concert is in your hostel. Aren't you excited about it?'

Even if I were excited about the SPICMACAY concert, I wasn't allowed to exhibit my excitement. For me and my friends, SPICMACAY was an organization you joined if you wanted to meet girls. Even the people who claimed they were really interested in Indian classical music were roundly derided and made fun of. Secretly, of course, we all envied the guys who did join. We grudged them the meetings that were said to happen on the lawns of a girls' college, we were jealous of the time they spent with the lovely dark salwar kameez-clad girls with social consciences who worked along with them in putting up banners and posters and making rangolis at the venues.

It wasn't as if I didn't like the music. I had enjoyed all the concerts I had attended. But the common perception was that you went to SPICMACAY concerts for the same reason you joined SPICMACAY: for the women. And to make such a public display of your frustration was not allowed.

As the evening progressed the banners came up. The hostel gate was decorated with marigolds. An elaborate rangoli was created in the lobby, thin well-directed streams of coloured powders poured out of clenched fists. White sheets covered moth-eaten mattresses. The hostel courtyard, previously the site of unmentionable, and unmentionably banal, activities, was transformed into a civilized setting worthy of staging something as wilfully sombre as an evening of Indian classical music.

I watched from the third floor balcony as volunteers worked down below. On the other balconies and out of the windows of their rooms I could see other guys watch the girls as they worked. My eye lingered on Aparna as she went around laying the mattresses and covering them with sheets. I hadn't noticed in school how slender she was. Her hair was longer now. Occasionally, as she laboured, a wisp of it would fall onto her face and she would tuck it resolutely behind her ear. By the time she was done, dusk had fallen on the hostel, and when she rose finally and stretched her arms, I could see her dark face glow in the fading light.

Eventually a white Ambassador drew up at the hostel gate and The Artiste stepped out. He was one of the new brigade, one of the young ones. 'They're much better. The old ones always want booze. They flirt outrageously and sometimes even paw the girls. This guy is nothing like that. He teaches at an American university, you know.'

A murmur ran through the crowd as soon as The Artiste came into view. The women sighed collectively and adjusted their hair, the men straightened their kurtas and their backs.

Our carrom room was The Artiste's makeshift green room. The carrom board had been hauled away, large bolsters and carpets had been dragged in. Incense had been lit. Its smell would linger for days, interfering with the concentration of at least a few carrom players.

A figure disengaged itself from the crowd just as The Artiste was about to be ushered into the carrom room. It was Kanitkar. I hadn't noticed him come in. He tapped The Artiste on the shoulder. 'Hey there, big man,' he said, in a ringing American accent.

'Prof!' exclaimed The Artiste.

They hugged. Not breaking the embrace The Artiste dragged Kanitkar into the carrom room. They knew each other from America.

The only kurtas I owned were the ones I slept in at night and sitting on the floor made my feet go numb. So, I watched the concert from the third floor balcony. Night fell, and with the mounted floodlights on I knew that people wouldn't be able to see me looking down, even if they did twist their necks up to look. The other guys who had been watching from above had long since dispersed, the novelty of the situation having worn off quite some time before the concert began.

The music took its sinuous way up to one climax after another. It was obvious that the audience was moved. Some listened with their eyes closed, others seemed mesmerized by The Artiste and kept their gaze fixed on him. Kanitkar stood at the back, his eyes closed, his crop of hair bouncing to life with every mini crescendo. The IIT guys in the audience, self-consciously crisp in their starched kurtas, stole glances at the girls.

When the show ended I saw Rocksurd sidle up to where Neeta and Aparna stood. He engaged Neeta in conversation. I remembered the story Johri had told of their trip to Goa that summer. 'Two Dutch chicks, yaar, giving it to whoever asked. Rocksurd shows up. Total Maggi Noodles scene, man. Done in two minutes!' If the story had been told as a put-down, it hadn't worked. Two minutes with two anonymous Dutch women seemed a whole lot better than my own lot.

An irrational urge to call out to Rocksurd struck me, to distract him in some way, to throw a spanner in his works.

I couldn't decide whether to go down and say bye to Aparna or not. The clean up went much quicker than the set up and before I knew it, the courtyard had returned to being a parking lot for rusting bicycles. Sometimes, when I remembered that evening, I would recall that before leaving, Aparna turned and looked around as if she were looking for someone. But other times the only image I would get in my mind would be her shapely back receding into the shadows that lay beyond the floodlit courtyard.

'Arindam! Rindooo! Arin-da*mmm*!'

My eyelids sticking together with sleep I reached for my glasses. The ceiling fan shuddered along in its hectic way. A thin line of late afternoon sunlight hit my eye through a gap between the two shutters.

'Riiiiiiin-*du!*'

I pulled on some underwear, looked for a T-shirt, then gave up. 'Who the fuck is it?' I shouted, then it struck me that it might make sense to open the window before posing the question.

'Rindu, come down.' It was Sheikhu.

'What? Why?' I said, realizing, despite my sleepy state, that something important must have happened to make Sheikhu come to my hostel.

'We have to meet Kanitkar,' he said, modulating his voice down to the point where it still wasn't his speaking voice, more like the sort of thing he would use to ask a question from the last bench.

'Kanitkar?' I repeated. The question I was asking was not, 'Who is Kanitkar?' or 'Why do we have to meet Kanitkar now?' It was more like 'Why are you not using our nickname for him? Why are you calling him Kanitkar rather than Kanti?'

'Yes, Kanitkar,' said Sheikhu. He was obviously not in the mood to answer unasked questions.

'Okay,' I said. 'Coming.'

He was waiting for me outside the hostel, next to my scooter.

'I was sleeping,' I said accusingly, turning the key.

'We need to talk to him about schols.'

'Schols?'

He didn't answer.

'We don't apply till December. Why do we need to talk to him about schols now?' I persisted, giving the scooter a hard kick. The engine coughed, then growled, as it came to life. I made as if to mount and then stopped and turned to look at Sheikhu. 'What's up, Sheikhu?'

'Nothing's up. Let's go.'

Reaching around to the right side of the handlebar, I pressed down the little red button. The dhuk-dhuk-dhuk of the scooter momentarily became a smooth voom and then cleared its throat to silence. I twisted the key out of the slot.

'What's going on, Sheikhu?'

'He called Neeraj to his room yesterday,' Sheikhu said quietly.

'Alone?'

'He told him to apply to Stanford, he said he'll get him in there despite the low CG.'

'Yesterday?' I said, the implication sinking in: A day later neither Sheikhu nor I had been invited for such a meeting.

'Yes.'

'How do you know?' I asked.

'Neeraj told me.'

Defeat, I was about to learn, comes in more than one flavour. When I played table tennis in school, I always fought till the last point, even when I was really far behind. On the cricket field, at a quiz, in the carrom room, at the billiards table, I would redouble my efforts when I knew that the situation was hopeless. It seemed to be the sportsmanlike thing to do, it was no more than what I owed my opponents. It made being graceful in defeat that much easier.

If I lost by a wide margin, I would accept that the other guy was a better player, there was no shame in that. After a close game I would feel that the next time would be different but I would never demand a rematch. Even losing thirteen straight boards to Pratap late one night in the carrom room didn't break my spirit, I had realized by then that there were some people who held a psychological advantage over you; they weren't better players but losing to them was inevitable. That explanation, not a very illuminating one in hindsight, served me well enough in facing up to the phenomenon. But what I was about to find out that afternoon when Sheikhu and I rode to the department to meet Kanitkar was that sometimes defeat came without any explanation, it sneaked up on you just as you were getting ready to play the game, like it must have with Choto Kaku the day the army doctor told him he was flat-footed. Defeat, when it came so unexpected and sudden, left you bewildered and shaken. It made you question your self-worth, it condemned you to years of fighting battles you might not otherwise have chosen to fight.

'It really doesn't matter where you do your PhD,' Kanitkar said. 'All that matters is who you do it with.'

Sheikhu and I stood with our backs against the blackboard, looking across the room at Kanitkar sitting behind his desk. We had come in a few minutes earlier, and hesitantly broached the topic of higher studies. Sheikhu had asked Kanitkar which universities were considered good places to get a PhD from. Kanitkar's one-liner had thrown the ball right back into our court.

'Is it possible to do a PhD here?' I asked. 'I mean, in India.'

'Sure,' said Kanitkar.

Neither Sheikhu nor I knew how to phrase the question we both wanted to ask. Kanitkar's gaze cut through the silence, bouncing from Sheikhu's face to mine. Later I realized that even before I asked the question he knew exactly what this interview was about.

'Sir,' I said finally, 'can we do our PhDs with you?'

'I don't know,' said Kanitkar. 'I don't know if you guys are PhD material.'

Whenever I thought back to that pronouncement in the years to come, what always struck me was the ease with which it was delivered. If Kanitkar's face softened, or if his voice turned apologetic, I did not notice it. In times to come I was going to find myself in his shoes, and in those moments I would sympathize with him, but for many years I was to struggle with the fact that Kanitkar showed no remorse.

'Do you think we have a chance of getting into a decent university? Should we apply for scholarships?'

'There's no harm applying. There's a non-zero probability of getting funded.'

And, the final blow:

'Will you give us recos if we apply?'

'I don't see what I can write in a letter for you guys that would actually help you.'

It was after five by the time we left Kanitkar's office. We were halfway across the ramp to block V, trudging slowly through the gathering evening, when Sheikhu spoke. 'I am not taking the GRE,' he said.

I didn't say: 'What bullshit, man, of course you are.' I didn't say: 'Fuck Kanitkar, yaar, we'll get other recos.' I didn't say: 'Don't be so fucking dramatic, behnchod, it's not the end of the fucking world.'

And by keeping quiet I allowed a tantrum to turn into a statement of intent, or it could have been that I didn't give Sheikhu the chance to retract his statement of intent. I regretted it often in the future, this sin of omission. The feelings I associated with that moment would transform into several different things in the years ahead. Sometimes I would feel guilty at the thought that had Sheikhu gone to Kanitkar alone, maybe things would have turned out different, maybe it was my presence that forced Kanitkar to turn both of us away. Sometimes I would feel angry at Sheikhu for acting so macho, angry that he felt that taking his anger out on himself would somehow make everything all right. And then there were other times when I felt abandoned by Sheikhu, when I felt he should have asked me if I was ready to give up before he decided he was.

Whenever I thought about that moment in the future I would tell myself that even if I had said something it would not have made a difference, Sheikhu would have stuck to his guns. Or maybe something would have happened later which would bring him to the same conclusion. But whatever tack I tried with myself, I could never get away from the fact that coming back from Kanitkar's office that evening, walking across the ramp to block V, when Sheikhu said that he was not going to take the GRE, I didn't say anything.

I hefted the spiral-bound report out of my bag and held it out.

'Where's Sheikhu?' I asked.

Neeraj didn't move to reach for it. He shrugged his shoulders.

The final presentation for our project was scheduled for the Friday after the major exams of the sixth semester, a few weeks before Kanitkar left India for good. There was a minute left to five. We went into the Committee Room.

'Which part do you want to present?' I asked Neeraj.

He shrugged his shoulders again.

After announcing that he was not taking the GRE, Sheikhu had fallen out of the project. I had tried to get him to discuss it a few times but he had kept putting me off. Neeraj and I had met a few times but he had been more interested in going off on his own complicated tangents. Nothing he had said related to our project, nothing of what I had understood of it in any case. At one point Kanitkar had told us to just code up some of the Algorithms we had studied and write a report so that we would have something to show the committee. Neeraj and I had spent a couple of long evenings writing programs, almost exactly a year after that first time we had met in the CompC. But this time it was just business, and I sat quietly by him while he coded, occasionally pointing out a typo or offering a small suggestion which he took or rejected without offering explanations for either. Neeraj refused to have anything to do with writing the report. 'It's a clerk's job,' he said, so I wrote it all on my own, padding it with printouts of our code.

'Where's Rakesh?' asked Kanitkar, striding into the Committee Room.

Neeraj and I looked at each other. I realized with a start that Sheikhu was not late, he had decided to miss the presentation.

'I think he's in the lab downstairs, sir,' I said. 'I'll go and get him.'

Sheikhu, to my surprise, actually was in the lab downstairs. 'What the fuck are you doing, man?' I almost shouted. 'The presentation is at five and it's two past five now.'

'I am not coming,' he said, not looking away from his screen.

'Sheikhu, what is wrong with you?' I said, jogging his shoulder. 'It's the final presentation. You'll get an F if you miss it.'

He brushed my hand off, not violently but firmly. 'So what?'

'So what ... So what?' I blustered. But I knew him well enough to know that he wasn't going to listen to me. I straightened, and in an even tone said: 'One last time, Sheikhu, come.'

'No.'

I found the two committee members standing outside the department office when I got back up the stairs. 'Just five minutes, sir,' I said to them. 'We'll be ready in five minutes.'

I ran into the Committee Room. Neeraj was drawing on the board. Kanitkar was sitting in the front row. 'Where is he?' said Kanitkar and then, even as I was trying to decide what to say, he went on: 'Ah, there you are. Thank you for deciding to attend.'

Sheikhu stood right behind me.

'Who do you think you are?' Kanitkar's was voice rising. 'You think you can come and go as you please? What is wrong with you? Let me tell you something, to do well as a researcher you need to be disciplined, you need to work hard.'

A thought ran through my mind: We were too old for Sheikhu to be given this tongue-lashing in the presence of his friends. Although Neeraj, Sheikhu and I were not a day older than nineteen at the time, there was something about that moment that made adults of all of us.

'When you first came and talked to me I liked your ideas, I liked the way your mind worked. But now I don't think you have what it takes to be a great theoretician.'

There was silence as that last sentence sank in. It was the most damning thing Kanitkar could ever say to Sheikhu, I think that was clear to everyone in that room even then. But it would be after many years, after I went out into the world and formed a clearer picture of the various levels of achievement that had been demonstrated in the world of Algorithms and theoretical Computer Science, when I had a chance to compare Kanitkar to the galaxy of researchers that made up our community, when I had seen people fail and succeed and pay for both with their health and their peace of mind, that I would realize that the quest for the title of 'great theoretician' was one which had caused great suffering to many people, and Kanitkar was himself, in all likelihood, one of them.

I went to Kanitkar's room the day before the grades were to be displayed. Neeraj was not interested, ostentatiously so, and I was afraid of mentioning Kanitkar's name to Sheikhu after what had happened before the presentation. So I went alone.

'You get an A-minus because you worked on the code and the report. Neeraj gets a B because he worked only on the code. Rakesh gets a D because he did nothing,' said Kanitkar.

The presentation itself had been disastrous. Sheikhu hadn't said a word. Neeraj had talked a little about some of the theoretical work, but that hadn't cut any ice since we had no concrete results. My attempts to plug the coding also hadn't impressed the committee, they were both theoreticians.

'Sir,' I said, 'I don't think Sheikhu deserves a D.'

'Hmmph,' said Kanitkar.

'No sir, he worked with us on the theoretical stuff. It isn't his fault that it didn't work out. I think he should get some credit for that.'

I had been class committee convenor for three years in a row now. When I wore that hat, my natural fear of authority got transformed. Facing up to a professor gave me the sort of rush that, I guessed, normally came with bungee jumping or skydiving, the sort of rush that came with driving into the face of your fear.

'After all, we worked for a whole semester on the Algorithms,' I said. 'And we spent only two weeks coding and writing the report. The weightage of those cannot be one hundred per cent. I think Rakesh should get at least a B.'

'You talk well,' said Kanitkar. 'You should get an MBA.'

When the grades came out, Sheikhu had a C. But I paid for my daredevilry. Someone had overheard Kanitkar telling me I should do an MBA. Within a couple of days everyone in my department was taunting me: 'Heard you're thinking of doing an MBA, Rindu. Makes sense, you talk so well.'

It hurt more than they realized.

The summer after my third year Kanitkar left for the US and never returned. A few weeks after he had left he sent Neeraj an email. 'My plans have changed,' it said. 'I have taken up a faculty position at the University of Chicago. I won't be able to supervise your BTech project next year.' It went on to say that Neeraj should apply to the University of Chicago for a PhD, Kanitkar would make sure he got through. Neither Sheikhu nor I got any email from him.

The disappointment I felt at Kanitkar's leaving extended beyond the fact that the chance of impressing him by doing good work in the fourth year was now gone. After the time he bluntly told Sheikhu and me that we weren't PhD material I knew that I had already blown whatever opportunity I may have had to impress him and win his favour. It was something more than that which left me unhappy at his decision and bitter at him for having taken it.

We had many role models at IIT: the famous alumni who headed large corporations, became civil servants, went to the US and became professors in eminent universities or researchers in big research labs. Their lives were our possibilities. And all of these possibilities carried visible markers of success. They were popular options people aspired to and discussed in the hostel and at the canteens. The paths to these summits were well mapped. Not that everyone could surmount the obstacles that lay on these paths but it was at least known that the qualities IIT was supposed to cultivate in you – confidence, rationality, competitiveness – would stand you in good stead as you pushed towards your goal. In that sense these incredibly difficult endeavours were actually the safe options to take.

But there were quieter possibilities that existed alongside these loud ones: you could get together with a few friends and start your own company; you could quit engineering altogether and become a writer or an event manager or an activist; you could study further right here at IIT, do your PhD in the same department; or you could finish your PhD abroad and return to teach in India. Each of these notions was risky. You could find yourself back where you began: a small flat in a crowded group housing society, worrying about the price of petrol and rising school fees. And precisely because of this danger each of these alternatives was exciting in a way that the safe options could never be.

When the pipe dream of 'coming back' was dreamt aloud, Kanitkar's case was always cited. He was the one professor who had a lifestyle that could compare with materially successful people. He lived in an upmarket South Delhi colony near the campus rather than in gloomy campus housing. He travelled to the US every summer for three months. He dressed well. And he was on first name terms with international superstar musicians. It looked like he had figured out how it was done, like he had it all: the respect of his peers, the adoration of his students, a noble profession, a charismatic, unfettered personality and, unlike his colleagues, freedom from middle-class poverty.

That was why Kanitkar's sudden departure came as a shock to those of us who had decided to make his brand of fantasy a reality.

Initially I felt that he must have left for the reasons my relatives who lived abroad always gave: he couldn't take the running after gas connections and phone connections, the corruption and pollution. After all, I felt, he had lived in the US for several years before returning to India. Maybe he didn't want to fight the good fight anymore. It was a discouraging thought. Even at that time, a year or so before I left India for the US, I already knew that coming back would be an uphill battle. Moving back physically was just the beginning. There were, after all, people who came back and stayed for a couple of years, often more, before deciding they couldn't take it and went back to the jobs that were held open for them in Seattle or San Jose or Stockholm. I knew it would be difficult to tell, even years into it, whether the battle had been won or lost. Kanitkar's decision to go to the University of Chicago was an admission of defeat.

But as time passed, I heard rumours about how Kanitkar had been looking for tenure at an American university all the time he had been at IIT Delhi. It seemed that the only reason he had come to India in the first place was because he had not been able to get tenure where he had been teaching in the US. At that time, the story went, someone in the Computer Science department at IIT had suggested that he should come and teach in India for a while, and he had taken up the offer.

My first reaction to this theory was disappointment and anger. Kanitkar's story was not a story of Indian defeat in a noble cause, it was just another partially interrupted story of American success. He had lied in his mail to Neeraj. His plans hadn't changed. They had just been implemented a few years behind schedule.

Only many years later when I was in Baltimore facing the rigours of graduate school, and still later when my own friends and collaborators were breathlessly running the race for tenure, did I begin to get an idea of how crushed Kanitkar must have felt when he had realized that the job in Delhi was his best option. Every time I heard a story of someone having to leave a job for a lesser one because of the tenure system, even when my friends left graduate school after years of trying unsuccessfully to get a PhD, I felt less resentful of Kanitkar.

The other rumour that had floated through about him after he had left for the US was of an American woman, one of his earliest students in fact, whom he wanted to marry. His moving to India had sabotaged those plans. 'Obviously, yaar, how can an American woman live in India?' It was after I had given over many sleepless nights to that question myself that I found the last of the bitterness disappearing.

Kanitkar's return to the US – and that was the true return, not his earlier move to India – taught me many things over the years. There were many moments in my own life that gave me a further insight into the complexity of that moment in his life. It was this intermeshing of our lives that taught me the meaning of the word empathy. Perhaps the single biggest lesson I got out of it was that it is a blessing to be understood, and that it is an even bigger blessing to be granted understanding.

*

The phone rang late the night before the first day of my fourth year at IIT. It was Neeraj.

'Hi Neeraj, what's up? When did you get back from Madras?' Neeraj had gone to Madras for his summer training.

'You didn't go to the hostel?' he asked.

'No, I thought I'd take my stuff in the morning and go to registration late. What's going on?'

'Can I come over?'

'Right now?'

When my mother asked me who had called I told her that it was my friend from IIT, Neeraj, and that he was coming over.

'At this time?' she asked.

'I think there's some problem,' I said.

She nodded, the quizzical expression changing to one of self-assurance mixed with concern. It was the face, I realized, that must comfort her students, make them feel like this person would take care of the matter, whatever it was. It was the face that had reassured me when I was younger.

Finally, around eleven thirty, the Maruti van appeared outside the gate. A pack of stray dogs set up a racket; this hulking intruder had chosen their watch of the night to visit the Society.

'What happened, Neeraj?' I asked once we were back upstairs sitting in my room.

'When did you get a drumset?' he asked. He looked tired.

'Summer,' I said. 'Some guys and I have been jamming. We might enter the rock show this time at Rendezvous.'

He toyed listlessly with one of the drumsticks, then put it back on top of the snare.

'Have some hot milk,' my mother said, appearing at the door.

'This is Neeraj, Ma,' I said.

Neeraj folded his hands. She favoured him with the wide warm smile that was reserved for my sister's friends and mine. 'Should I put a bed in the drawing room?' she asked.

Neeraj's head was bent over the mug of Bournvita. He didn't say anything, so I did: 'Yes, Ma.'

Then, unexpectedly, she rubbed his back and said: 'Drink up, it's hot.'

When the milk was drunk we went down for a walk. It was a quiet night in the Society. The chowkidar tap-tapped his stick as he walked his rounds. Occasionally, a dog howled outside the Society's boundary wall. In the distance, where the tracks crossed the river, passing trains sounded their deep whistles.

'He took my niece out of school,' Neeraj said finally. 'I was away in Madras and he took her out of school. What will she do in school? he says. What's the use? he says. Just a waste of money. I thought things were improving, I thought things were better now but they're worse, much much worse.'

I didn't know what to say.

'I am not going to register tomorrow,' he said. 'I am going to spend this year running the shop, taking care of things. I owe it to my niece. I can always come back and finish my degree next year.'

'Seriously?'

'Yes,' he said. 'I've thought about it. In one year I can turn the shop around, I can make a profit. It's such a good location. We can easily make two lakhs a month there. But my brothers, my father, all they want to do is drink. They don't even pay the bills, do you know? The dhaba's light has been cut for the last six months, I just found out today. They have been drawing a line illegally for six months.'

'But you can't quit IIT now,' I said, grasping at the one thing that made sense to me. 'Kanitkar has promised you a schol to Chicago.'

He sat down on the bench behind C block, the one where Kartik and I would sit and talk when he visited me in the Society, where Bobby waited when I made my first hesitant rounds of the Society on his Vijay Super.

'No, Rindu, no,' he said. His body shook, then convulsed in sobs. 'Why did he have to hit her? She's just a child. What has she done to him?'

'It's okay, yaar. It's okay.' I put my arm around his shoulders.

'My mother … my mother,' he sobbed. Then he said a garbled sentence in Hindi.

'What did he do to your mother?' I asked.

His body throbbed as he wept silently. Then, with an effort, he stopped. I removed my hand. 'Let's go up,' he said.

Neeraj did not spend the night at my house. At around three in the morning he woke me up and told me he was leaving. The next morning I saw him at registration. He acted as if we hadn't met the night before.

Several times in the future I tried to reconstruct the sentence that I hadn't completely heard. He could have said, 'He beat my mother' or he could have said, 'He killed my mother.' I never asked him about it. He never mentioned his mother again.

Aparna's hand curled around my waist. It settled on my T-shirt just above my belly button, making me painfully aware of the folds of flesh that lay beneath. Slowly, deliberately, I exhaled, hoping she wouldn't notice the expansion. 'Are you okay?' I asked.

She adjusted her sitting position, pushing further back onto the pillion, her thigh grazing my tailbone. 'Yes,' she said. 'Let's go.'

It was a few months after the SPICMACAY concert, early in my fourth year at IIT. I had stopped by Connaught Place on my way back to the hostel one breezy overcast Sunday evening. The new Extreme album was out and I had to get it, Pandit had said we might do some songs from it. I had been hurrying past Eastern Court, the clouds were looking ominous, when I had seen Aparna standing at the bus stop.

'Do you want a ride somewhere?' I had said, stopping my scooter a few paces ahead of her after having debated in my head whether to stop exactly where she was or just before and having overshot her in the process.

She had kept looking in the other direction.

'Aparna,' I had said. She had turned but still not moved. 'It's me, Arindam,' and I pulled my helmet off my head with a flourish, involuntarily passing my hand through my sweaty hair.

'Oh, hi, Arindam,' she had said. 'What a surprise!'

When I looked back to check if she was settled on the scooter I saw the men at the bus stop give me dirty looks.

'Are you okay?' I asked.

'Yes,' she said. 'Let's go.'

When we had gone some distance she leaned forward: 'Sorry for not turning the first time you called, all sorts of people say all sorts of things at these bus stops.'

'It's okay, I wasn't offended,' I mumbled, turning my head slightly into the slipstream.

'What?' she said, moving further forward and raising her voice. 'What did you say?'

'Nothing,' I said, squirming in my seat. Her breasts were pushing into my back. I remembered the time Bhats had come into my room to return my scooter keys: 'Shit Rindu, this really sexy girl took a lift from me today. Fuck, she had huge boobs, man. I just kept jamming on the brakes. Major hardon!' Here I was, in roughly the same situation, minus Bhats' habitual exaggeration, and all I felt was exceedingly self-conscious. I slowed the scooter down and inched forward on the seat. I didn't want to jam on the brakes, I didn't want Aparna, accustomed as she was to all sorts of people saying all sorts of things to her at bus stops, to think that I was jamming on the brakes deliberately.

We had just got to Chanakya Puri when the rain came down. Within seconds my spectacles were a windshield with no wiper. 'I am really sorry,' I said, once we were safe under the bus stop, my scooter parked under a nearby tree.

'Oh fo,' she said. 'It's not your fault, yaar.'

Her hair was shining wet. Little drops of water curled up at the ends of the strands, not big enough to fall. She looked into her jhola to see if her books were okay. Then she took hold of the free end of her kameez and started wringing the water out of it.

The rain settled into a heavy drizzle and the two of us settled into the bus stop. We talked at first about common acquaintances from school, and then about our colleges. She had finished at Delhi University and started her MA in history at Jawaharlal Nehru University.

'No choice only, either vote for extreme right or extreme left,' she said. 'What to do?'

Her slang, it seemed to be a parody of the way Hindi-speaking people spoke English, was very different from IIT slang. It sounded like a minor functionary at a museum telling a foreign tourist what to do, or like a self-important clerk dismissing a petitioner to another window. At IIT our linguistic gymnastics sprang from caricaturing each other. We especially made fun of faux anglicization or Punjabi crudeness. And we had a fund of hand-me-down lingo whose provenance was unknown. Sometimes it was easy to infer where a word came from; funda came from fundamentals, which was what IIT was all about, fight came from sporting events where players used it to psyche themselves, max came from a maths textbook. It was impossible to tell when these words entered the language but it was clear that most of the slang was born inside the walls of the campus, or at least it was given its final form there. Listening to Aparna speak, I realized that campuses like the ones she had been to, DU and JNU, were much more porous to the rest of the city than IIT was. My three years in IIT had made me a foreigner to that city. I could speak its language, but it was not the language I spoke most often.

As I sat there speaking to Aparna I had a strange sensation. It was the feeling I was to have when I sat talking to a close American friend. It would usually come in the middle of an intense or intimate discussion, just after a moment of connection. I would suddenly think, there's a whole country within me that this person can never travel to.

Aparna and I could laugh and joke with each other in DU-speak, we could fight and make up in it, we could philosophize and complain in it, but I could never expect her to fully enter the room that was IIT slang. It was too cluttered with in-jokes and engineering references. It shifted shape too often. And it was too suffused with the stale smell of male sexual frustration. It sickened the stranger who wandered in.

'JNU is a hysterical place, totally hysterical,' Aparna said. 'Either you are extreme right or extreme left. My friends are mainly lefty so junta thinks I am lefty too. But the funny thing is that the most ardent supporters of the ML on campus spend two hours in prayer everyday. So pomo, na?'

I laughed along with her, it was impossible not to, although I had never met a Marxist-Leninist in my life and didn't know what pomo meant.

'Major angstiness keeps happening all the time. Makes me feel like a total Trishanku. What to do, Arindam? I can't shout, Ho Ho Ho Chih Minh, We Will Fight, We Will Win, with a straight face.'

She talked and talked, and I laughed and laughed with her. The manner in which she said words like 'yaar' and 'Trishanku' – as if she were a guy – charmed me completely. I was really enjoying myself when through the rain I saw a 615 trundling towards us.

'There's a 615,' I said. 'That'll take you to JNU.'

She turned to look at it. Her hand moved to adjust her jhola on her shoulder in preparation to clamber on, then it fell back. 'I'll take the next one,' she said.

A middle-aged lady, probably a clerk in a government bank, got off the bus. Her powdered primness had been rendered defunct by the rain and the wind, but she nonetheless opened her umbrella with a practised dignity and, before walking off, cast a glance at the two of us standing at the bus stop. She paused for a moment and then something about the silence Aparna and I stood sharing, sheltered from the rain on that grey drizzling day, made that bank clerk aunty smile.

'Yaar,' said Neeraj, dumping the hardback of *The Shadow Lines* I had lent him on my desk, 'this Amitav Ghosh's fundas are totally gol.'

I had lent *The Shadow Lines* to him a week ago so that he could make a presentation on it in the Indian Writing in English class he was taking to fulfil his Humanities requirements.

'Amitav Ghosh's fundas are gol? Are you sure?'

The book lay quivering on my table. He glared at it balefully, like he was silently challenging it to battle. 'Totally gol. Look at this.'

He opened out the page somewhere near the end of the book where the narrator draws a circle with Khulna at its centre and Srinagar on its circumference.

'See,' said Neeraj. 'So because of this problem in Srinagar there are riots in Khulna and people get killed in Dhaka. So, Amitav Ghosh draws a circle on a map…'

'Not Ghosh,' I broke in, 'the narrator.'

'Haan, haan, same thing. And then he says all this, that place is closer than this place and this place is closer than that place. How can he claim this?'

'What's wrong with it?'

'Well, basically he is claiming that this projection is conformal,' he said. 'Scale is preserved in every direction.'

'Isn't that true of these atlas maps?' I asked.

'For completeness' sake he should say which projection has been used.'

'So you aren't saying he's wrong,' I said, trying to figure out exactly what he was getting at. 'Just that what he has written is incomplete?'

'Yes,' he said. 'Especially since the earth is an oblate spheroid.'

'Let me guess,' I said. 'You haven't prepared your talk.'

'I couldn't understand anything,' he said, grinning broadly.

I sat him down and we started planning his presentation. Plot, characterization, the significance of the various women in the novel, all seemed to do little to pique his interest. Finally, I drew a time-space grid in which I put cities on one axis and time on the other.

'If you put Dhaka, 1964 in the centre,' I said, 'you can see that the narrative circles around this point. It goes forward and backward in time, from the Second World War to the 1970s, jumps from one place to another, London, Delhi, Calcutta, but the riots in Dhaka in 1964 are the central incident around which everything revolves.'

'Yes, yes,' he said, enthusiastic at last. 'That's true. He doesn't tell the story in one line.'

'It would be so boring, wouldn't it?' I said. 'Some guy writes dirty letters to a girl he met in London when she was an infant. She comes to see him in Calcutta and they go to Dhaka where they get caught in a communal riot.'

'That's true,' he said, absently, like he would when we discussed Algorithms and he was off into one of his deep thinks. 'But Rindu, tell me, how did he decide to write it in this way? How did he say, Okay now this comes, then that, now we go to the flashback in London, now we talk about Calcutta, now we go back to London? What's the logic of it?'

'There is a logic,' I said weakly.

'Haan, I know there is a logic. But what is the basis of the logic? What does it mean?'

Neeraj had, as usual, broken the problem down to its fundamentals.

'If I knew,' I said, 'then I would be Amitav Ghosh myself.'

He looked at me like he had found the answer to a question he had been asking for a long time.

'Rindu,' he said, 'why do you want to do research in Computer Science?'

'Why do I want to do research in Computer Science? What has that got to do with *The Shadow Lines*?'

But I knew what he was getting at, and I felt my heart sinking as I anticipated what he was going to say next.

'Why don't you become a writer? Study English Literature and write novels. That's your real interest, isn't it?'

'I like Computer Science,' I said, fighting down the anger that was rising within me. 'I like theory. I might not be as good at it as you are but I enjoy it. That's why I am doing it.'

'That's okay, Rindu,' he said, taking on an infuriating tone of certainty. 'I am not saying that you don't like it. But is it your passion? Is it what you really want to do or is it just something you feel you should do when what you really want to do is be a writer?'

'Me, a writer?' I said, making an effort to lighten my tone. 'No scene, yaar. What will I write? And who will read my books?'

He made as if to say something, then changed his mind. 'Okay, Rindu, he said, 'I'll go back to my hostel and write it all out for the talk tomorrow. If I don't write it all, I'll just forget it.'

The next afternoon I was hanging out near the Nescafé booth when Bhats came up.

'Neeraj gave a talk today,' he said. Bhats was in the Indian Writing in English class as well.

'Yes, yes,' I said. '*The Shadow Lines*. How did it go?'

'It went off so so. At the end he said: I want to thank my friend Arindam Chatterjee for helping me with the talk.'

'He actually said that?'

'Yes,' he said. 'We were all shocked, thought he would get a big fat zero but the prof, she just smiled.'

I smiled myself on hearing this. One year earlier I had topscored in the same class and I knew the professor well. In fact, I had overheard her saying that I was the brightest student she had seen for a long time.

*

We got off the bus on Kasturba Gandhi Marg, not half a kilometre from where I had spent the first fifteen years of my life.

'Where are we going?' I asked.

'Shhh,' Aparna said. 'You'll see.'

She turned into a side lane, stepping briskly through the early winter afternoon. Large leafy trees had laid out a patchwork of sun and shade on the asphalt. I skip-stepped from one wobbling island of light to the next, following in Aparna's wake.

'Are we going to USEFI?' I asked. 'Do you want GRE forms?'

'Oh fo, Arindam, so curious you are. Just wait, na?'

We turned before we reached the USEFI office, right near the riotously overgrown grounds of an old New Delhi bungalow which proclaimed itself the embassy of some small country. And then, just around a shallow bend, was the building we had come to see.

'Wow!' I said, taking in the large stone wall, the steps, the rusted Archaeological Survey of India signboard.

'It's Uggarsain ki Baoli,' she said, obviously delighted by my reaction. 'Isn't it great?'

The rickety iron gate blocking the entry into the old step-well swung open on pushing and we were in. A few pigeons jumped up at the disturbance, but weren't perturbed enough to actually take flight. The crows cawed halfheartedly. In the far corner a man was sleeping on his back, his face tucked into the crook of his right elbow.

The baoli descended away to the north, about fifty metres down. There was no water visible, only a thick dry layer of mud at what seemed to be the fourth level. Grass grew on it in patches. The front wall was a large arch inset with several smaller arches.

'That's where the shaft is,' Aparna said, following my gaze. 'The well is behind the arch. It's typical of Delhi's baolis. There are twenty-six of them scattered all over the city.' The slang had slipped away. Her eyes were shining with excitement.

'Do you want to go and see the shaft?' she said.

I did, but instead I said: 'Let's sit here for a while, it's beautiful.'

We sat on the steps halfway down the baoli. A hint of breeze swept in from the east and cooled my neck. I looked sideways at Aparna. She was looking up at one of the arches in the north wall. Her body sat loose and tranquil, her face was at peace and happy. I didn't speak, although I wanted to, or touch her, although I wanted to. I just sat there on the stone step and shared that moment with her.

'You know, Arindam,' she said finally, 'I love this place. When I was in DU, I would often get off the Special on my way home and come here for a while. Some days I would go to Old Delhi and wander around in the galis there. Other times I would go to Red Fort and sit there. But whenever I was in a really bad mood I would come here.

'My parents were so relieved, you know, that I like history. Anything, they said, as long as it holds your interest. You don't have to be a doctor or an engineer, just do something you like. I used to worry that I'll never find something that I like. It was scary.'

Then she turned to me: 'Do you like Computer Science?'

If that question had been posed to me a year earlier, before I took Kanitkar's class, I would have simply shrugged my shoulders and made a face. That day, a few months after Kanitkar had left, if someone else had asked, in some other place, I would have answered a fierce defensive yes. But the honest directness of her question gave me pause.

'Yes,' I said, finally, quietly. And I knew then that it was true.

'Five o'clock, this place closes,' said a disembodied voice from above. I turned to see that the sleeping man had woken and was now considering the two of us with suspicious interest. From his expression it was clear that he had classified us as one of those young couples who came to historical monuments in Delhi to fool around. His body language made it sufficiently clear that no fooling around was going to take place on his watch. I edged a few inches away from Aparna, attempting to set his mind at ease. Secretly I desperately wished that what he thought about us was true.

'Let's go and see the shaft,' I said. We got up and went to the ledge on the east wall.

'Hey, where are you going?' the man shouted. I looked up at him, put on the most superior expression I could manage, and motioned with my hand as if I were a Mughal emperor asking a talkative minister to shut up. His head jerked forward a bit, as if he couldn't believe what I was signalling. Then he dropped his shoulders and turned away, suddenly tired of the moral policing that had become the most important part of his job.

Up the steep staircase we came to the high platform behind the north wall of the baoli. A large circle was cut in it. I peered down into the blackness below. Picking up a little pebble I let it drop into the shaft.

'It's there,' said Aparna, a split-second before we heard a muted splash. 'It's one of the few remaining baolis with water in it.'

Looking up I saw the skyscrapers of Connaught Place towering over us to the north. 'All those people in all those windows,' I said. 'They can just look down here whenever they want and see this place. It probably makes their shitty jobs worth doing.'

Aparna came and stood next to me. 'The nicest thing about you,' she said, and there was laughter in her voice, 'is that you set out to be oh-so-profound but always get distracted into sounding smart-alecky.'

She slipped her hand into mine, casually, as if she had been holding my hand for years, as if it were not the first time we had touched each other with intention. I could hear my heart beat faster, I could feel my stomach contract with nervousness. When I finally looked around at her, she was looking at me.

'You know,' I stammered. 'You know, I don't think, ummm, I don't know, you know, I haven't, you see, actually, ummm, I don't know how to say this but, uh, what if that guy, ummm, you know, er, sees us ...'

And then I was quiet because she had shut me up with a kiss.

The International Happy School (registered) turned out to be a pink-washed concrete box nestled between godowns and shops on a small hill by the side of Mathura Road. Parking my scooter outside, I followed Neeraj in. He went to the office and I wandered down the hall into one of the classrooms. The desks were old and broken, too small for anyone older than six. There was less than a foot of space between the unevenly arranged rows. A large corner of the blackboard had broken away, baring the grainy wall behind it. This was the school in which Neeraj's niece studied.

I had missed the afternoon films at Siri Fort, it was the fifth day of the film festival. There had been a class I had wanted to attend. Neeraj had caught me outside the class and told me he needed a ride to Ashram. He had to pay his niece's school fees he said. After many arguments with his father he had managed to get her re-admitted to school, promising to pay her fees himself.

'Where are you going to get the money from?' I had asked.

'I'll borrow it,' he had said. And, anticipating my next question: 'Once I am in America I can repay it easily. Even if I save a hundred dollars every month from my stipend I can pay it all back in less than a year.'

It made perfect sense but when he had said it I had been shocked. I hadn't been able to conceive of debt on such a scale, gambling on a stipend which I may or may not get in a distant country which I may or may not reach.

We had reached the school by four thirty, the class finished at four. I had planned on dropping him back to IIT and getting to Siri Fort in time for the six o'clock screenings.

The huddle of desks in the tiny classroom was making me feel uncomfortable, so I stepped out into the sunlight. Mathura Road was in fine voice down below; trucks and buses thundered past, lorries brayed in their high-pitched tones, auto-rickshaws danced between their larger adversaries, growling like dogs attacking an elephant. Across the road was Hotel Rajdoot. Its fading exterior, and the large sign in an outdated font proclaiming its name, added a touch of anachronistic sleaziness to the landscape.

Someone had emptied a bucket of waste water on the pavement in front of the school. The water trickled down towards the road below, splitting into streams and recombining as it went. I was mapping this microcosmic riverine system, from watershed to scummy watershed, when Neeraj emerged.

'What do they think of themselves?' he burst out as soon as he saw me. His small frame was tight with rage, his large head leant into the expostulation.

'What happened?'

'I had given her last month's fees but the school people say it wasn't deposited. Either my father or her father must have taken it from her.'

'Wouldn't she tell you if they did?'

'She's scared of both of them,' he said. 'Very scared.'

Then the anger began draining out of his body. His thin moustache quivered with the hint of a sob. Taking a step towards the scooter, he said: 'Let's go, no point standing here.'

But we didn't go back to the hostel. I took him to a nearby dhaba instead and bought him some tea. The tea was boiling hot when it came and I could see that the small sips he was taking were soothing him from the inside.

'The whole problem began at the wedding itself,' he said. 'I was only about six or seven at the time so I don't remember the incident, but I have heard the story many times. When my father led my brother's baraat to the girl's house he found no preparations had been made. There was no shamiana, no food, not even a priest! It was a big insult for him. But he didn't call the wedding off. He arranged for a priest and the marriage was conducted, but he made it very clear that his daughter-in-law would never be allowed to visit her father's house. I think he knew that this would be a much worse punishment for her and her father.'

'But why were there no arrangements made for the wedding?' I asked.

'I don't know,' he said. 'I always asked that question but no one gave me a good answer.'

It was, I realized later, like the opening of a story from the Ramayana or the Mahabharata, complete with insults and wedding processions and fearsome vows.

'Anyway, she came to our house and everything was fine. My niece was born a year later. My second brother was getting ready to marry when one day a woman came from my bhabhi's house.'

'A woman?' I asked.

'Yes. Some woman, she was related to my bhabhi somehow, not directly. And she started saying that it was unfair that a girl should be kept away from her father's home, it was against the custom.'

'What did your father say?'

'He made it very clear that if bhabhi wanted to go she could go, but once she went she could never come back. He said: If you cross the threshold of this house once, it will be the last time.'

'He actually said that?' I asked. 'That's like something out of a Hindi movie.'

Neeraj looked puzzled at my amusement.

'Anyway,' I said, quickly, before his puzzlement turned to hurt, 'what happened then?'

'At first my bhabhi didn't want to go but that woman kept working on her till finally she agreed to go. At this point my father said: You can go if you want but your daughter will stay here. She cried and fought for two days but he would not budge. Nothing anyone said could make him change his mind. Your father insulted me in front of the whole world, he kept saying. Now he will pay for it.'

My eye fell on my watch, it was almost five-thirty. There was just half an hour left to the screening.

'Finally,' Neeraj said, 'she left and my niece had to stay. No one cares for her in my house, Arindam. Her father beats her. My father doesn't talk to her. Her grandfather insulted me, he keeps saying, Why should I talk to her? I am the only one who cares whether she lives or dies.'

I could feel a restlessness rise within me. There was not enough time to go to the hostel and then get to Siri Fort, I would have to take Neeraj along with me. But I didn't know how to bring it up. In this confusion I asked a tactless question. 'Why do you care so much for her?'

'Yaar,' he said, like he was explaining a complicated theorem to a dunce, 'she's my niece. I love her. I can do anything for her. Anything. Rindu, if you really love someone, it doesn't matter what the cost is, it doesn't matter if they can repay you or not, you have to do whatever you can for them. Besides, apart from me she has no one else in this world who will care for her.'

It sounded like a Hindi-film dialogue. But I didn't stop to figure out if he actually believed it. All I could think of was the film I was getting late for.

'Do you want to come to the film festival?' I asked.

'Do you have an extra pass?' he said, brightening up a little.

'Well, Sheikhu and I have delegate passes. We went to the directorate's temporary office in Siri Fort and they told us that there are three delegate cards for IIT students. All you have to do is get a letter. So we went to the Film Series Committee president who happily signed the letter with Sheikhu and my name on it. Now we are both delegates.'

'But how will I get in?' he asked.

'It's simple,' I said. 'Sheikhu and I go in, then one of us comes out with both the passes and gives you one. Then you go in. It's very simple, they never look at the photo.'

'That's fraud, I am not going to do that.' His voice was firm with moral conviction. I knew that the only way to get him to change his mind was to argue that cheating to get into a film festival was not wrong in the larger scheme of things. There wasn't time for that. And, besides, I had never won an argument with Neeraj.

'Okay, then,' I said. 'I'll drop you at the hostel and then go. At most I'll be fifteen, twenty minutes late.'

'Don't go, Rindu,' he said, and caught hold of my wrist. When I looked up at him I saw his eyes were bright with unshed tears.

If I had been a different person, if I had been Bhats or Kartik, for example, I would have laughed that moment off. I would have said something like: 'Don't maaro this senti on me, I have to go.' If I had been someone more like Neeraj himself I would have probably forgotten all about the film and answered his direct cry for help.

Instead, I looked away, wrested my wrist from his and got up. The intimacy of that moment was pounding at my chest like fear, and I wanted it to stop. 'I'll drop you at the hostel,' I said, looking away from Neeraj. 'Come.'

'I'll take a bus,' he said.

I waited till he had left and then ran to my scooter. Weaving and blustering my way through rush-hour traffic I got to the auditorium on time, that much I could recall when I thought about it later. But, try as I might, I could not recall what film I saw.

Three days after the film festival ended, its images were still swirling around in my head. All night I would dream elaborate montage dreams. Scenes from the films I had seen danced through my head while I slept, the actors replaced by Neeraj and Aparna and Sheikhu and Jatty-Jat and Kartik. When I awoke, tired and lightheaded, it would take me a few minutes to unravel the tangled threads of dream-reality from the knotted strands of the waking world.

It was in these foggy states of mind that I often found myself writing. Normally, I would carefully file away the pieces that came from these moments. Digging those pieces of paper out of their file would be like opening an old photo album.

That vocabulary was like an old shirt that I still had but was now ashamed of wearing; those ideas were like friends whose email addresses I still had but never used; and that intensity of emotion was like the moustache I used to have, it lived only in the snapshot.

But the piece I wrote that weekend right after the film festival, lived briefly in its present before it went into the file to become the past.

In the past whenever I wrote something I would always daydream that I had a girlfriend whom I could read it to. I would imagine her enraptured by my voice as I read, praising me when I stopped, loving me all the more for the beauty of my mind. And now I had a girlfriend. I dialled her number with nervous fingers and shuffled and reshuffled the pages in my hand as the bell rang.

'Dreary sunlit mornings slip unnoticed into overheated afternoons. Afternoons wear off, leaving behind a hot, sticky feeling which the gloom of the evening heightens. Even the clear darkness of the night cannot drive away the wet heat that bearhugs my mind. Day follows unmemorable day, with a monotony and dull inevitability that seems to cover everything like a layer of dirty snow. Long walks, spent ruminating, bring me to the same point again and again, physically and mentally. In the lustreless light of the evening, as I walk past drooping leaves and dead shrubs, I pass people coming from work. They seem to be serving a sentence. Confinement in isolation.'

'It's nice,' she said.

I cleared my throat. 'There's a little more.'

'I dreamt of you last night,' I said, switching back to my reading voice. 'I saw you in a temple. Your dark complexion glowed with energy, your big black eyes overflowing with the reflected light of the chandelier. You arched your neck slightly, turning it to one side. Placing your hands on your shoulders you moved them down your glistening wet body over your small breasts, touching your dark nipples with the tips of your fingers as you passed them. You flattened your palms inwards over your stomach, pressing it in. And then, you began dancing. You danced with abandon, your hair open, billowing and jumping and dancing. It had a life of its own, your hair. You danced and you danced and you danced and I realized that you wouldn't stop dancing. This would go on and on. But then a grey curtain seemed to fall in front of you, or maybe it fell in front of me and I awoke to find it was the middle of the night.

'That was two hours ago. Since then I have walked and walked. I thought at first about nothing. But the mind is an unstoppable machine. So, I thought about you. I thought about your body, so soft and yielding to the caress of my gaze. So living, so rich and resonant in the temple in my dream as it was when we talked. If only I had touched you then ...'

Through the low electronic whine of the phone line I could hear Aparna breathing.

'What do you think?' I asked, finally.

'It's nice,' she said again.

'You didn't like it?' I asked.

'I said it was nice, didn't I?' she said.

'What's wrong, Aparna?' I asked.

'Why is it so despairing and hopeless?' she asked.

'I don't know,' I said. 'Sometimes it's just like that.'

'Okay,' she said, sounding as if it were not okay, 'that's fine.'

'Didn't you like the description of the girl?' I asked, ignoring her attempt at defusing the situation. 'It's based on you.'

'Did you seriously think I would like it?' she exploded.

Despite my confusion I realized it was a rhetorical question.

'Do you have any idea how … how … how weird I was feeling when you were reading those descriptions? Like I had seen some photos of myself taken while I wasn't looking.'

'I didn't mean it like that,' I said quietly. 'I thought it was a romantic thing to do.'

'Listen,' she said, softening a little at the sound of my voice, 'I am not one of those film heroines who melt on hearing Urdu poetry. Read the stuff you wrote again, it's not about me, it's about some image of me that you have in your head.'

The truth of what she said rang through my mind like the proof of a theorem. It was the first time I was made to realize that to write about people meant having to leave oneself behind and enter into them. It was also the earliest point in my life when I learned that to love someone also entailed roughly the same thing.

As I put down the phone that evening I got the sinking feeling I would never be able to do either.

Evenings at the hostel are for hanging out, gossiping, sitting around. It's called paloing, the Hindi verb palna, to be nurtured, conjugated in a Hinglish way. It's deployed every evening. The quizzers go quizzing, the debaters go debating, the sporty types go sporting. Everyone else stays in the hostel, paloing.

I come back from the Institute around five, park my scooter in front of the hostel and head to the mess. It's time for tea – hot, sweet tea.

The mess is a big gloomy hall. Seven large thermocol letters on the front wall proclaim it to be 'OVR MESS'. A lazy mess committee volunteer, in an effort to create a sense of ownership amongst the hostel's residents, has ended up creating a new name for this place. 'Where are you going?'

'To the OVR, yaar, it's dinner time.'

Three long black tables carve up the eating space. People sit in clusters of eight or ten along these tables. Seeing me come in, one of these clusters hails me: 'Rindu!' Or, if it has been a good day, 'Okay, all right!' During the exams, being hailed is a rarity. The other groups acknowledge me as I pass them on the way to the serving area.

Picking up the fattest steel glass, or the thinnest one if I am not really in the mood, I check my hip pocket for samosa coupons. Both hands full, I hurry to the table. The steel burns my hand as I go.

'… So, you are at a crossing and you ask one guy, Bhaisahab, where is Vikaspuri C block and he says, Going to C block? No problem. I am going there too. Just follow me, put your scooter behind.'

'No, no, yaar, the best is when you ask the guy next to you, Bhaisahab, where is C block and the guy behind him butts in, Arré, let me tell you, I go there twice every day.'

'Come on, yaar, haven't you heard those guys: C block, hain? Just go straight till you reach the flyover. When you cross the flyover there is a red light. I normally just go right through, you can stop there if you want. From there I know a gali which starts near Sharma Electricals, but I think you should just take the main road till you get to the roundabout. Once you reach the roundabout, just ask anyone. It takes me about ten minutes from here, it will take you about twenty.'

This goes on till it's too dark to see each other's faces. Tea is no longer being served. Eventually someone gets up and that's the signal. People pick up their bags and file out from different doors, depending on which wing they live in. It is dusk in the courtyard by the time we leave. As we start on the stairs up to our rooms, the mess lights come on with a dull resounding click.

I go to my room and dump my bag on the bed. Then I come out and look around to see which other room is open. Spotting one I go across. Every evening there is one room designated for paloing.

A much used Deep Purple tape is grinding out Black Night or My Woman from Tokyo or Child in Time. Depending on how intense the drum parts are, Rocksurd is, or isn't, sitting on a chair waving his hands as he plays an imaginary drumset. Bhats is lying on the bed smoking a cigarette if it is a room where smoking is acceptable, just lying on the bed if it isn't. Kartik is pacing around, to the extent it is possible to pace in such a crowded and cramped space. Suraj is sitting on the floor with his back against the wall, his cigarette drooping from his fingers poised in front of his mouth, a half-solved crossword torn out of the *Times of India* lying on his lap.

I find a place and settle in. There's an hour to kill before dinner.

'Sheikhu's got the call, man!' Bhats exclaimed, his right hand raised for a high five. 'It's A, baby, okay, all right, Sheikhu's got a call from A.'

'Sheikhu? Which Sheikhu?'

'Fucker,' said Bhats, his arm beginning to show the strain of an unanswered high five. 'How many Sheikhus do you know? Compguy Sheikhu. Your Sheikhu.'

I looked down at Suraj. He nodded absently, murmured 'Yes, compguy Sheikhu, A, final call, ' then began to scribble something into the black-white grid lying on his lap.

We were in the second half of our last semester at IIT. A month or so had passed since the interviews for the IIMs. The daily excitement of interview calls coming in was fresh in my mind. Each evening would be a litany of names and campuses. Ahmedabad was the most sought after, then came Bangalore, Calcutta and finally Lucknow. And it was in this order that the interview calls were relayed. 'Did you hear, KD, he's cracked ABCL. All four!' 'Rindu, I got calls from ACL.' In all that time I had not heard any mention that Sheikhu had taken the CAT. Neither he, nor the CATwallahs from my hostel, had ever let slip that he was in the running. And now the first of the final calls were coming in and Sheikhu had a call from A. He had taken the CAT, he had got an interview call to A, he had filled his interview forms, written all those essays about career goals and personal strengths and weaknesses, he had taken the interview and participated in the group discussion. And I hadn't the slightest inkling that this had been going on.

I should have seen it coming. After all, the possibilities that lay before us were limited and Sheikhu had eliminated two of the major options: He had declared that he was not applying for schols abroad and the civil services were not a serious option for a funda guy like Sheikhu. That left just two possibilities: a job and IIM.

Every year several people took jobs in the various software companies that came to recruit on campus. Their annual pay packages were larger than anything my father had earned even after a lifetime in the government. They sent young, articulate recruiters who wore suits and sarees and asked difficult technical questions. There was one major problem: unlike the IIMs or American universities or the civil services, there was little danger of rejection. This counted severely against these places. When I thought of these companies I thought of cheap sunmica furniture, boring conversation in a second-rate canteen, years of toiling through routine jobs and a slow ascent up a crowded corporate ladder. Taking a job was a dull, stable option. It was what we were all supposed to be doing, as engineering graduates, but it was what very few of us really wanted.

Having known this I should have realized that going to management school was a very real possibility for Sheikhu. Every year the salary figures for graduating classes from IIM A seemed to climb higher and higher. They were beginning to get direct job offers from American companies with six-figure salaries in dollars. But it was this staggering amount of money, coupled with the notion that it was undeserved – it was given for being able to bullshit with élan – that had made going to IIM a disagreeable idea for Sheikhu and me. We had talked about it at length in our third year, secure in the knowledge that the work Kanitkar was preparing us for was the antithesis of the IIM model of success: low-paying and worthwhile. This was the only excuse I could offer for not having guessed that he would take the CAT and it was probably why he hadn't told me that he was taking the exam.

Having satisfied Bhats with a perfunctory slap on his palm, I turned and headed down to my scooter. The most uncomplicated feeling that rose to the surface was one of hurt: Why had he not told me? Why had he kept this really important thing from me? Doesn't he think I am his friend? Following close on its heels was the feeling of having been left out: I could have helped him with his essays. I am good at that. And as that cleared, came the keen feeling of sadness: He must be feeling terrible, like he sold out, like he gave up.

I came through the reception, casting a glance at the big table on which the mail was kept. Like on every other day, my eye searched for the stiff-papered envelopes from American universities that would bring news of my applications. There were none. The quotidian disappointment stirred up one last emotion whose viciousness surprised me: He gave up. I didn't.

Sheikhu was sitting on someone else's scooter outside his hostel. I parked right next to him. 'Congrats, yaar,' I said, trying to inject the correct note of jubiliation into my voice.

He looked up at me. His mouth was set in the typical way he had, the expression which made people think he was an arrogant fuck. That day it struck me that this disdainful face of his was a way of hiding what he truly felt.

'Thanks,' he said quietly, his eyes scanning my face.

A band of guys heading back from the Institute spotted him sitting there. 'Cool crack Sheikhu! IIM A! Fucking crack, man! Shit, I knew you would blast through CAT and the interview! Treat, treat, treat!'

Backslappers engulfed him. He made an effort to smile. It would have been insulting not to. Not to be happy at having breezed into IIM A was to make a mockery of all those who worked for months, who attempted the CAT year after year, and still couldn't make it. So he battled through his crowding emotions and smiled.

After a while he got off the scooter, and went and sat on the grass. I sat with him as he pulled blade after blade of grass out of the hostel lawns and dissected it. The hostel's lights came on eventually. Sporty types started returning for dinner, squash rackets or volleyballs in hand, fanning themselves with their T-shirts as they walked, laughing and chatting about the game just done. If they had seen Sheikhu sitting there on the grass they would have come across to congratulate him, word of his achievement must surely have made its way out to the playing fields as well. But it was dark where we sat so they walked by, into the well-lit hostel where a shower and a hot meal awaited them.

And as they strolled into the hostel to perform the rituals of yet another evening at IIT, Sheikhu and I sat on the lawns, in the dark, silently plucking the yellowing grass from the dry earth.

In the two hours between the GRE general test and the GRE Computer Science subject test, fifteen compguys could be seen running helter-skelter on the dry turf outside the examination centre. They seemed to be playing some sort of game involving one person running around touching the others. The touch of this person was poison and, like most poisons, would cause the touched to sit on his haunches till one of the others came by and administered the antidote, another simple touch.

Neeraj ran the hardest and got pushed down most often. Whenever he was touched he laughed loudly and sat down uncomplainingly. He weaved and dodged as hard as he could but of this unathletic company he was easily the least robust. At the GRE centre, when a group of twenty-year-olds played this game of vish-amrit, as a joke, or maybe as a way of bidding farewell to a childhood fast slipping away, they seemed to have, by unspoken consensus, eliminated the cruelty that had always been its concomitant in the past.

Earlier in the day we had taken the general test. Over a three hour period we had sailed through the quantitative sections, wrestled hard with the analytical sections and taken our chances with the verbal sections along with various other people from different colleges or from other departments at IIT. Now everyone else was gone, only the compguys were left. Many Computer Science departments didn't need to see a subject test score. But all the good ones did.

That afternoon between the exams, fifteen compguys running on the grass, was the launching pad for a long association that would carry itself forward to America. We would marvel together at how different our lives had become, and react to that difference in remarkably similar ways. In the course of hundreds of fierce, intimate battles conducted over email we would watch each other grow into men. Slowly our energies would get diverted – wives, children, professions, institutions – and the intensity of the engagement would wane. But much would be said and done before then. And that afternoon before the GRE subject test would always return to my memory as the beginning of this long shared journey.

Like the JEE, four years in the past now, the subject test was an exam we respected. 'You can't study for it, yaar, it's all fundas. If your fundas aren't clear after four years of CS, they aren't going to get cleared in two weeks of study.' The result came as a percentile and it revealed your fundas as clear or gol once and for all. It was like getting tested for a fatal disease, there was nothing you could do to change the result.

Most of us had not studied for the exam. We had looked around halfheartedly for guidebooks but there were hardly any around. So, we spent the afternoon playing vish-amrit, a game, I thought, that captured my idea of the way the world itself worked. There were people out to poison you, to push you down. But when you were down there were others who would help you up, who would heal you with their touch.

There was a fundamental difference between the way Neeraj played the game and the way I played it. When he got pushed down he would yell and shout at the others: 'Give me amrit! Come on, yaar, give me amrit.' I found this behaviour childish, undignified. When I got pushed down I would sit quietly on my haunches waiting for someone to come by. I was never able to recall whether he got helped up more than I did.

The day after the GRE was a quiet Sunday in the hostel. I returned in the afternoon, feeling rested after having slept for ten hours at home the night before. Even before I had finished taking my underwear out of the backpack, there was a knock on the door.

'Hi Rindu, going to wash your clothes?' It was Neeraj.

'Umm, no,' I said, putting the underwear down. 'I just got back from home.'

Neeraj came in and sat on my bed. I felt my stomach tightening with bitterness as I waited for him to say something.

'How was the exam?' he asked.

'What the fuck do you mean how was the exam? Why did you do that?' I asked.

'What?'

'You know well enough what,' I said. 'I saw the way you were sitting, with your back turned towards me, hiding your paper from me. Why did you do that? And if you hadn't done anything, why did you run off without talking to me after the exam?'

Neeraj and I had seats next to each other in the subject test. All through the exam he kept his paper out of my sight. It wasn't as if I wanted to cheat off his exam, I had given up copying on homeworks and exams around the time I had decided I wanted to do a PhD. At the GRE subject test I had wanted to go it alone, but an old instinct had led me to survey the terrain around me. I noticed Neeraj sitting in a strange way, as if to make sure I didn't copy. At first I had thought it was just idiosyncratic exam behaviour but something had made me keep checking his posture, and then, to take the test further, I had leaned over in his direction. The way his body had scrunched up in response had confirmed my suspicion.

'I wanted you to do it on your own, Rindu,' Neeraj said, his sanctimoniousness making my skin bristle. 'Sooner or later, you will have to learn to pull your cart yourself.'

'I didn't want to cheat from your paper, okay? I am just angry that you thought I would.'

'Rindu, you prize grades over knowledge, yaar,' he said. 'You always have. Scores are not important, it's how much you understand that matters.'

Anger took a tight vice on my head. As I tried to shake it off I felt the words erupt from my mouth. 'Fuck you, Neeraj! You didn't want to show me your paper because you wanted to top the exam. You wanted to prove to everyone that you know more than they do, that you are a fucking genius. It isn't enough for you that everyone already thinks you are the smartest guy in the world. Your classmates, professors, everyone. You just can't get enough of their praise. So listen: you are the most intelligent man ever, you are the smartest theoretician in the world, you are a genius. Happy? That's what you want to hear, isn't it? Fuck you and your "scores aren't important" bullshit. Knowledge means nothing to you either.'

Neeraj's face was expressionless. Something glistened in his eyes, but in the shadowy light of the afternoon I couldn't tell if it was a tear. My wrath spent, I immediately felt sorry for what I had done.

'Listen,' I said, sitting down on the bed, reaching across to touch his shoulder, 'I'm sorry. I didn't mean all that.' But as I said it, pausing between phrases, waiting for him to interrupt me and say that he was sorry too, I felt my contrition fade away.

'Let it go, yaar,' he said, forcing a cheerful tone, shrugging my hand off his shoulder. 'Tell me how the exam went.'

'Okay,' I said.

'What did you do for that question with M memory modules connected by a ring?' he asked.

'Oh that one,' I said. 'I think I took every alternate module and passed a message around this subring. That gave me a lower bound of M.'

'But if you take them in pairs and contract them repeatedly,' he said, 'you get M log M.'

'Really?' I said, trying to work out what he was saying in my head. 'So you take a pair, send a message, then look at the pair as a single unit ... Oh! Yes. That's right. Shit, I fucked that up. That's negative one fourth right there.'

I tried to laugh at myself, but the disappointment was keen and the self-deprecating chuckle ended up as a snort of disgust.

'What about the recursive language question?' he said.

And then, one by one, he began bringing up problems that he somehow seemed to know I had done wrong. Each solution was characterized by the subtlety that the subject test was famous for. I had been looking for this level of intricacy, but I had not been able to spot it. Neeraj had seen right through the exam, had cracked the questions in all their hardness, and had guessed that I would not have figured them out.

I tried to cut the conversation short, or postpone it. 'Fuck it yaar, it's over now,' or 'Let's discuss this later, I am not in the mood right now.' But he kept coming, question after question. It started feeling like a dream in which I run to escape the desert but the faster I run, the vaster the desert seems. A voice inside me started saying: Make this stop, make this stop.

'Why are you doing this, Neeraj?' I said, finally.

'Doing what?' he said.

'Why are you torturing me like this? I thought you were my friend.'

The mask of normalcy he had been wearing came off with a suddenness I had not expected. 'Friend?' he said. 'You. You thought I, I, was your friend?' His big head was rocking back and forth over his little frame. 'Do you remember the time in the lab when you helped write my SOP? Do you remember what you had said then?'

I remembered that I had sat with him and rewritten his statement of purpose. His grammar was terrible and I knew that if any admission committee in America looked at what he had written, they would have laughed till they burst. That's why I had helped him. And, of course, because helping people with their essays allowed me to show off my English skills.

'What did I say?' I asked.

'I said, Thanks for helping me with this, and you said, No problem, yaar, you help me with CS, I'll help you with English.'

It must have been an off-the-cuff statement because I didn't remember having made it.

'So,' I said, 'what's the big deal?'

'That's not friendship,' he howled. 'I don't want your help in exchange for my help. That's not friendship. If you were my friend, you would have never said that.'

'But, Neeraj, I just said that I was happy to help you because you helped me in other things. What's wrong with that?'

'That's not friendship, Rindu,' he said, his voice thick with tears. 'If you were really my friend you wouldn't have even thought such a thing. You would have helped me just because I was your friend. That's what friendship is.'

In my world you talked about things with friends, and you were there for them in emergencies, but there were certain limits, certain things you did not say – especially with male friends. The Hindi-movie world Neeraj was coming from, full of stories of violence and greed and lifelong grudges, seemed to involve friendship as fierce as the hatred it bred. It was nothing like the world I knew, where violence was quickly swept under the carpet, hatred got converted into petty jealousy, and friends didn't ask for more than their friends were willing to give.

'I am your friend, Neeraj,' I said. 'Maybe I can't express it in the same way, but I am your friend.'

'If you were my friend, you wouldn't have left me that day we went to the school,' he said, scratching the scab that had formed over my guilt.

'I'm really, really sorry about that,' I said. 'Really sorry.' An intense feeling of remorse spread under my skull like the beginning of a headache. 'Really, really sorry, Neeraj.' Every 'really' was like pressing down on an aching muscle, a temporary relief. The moment it was said, the pain flooded back.

'You don't know what friendship is, Rindu,' he said, sounding calmer now. I got up off the bed, my legs feeling stiff, my stomach tying itself in knots. A large wave of self-pity crashed down on me. What about me? I thought to myself. Who tells me I'm good enough when I feel I'm not? Who looks at me when I need attention? And as I articulated these questions to myself, I felt anger rising and salving the guilt and the pain I had been feeling.

'Yes,' I said. 'I don't know anything about friendship. And if you're done with your friendly questions, why don't you go back to your own friendly hostel?'

A few weeks later the subject test results came out. Neeraj was in the ninety-ninth percentile. He had scored higher than any of us, some people said higher than anyone else in India. My own score put me in the ninety-fifth percentile. 'That's a good score for you,' Sheikhu said when he heard. He was right. It was a good score.

For me.

It's the sweat accumulating on my neck that wakes me up finally. I flap my hand over it. There's a blanket of air lying heavy on me. It doesn't budge.

My ears slip into wakefulness before my eyes open. A viscous silence fills the room. The fan isn't whirring. Outside, the hostel is buzzing. It doesn't have the urgency of morning or the weariness of evening. This means one of two things. And since there are no exams on right now it can mean only one thing. I open my eyes with a groan. The electricity is out.

The darkness is as absolute as it will ever be. No orange glow leaks in through the gaps in the black chartpaper covering my window. The slit beneath my door is invisible, the white neon of the hostel corridor is absent. A stab of panic: Have I gone blind? Shaking off the feeling I snake my arm out towards where I normally leave my spectacles. Putting them on doesn't make the darkness light, but it does sharpen it. I begin to roll out of bed, realizing suddenly that I have no clothes on.

The floor isn't littered for a change. In this weather the only way to cool the room at night is to pour a bucket of water on the floor before sleeping and turn the fan on full blast. And if this involves displacing the tutorial sheets and underwear and soapcases and shreds of magazine covers that make their home on the floor, so be it.

Gingerly placing my foot on the floor I find it dry. In the recesses of my sleepy mind, surprise at the dryness takes a full two seconds to register. My head turns to the clock after another two seconds. Its fluorescent arms proclaim three-thirty.

'Oye Mozu! Oye Lulli! Oye Champi! Oye Panty! Oye Rindu! Oye Bhats!' Rocksurd's voice comes thundering down the corridor.

'Calm on, fuckers! Calm on!'

The sound of doors being kicked grows louder as he walks down the row. I scramble for a towel. I have just managed to wrap it around me when my door explodes inward.

'Calm on, baby,' he bellows. 'Calm on!'

'I'm coming,' I grumble.

He moves on to the next door.

I hold on to my towel as we make our way up to the highest floor of the north wing. Dark figures scurry up and down the stairwell. A bucket hits me in the thigh on its way up. Too sleepy to curse, I take a halfhearted swat at its owner. Too late.

We walk around to the side facing Jwalamukhi hostel. From here I can see all the boys' hostels. The distant ones seem quiet. They aren't, of that I am sure. It's just that I can't make out what's going on there. But across the way I can clearly see that Jwala is on the boil.

'Kumaon ki le li. Zigzag zigzag,' a faint cry emerges from the wing closest to our hostel.

'Jwaala waalon!' calls Rocksurd.

'Gand mara lo!' we respond.

The shouting match intensifies. More people join on both sides. Jwala is asked to get its collective ass fucked. Kumaon is declared Jwala's sister and Jwala proclaims itself a sisterfucker. Kumaon fucks Jwala, zigzag zigzag. There's even a rhyme that talks about half a field being sowed with radish, half with shehtoot, and then follows this up with a bird sitting on a tree making an indelicate reference to Kumaon's mother's privates.

All of a sudden there's a flash of light on the south wing's roof. There's the sound of a projectile sailing through the air and then, on the other side, the smashing of glass. Tomorrow we will discover that some science-minded Kumaonite has attacked Jwala with a tumbler stolen from the mess, launching it with a large firecracker. In doing so he has given a fittingly innovative expression to an age-old hostility.

Jwala's carefully orchestrated abuse dissolves into a long 'oye' carried by a few hundred voices. It rises in pitch and volume till it crashes and breaks. A loud angry gurgle replaces it.

I flee the north wing balcony, as do the others I was shouting with. We run to the lawn in front of our hostel. Not to engage with a possible invasion but to build ourselves an alibi. 'Yaar, I have been down here since the light went.'

A few hundred feet away we see a crowd of Jwalaites. It rumbles and churns but it doesn't move towards us. Later we will find out that their house secy and mess secy are talking to them, calming them down. Finally, the mob turns towards Kumaon. But instead of charging, they yell obscenities at us. We don't answer. Their anger is legitimate.

The excitement subsides and we sit around waiting. Lit cigarettes glow and fade like fireflies. The darkness here is not total, it's coloured a faint silver by the moon and the stars. Dark shapes doze on the lawn and on the steps and on people's scooters. Occasionally someone fans himself with a newspaper. My neck keeps rolling back with sleep but the pressing humidity keeps me awake. The ground is soft and cooling, the grass itches my skin.

The eastern sky is beginning to look lighter than the west. It's well past four. Someone starts snoring. I want to get up and locate the culprit but my body feels too heavy.

With a loud hum a hundred fans come on suddenly. Tubelights flicker to life. A brief cheer resounds through the campus and then we all hurry back to our rooms to retrieve what is left of our sleep.

'Hey Rindu, just wearing a towel, haan?' I don't answer, continuing to walk towards my room. A pair of hands tugs at the towel. I don't resist.

Naked and sleepy I keep trudging towards my room till the perpetrator, his prank having totally misfired, comes running up and returns my only covering.

'This is Chanda,' says Neeraj. 'My niece.'

Aparna smiles at Chanda. She puts out her hand as if to pat the younger girl's head, but then lets it drop to her shoulder. She isn't old enough to pat people on the head.

Chanda is small for her fourteen years, a shapeless, sexless girl with delicate fingers. Her face is crafted to express sadness, an innocent, spontaneous sadness. But at that moment it is reshaped into cautious delight.

'It's a lovely name,' Aparna says. 'So fitting.' And no one who sees Neeraj's niece warm to Aparna's touch can disagree, no one who sees her smile shyly at the compliment. Her face is lambent like a tadbhav moon.

A month before I left India for the US, left Delhi for Baltimore where I had been accepted to a PhD programme in Computer Science, Aparna and I went to meet Neeraj. He was leaving that day, a few weeks before the rest of us. Kanitkar had asked him to come to Chicago before the semester began. 'I agreed immediately, I want to finish my PhD in three years maximum.'

Neeraj hadn't told his father he was leaving for America till his visa came through. There had been a fight, his father had thrown him out of the house. He had rented a small apartment in Parkash Mohalla, a village behind East of Kailash. All the times I had gone to watch films at Sapna, I had not known that a place called Parkash Mohalla existed just a few hundred yards in from the main road.

'I've never heard of Prakash Mohalla,' I had said over the phone.

'It's Parkash Mohalla,' Neeraj had said. 'Just ask anyone at Sapna Cinema. Once you find it, ask for Gandhi's house. I am renting the first floor.'

Asking for Gandhi's house had led us to the wrong place. Twisting through narrow streets, looking down even narrower galis for a clue to our destination, we had arrived at a computer training institute that promised to train its students in operating several important pieces of commercial software. A young man dressed in jeans and a clean white shirt loitered outside it. Despite suspecting that he was an outsider to the mohalla, I had followed his directions up the street to Gandhi's house.

'Who are you looking for?' I had been asked by a man who had seen us trying to find a staircase.

'My friend is renting a room on the first floor here,' I had said.

He had thought for a second then said: 'Is he short, with a moustache, has been renting for one month?'

'Yes.'

'Go up the street, turn left at the dairy, then left again at the end of the road. Then right near the PCO. It's the second house on the right. He is on the first floor.'

'But,' I said, 'he told me he was in Gandhi's house.'

'Yes, yes,' the man had said. 'That is also Gandhi's house.'

The flat had two rooms, one leading into the next, and a kitchen in the back. The outer room was entirely bare. In the inner room sat two large suitcases on one side and a thin mattress covered by a faded sheet on the other. On this sheet lay a canvas schoolbag and a water bottle. Gandhi had built shelves into the walls, and created a concrete alcove above them. Neeraj had kept his air ticket, his passport and the envelope containing his I-20 on one of the shelves. In the alcove sat a small hand mirror.

'This is Aparna Chachi,' Neeraj said.

'No, no!' I had exclaimed. 'She's no chachi-shachi.'

Aparna grinned.

Chanda looked up at her obliquely. 'Chachi is beautiful, looks just like Smita Patil.'

At this Aparna blushed and I burst into gotcha laughter.

Neeraj and I settled down on the mattress. Aparna and Chanda went into the kitchen.

'Does your father know she's here?'

'No,' he said. 'He thinks she is at school.'

'Good that she came to see you off,' I said.

He looked down at the sheet on the mattress, reached for a corner, rolled it around a finger, then unrolled it.

'All your stuff packed?' I asked.

'Haan.'

'How many hours at Heathrow?'

'Six or seven.'

'And then direct to Chicago?'

'Haan.'

The sound of something hitting oil filled the room. I looked through the grille window into the kitchen. Aparna was at the stove cooking a paratha. Next to her at the counter stood Chanda, rolling out the parathas, stuffing them with paneer, then folding them over and rolling them out again into perfectly round pieces. The ease with which she worked made her look much older than she was. Her schoolgirl's pigtails made her look younger than she was.

Aparna reached for the paratha with the slender index finger of her left hand and her thumb, an artistic gesture. She flipped it over, then seeing it wasn't done enough, flipped it back. I saw her in profile, her brown shoulder pointing at me out of the red sleeveless cotton kurta she wore.

'This kurta is very pretty, Chachi,' Chanda said.

'Come with me some day,' Aparna replied, turning from the stove and looking her up and down. 'There are lots of these in Sarojini Nagar.'

Chanda smiled a wide toothy smile in response.

Lunch was ready fifteen minutes later. Chanda came out with a single plate piled with parathas. Aparna was carrying a bowl with some sabji in it. They put the food down in the middle. I was looking around for some newspaper to put my parathas on when Chanda broke off a piece, picked up sabji with it and brought it to my mouth. Blushing a furious red I pulled back.

Neeraj burst into laughter: 'He's blushing!' Aparna laughed too, but I could see that she had been taken by surprise as well. Chanda's hand didn't follow me but it didn't fall back either. It just bobbed up and down like it would in front of a recalcitrant three-year-old.

Intensely conscious that my mouth was touching another person's fingers, I took the food Chanda was offering me. Even as I began chewing on it, Aparna reached for the parathas, formed a bite like Chanda had, and offered it to her. She took it happily. Aparna started to bring her hand back, then reached out once again and caressed Chanda's head, stroking it softly as she ate. Chanda smiled as she chewed, first at Aparna, then at me and finally at Neeraj, who looked closer to crying than he had at any point that day.

We worked our way through the stack of parathas, each one feeding the other. In my head I found myself calculating the number of different ways in which four people could feed each other. At first I thought it was six, but when Neeraj fed me and I fed him back I realized that these two were two entirely different actions, so I had to change the answer to twelve. We sat there eating paratha and sabji in twelve different ways, and I wondered how Aparna and I would explain to our friends in the Delhi that lay outside Parkash Mohalla what had happened at lunch that day.

Afterwards Chanda opened her schoolbag and brought out a sketchbook. She flipped through the pages, showing Aparna her pencil drawings.

'These are lovely,' Aparna said. Each one of the drawings depicted an empty room. Some had chairs, other's simply had windows through which one saw nothing. The lines were controlled sometimes and sometimes they sprayed across the page.

'I love drawing,' Chanda said.

'Do you have a pencil?' Aparna asked, opening out a blank page in the sketchbook.

Aparna took the pencil in her left hand and started scratching away at the page with the flat part of the lead. Her hand moved continuously and quickly. Seeing her bent over that sketchbook, her face cast in the focused tranquillity of a person at work, her back bent, her neck extended forward, her legs folded away behind her, her right hand supporting her weight, I wished I could draw too so that I could sketch her like this.

'Here,' she said, when she was done.

Chanda took the sketchbook from her. It was the silhouette of a girl, sketchbook in hand, standing in a light grey fog. 'Chachi drew me,' said Chanda, handing the drawing to Neeraj.

I drove Aparna to the Sapna Cinema bus stop. We wanted to give Neeraj and Chanda time to say their goodbyes before Chanda returned home. Aparna too had to get back to JNU. Before leaving, Aparna gave Chanda her hostel address and told her to come and meet her.

'Thanks for coming, Chachi,' I said when Aparna got off the scooter at the bus stop.

'No, Rindu,' she said, laughing weakly at my joke. 'Thank you.'

'That was a lovely sketch,' I said.

'It was nothing,' she said. 'When I was small, that was my favourite doodle. That's why I can do it so fast, almost without thinking. My mother would come in and see it and say, Again you're drawing yourself. Draw someone else for a change.'

I put my hand on her arm and rubbed it.

'It's so sad, Rindu,' she said, her voice breaking. 'She's such a lovely girl. It's so unfair.'

Neeraj had a suitcase open and was moving clothes around when I got back to his flat.

'Chanda's gone?' I asked.

'Haan.'

He took out a towel, a new pair of trousers and a shirt. 'I'm going to bathe.'

I sat on the mattress and waited. Outside, day began to turn to night. I sat on the mattress trying to imagine what Chanda must be feeling now that the last person who cared for her was gone. 'It's so unfair,' I thought, and that phrase made me think of Aparna, picking up a paratha, stroking Chanda's hair, sketching a lonely little girl in the sketchbook.

'Why are you sitting in the dark?' asked Neeraj, flicking on the light switch as he came in.

'What's going to happen to Chanda?' I asked.

He averted his face. Folding the towel slowly, he put it into a polythene bag.

'I'll come back and get her once she's eighteen,' he said, stuffing the bag into the suitcase. 'My father won't be able to say anything then.'

'But that'll be years from now,' I said.

'Then you tell me Rindu, what should I do?'

I washed the dishes and packed them in newspaper. He put them into one of his suitcases. We put the garbage into a plastic bag and deposited it outside the flat. The taxi had been called at eight, and it was almost seven thirty when Neeraj put on his new shirt and his new pants.

'This belt is too big,' he said. 'It needs two more holes.'

Dusk had brought Parkash Mohalla to life. Lights had come on at the PCO booth. The operator sat inside, his feet up on the table, his eyes closed, waiting for nine o'clock, when STD rates would fall and people would file in to call their families in Palwal and Meerut and Gwalior and Muzaffarnagar. Further down the road, there was a knot of people standing outside the computer training centre. Old men were walking in twos, their daughters-in-law were out in their verandas watering their plants.

We turned a corner and went through a gap in the boundary wall into the larger market beyond.

'Where's the mochi?' I asked.

'I don't know, we'll have to find one.'

Many of the shops had signs in Bengali. A couple of them sold sweets. They looked just like the sweet shops in Chittaranjan Park, except these were run down whitewashed affairs with naked bulbs for lighting, no marble flooring or bright neon lights.

'I didn't know there were Bengalis here,' I said.

'Bongolis are everywhere,' he said. 'Do you want a shondesh, you bhooka bangali?'

I laughed.

We found a mochi finally.

'How much?' I asked, when he was done.

'Give me whatever you want to,' he said in Bengali-accented Hindi, a mirror of my own Hindi-accented Bengali. I brought out a five-rupee note and gave it to him.

'You are spoiling the rate,' said Neeraj once we were out of earshot.

'What do you care? You are leaving tonight.'

'That's not the point,' he snapped.

We walked in silence for a while.

'So what are you planning to do in Chicago?' I asked.

'I want to finish my PhD in three years maximum,' he said. 'I can do it in less but they won't let me.'

'Who won't let you?'

'The university.'

'But you haven't even started, Neeraj,' I said.

'I know I can do it, Rindu. I have lots of ideas. If even one of them works out, it could be whole PhD dissertation.'

I found myself walking a little faster.

'You know, Rindu,' he went on, 'sometimes when I am unhappy I think of a theorem as I lie down to sleep. When I wake up in the morning, I have the proof.'

It felt like we were back in my room with him throwing answers to the most difficult subject GRE questions in my face.

'It's eight already, Neeraj,' I said. 'The taxi must be here.'

We slipped back into Parkash Mohalla through the cut in the wall and were about to turn the corner when a large Sikh came around it.

'You called for a taxi?' he said.

'Yes.'

'Where were you? I have been looking for you for half an hour. Finally the PCO wallah told me that one big guy and one small guy went to the market a little earlier, they must be the ones who called you. That's why I was going to the market to find you.'

Suddenly I saw Neeraj and myself through the eyes of the PCO wallah: one big guy and one small guy. I saw us walking in the campus, me looking at the ground hunched slightly to prevent my stomach from sticking out, Neeraj walking his brisk bouncy step. And in that moment I missed Neeraj more strongly than I ever would in the future, more strongly because he was right there, right next to me.

'Chal, Rindu,' he said once the suitcases were loaded into the taxi and the keys deposited with the downstairs neighbour. 'I'll go.'

'I'll be there soon,' I said. 'I'll email you as soon as I get an email account.'

I knew this wasn't really a parting, we would meet several times in the future. Professionally and personally our lives would remain intertwined, we had too many things in common for it to be otherwise. But as we hugged tightly it felt like the end of something, and like a long awaited release, like freedom and sadness tightly woven into one another.

After the taxi had trundled around the corner I put my helmet on and went to my scooter. I sat on it for a few minutes, my mind absolutely blank, before I kicked it alive. I turned the throttle a few times, letting the engine roar idly. Finally I put it into gear and left Parkash Mohalla.

8

I Climbed Mt. Rainier in Jeans

SHE STOOD AT THE MOUTH OF THE ARBOUR, UNDER THE ARCH, her gaze fixed in the direction of the parking lot. Her complexion had deepened into a richer brown, or it could have been that a year-and-a-half of being surrounded by black and white people had dulled my sensitivity to brown. I paused at the turnstile and looked at her, conscious even at that moment that this scene was being graven into my memory, that it would come back again and again with differing intensity, in black and white or colour, newsreel grainy or Technicolor glossy.

College kids cutting class clustered in the space between her and me. Denim blues and T-shirt reds, a parrot-green dupatta, a bright pink top, gleaming leather shoes; the handloom beige of her shawl thrown into soft perspective. Her jawline – sharp-soft, young – made my heart lurch like it had lurched the first time she had climbed onto my scooter behind me.

The turnstile rattled against my knee.

Her smile, when it came, was pure joy, alight with an intelligent, innocent affection. My own face creased into a broad dimpled grin: involuntary at first and then, when the sadness came flooding back, sustained by clenching my cheeks.

We didn't eat at Nirula's: 'This place is too much yaar, all these shady lovebird types.' Walking towards the bus stop – past the cinema hall's marquee, past stairs leading down to a defunct video game parlour, past momo shops and leather stores, past pasty Russian women, possibly prostitutes, through the municipal shopping centre-cum-office complex – I took refuge in telling stories of the guys from NOIDA who I used to take the school bus with. 'Get off the bus, head through RK Puram to Karnataka Sangam for a dosa. Then Moti Bagh Railway Station. It takes two hours for the ring railway to go all around Delhi. Plenty of time to catch an eleven o'clock show at Chanakya. Out at one, just in time to catch the school bus back to NOIDA.'

'Too much, yaar,' she said. 'Sounds like a lot of fun.'

'I never went with them,' I said.

'Too bad. It would have done you good.'

We caught the bus at the stop across from the one where we had once taken shelter from the rain.

'Connaught Place,' I told the conductor. He tore off two tickets without asking me if we were together. Aparna made her way through the bus, elbows up. I followed.

'Must be strange for you to travel DTC again, na?' she said.

'Not really,' I said. 'It's a little strange to travel with a girl though, always wanting to run to the front. I normally stay at the back, get off from there.'

'That's because you don't get pawed when you do,' she said, and there was a fight in her voice. It was as if she had said: 'You are an insensitive bastard.' That in itself would have hurt but there was more: 'You aren't my boyfriend any more. No more immunity.'

I was quiet all the way to Connaught Place.

Loneliness is a disease whose symptoms grow worse at night. They would begin to creep over me once my roommates went to sleep. I would find myself going to the department at midnight, aimlessly surfing the web, trying to read what I was supposed to have read during the day. I would walk the corridors looking into other offices hoping to find someone to talk to.

If I stayed at home I spent six hours at a time in front of the television, getting up only to eat or pee, till my limbs grew stiff and my head hurt. And sometimes, tired of infomercials and sitcom reruns, I would find myself sitting in the living room late at night with the lights off, playing the outgoing message on my answering machine over and over again. 'You've reached Manas, Vijay and Arindam's number. Please leave a message.'

In the first few months of my stay in America there had been correspondence with Aparna to look forward to. I would write her a long email every day, telling her about the films I had seen and the classes I was taking and how adrift I felt. She would write back once in three days, a short disjointed email typed hurriedly at a cybercafé or a friend's place. The sentences would begin with lowercase letters, she would misspell everything and punctuate nothing. In the first reading the email would make me feel better but it would always be too short and by the time I read it a fifth time I would feel resentment crawl biliously up my throat. My own paragraphs became even neater, I'd rewrite and polish each line, running a spellcheck before sending out each email.

When I called her on the phone she never had time to talk. Her parents had moved away from Delhi and she was living in the hostel now. This new freedom was full of friends who visited her and relatives she visited, both of which were missing from my new life in America. When she was at the hostel it took several attempts to get through, a lot of shouting in English and Hindi and then many minutes before she came down from her room to the phone. The girls waiting in line for their own long distance calls would keep asking her to hurry up and she herself would be getting late for a film or a political meeting. 'How much is this costing you, Rindu?' she would keep asking. 'It's in the budget,' I would reply, but the question would return again and again till I began to dread it and started cutting the conversations short myself.

The big fight came in winter. It was precipitated by my decision to not go to India for the break. 'It's too soon,' I told her. 'People here will laugh at me if I go back to India four months after arriving.'

I was utterly confused when she raged and cried and begged and pleaded. She had been so distant on the phone and on email, and now she was accusing me of being selfish and not wanting to see her. The argument proceeded at an agonizingly slow pace: one email a day. Finally, my anger boiled over into a one-line missive.

'I can't come because I have spent all my money on phone bills.'

A week of phoning and not finding her at the hostel and sending apologetic emails later she did write back. A cheerful email saying that it was fine if I didn't want to come and that I should take care of my finances. 'There's still time,' I wrote. 'I can still buy a ticket.' But she wrote another sunny email saying that the city was looking wonderful in the winter and that the shakkarkandi vendors were out on the streets and that Derrida was visiting Delhi soon, which had everyone agog.

Slowly the frequency of her emails went down to no more than one a week. I would immediately type out a long reply and then go into school early the next morning to see if she had written. My email program would remain open all day while I sat at my desk, and every time it beeped my stomach would clutch in anticipation. At night sometimes I would get a strong feeling that she had replied and I would bundle myself up in my winter gear and trudge to school through the snow at three in the morning, battling the cold and my fear of getting mugged, only to find that my inbox was bare.

In late February she started emailing me more often, longer chattier emails. Increasingly she talked about this friend she was spending a lot of time with. The campus was in turmoil over the killing of a former student union leader. Her friend, Bijit, was very involved in organizing protest marches and rallies. On one occasion the two of them had been part of a demonstration and the police had lathicharged the crowd.

When she finally told me that Bijit had said that he liked her and that she thought he was a very nice guy, I felt no jealousy. I never seriously believed that she would actually want to be with anyone but me. We shared something so special, we vibed so well, that I thought it was impossible that either she or I could ever recreate our kind of intimacy with any other person.

For a few weeks after this revelation the winter freeze thawed between us. She was nicer and nicer to me, and more intimate in her emails and on the phone. We would talk about the Bijit situation and I would be understanding and try to say wise, calming things. She had talked to him, she said, she had told him that she liked him as a friend and that was all. I thought nothing of the fact that her distress regarding him kept returning. When, in April, I said that I had decided not to go to India so that I could start some research in the summer, she didn't say anything.

A few days later she wrote to me saying that it would be better if we took some time off. She would like us to not talk or email for a while.

Seven months of backbreaking loneliness and more than twenty unsent emails and hundreds of half-dialled phone calls later, just before returning to Delhi for the first time, a year and a half after I had left it for good, I broke the agreement and emailed her.

The thought of losing my vapid rituals – TV, films, the internet – even for a month, the thought of pretending to be happy for the benefit of my friends and family, the grief of having lost my life in Delhi, all got together to break my resolve.

'I know you said that we shouldn't talk or email,' I wrote, 'but I am coming to Delhi this Friday and I really want to meet you.'

My fingers tingled at the thought of reaching out to a Friday in Delhi sitting in front of my computer in Baltimore on a Monday: across a grey dawn at an empty European airport, across a twenty-four hour journey through dehydration and claustrophobia.

Tuesday brought no reply so I had to run to the department an hour before the shuttle came to take me to the airport on Wednesday.

'Hi Rindu! Good to hear from you! Of course we should meet. Ring me up when you get to Delhi.'

The exclamation points were like slaps to my face, punishment for having broken the pact.

*

Balancing two cups of coffee and one plate of sambaar vada on a tray I walked through the large shedlike structure of the Coffee Home. Late morning sunbeams, heavy with dust, sloped in through the door as I slipped out. The courtyard was packed with an early lunch crowd: groups of white-haired men drinking tea and discussing politics; plumpish saleswomen from the nearby handloom emporia in brightly coloured saris and overly made up faces, gossiping about co-workers; cigarette-smoking, tie-wearing young men eyeing young girls in salwar kameez. Aparna was the only one sitting alone.

'Oh,' she said, as I set the food down, 'I forgot to tell you. Chanda called me at the hostel a few months ago.'

'Neeraj's Chanda?'

'Ya.'

'What did she say?'

'She talked about this and that. I told her to come and see me, that we could go shopping and she promised she would. But she never came and she never called again.'

'That's strange,' I said, trying to pretend I was interested.

'How is she now?' she asked.

'Don't know,' I said. 'I haven't had much contact with Neeraj since I left India. He sends emails occasionally on the class list but I haven't talked to him directly since the summer we left.'

'Oh,' she said.

'How is Bijit?' I asked, blowing on my coffee.

'He's fine. Gone to Bangalore for a month,' she said, dissecting her vada as she spoke.

'For work?'

'No, parents,' she said, slurping sambaar over the second word, making it sound like play-rents.

'Oh,' I said.

She swallowed the piece of vada in her mouth, dabbed her lips with a napkin, then looked up at me and said: 'I am going too, day after tomorrow.'

'To Bangalore?'

'Yes,' she said.

'For how long?'

'I'll be back after Republic Day.'

'But I am leaving on the twenty-fifth,' I said. 'I won't get to see you before I leave.'

'Oho,' she said, like she was commiserating with a child who had dropped his ice cream. 'When are you coming to India next?'

'Don't know,' I grunted.

She ignored the petulance in my tone, looking away at the water tap instead where a karamchari was stacking clean glasses in neat towers of six each.

I waited for my annoyance to dissipate and then I asked: 'Are you seeing him, this Bijit? Are you with him?'

When she looked back at me her face looked like it was aching with compassion. In the gentlest voice I had ever heard her use she said: 'Yes, Rindu, I am.'

We walked all over Connaught Place in the next few hours: tourist junk shops, pavement magazine stands, art galleries, fancy book stores, pirated CD shops. We talked like old friends, like two children of the same city, like former schoolmates with tens of common acquaintances. Sometimes it felt like we were lovers again, walking close, almost touching. Other times we fought, snapped at each other, wounded each other with the precision that comes from having been closer to each other than anyone else. But most of the time it felt like we were sharing a last futile intimacy, like a child trying to drink the leftover froth in the glass after the milk itself had been drunk.

Dusk had fallen by the time we found ourselves at the Eastern Court bus stop. 'When are you coming to India next, Rindu?' she asked again, this time to signal that the meeting was over.

'Probably next winter,' I said.

'Good, good,' she said. 'I'll be in Delhi only.'

Scooterists trundled past on their weary way home. I thought of the day I had stopped here to pick Aparna up on the way to the hostel.

'Why so quiet?' she asked.

'No, nothing.'

The light changed upstream and a blueline bus appeared in the distance. Aparna stood up.

'That looks like a 615,' she said. 'I'll go.'

Take the next one, I wanted to say. But I didn't.

She hugged me tight. I felt it was unfair of her to compress this moment of parting into the ten seconds it took for the 615 to get from the traffic light to the bus stop, but I returned the hug as best as I could: I didn't want her to sense my annoyance.

'Bye Rindu,' she said, stepping back and looking up at me. I wanted to pull her back into my arms and kiss her, hard and full on the lips, to make her come back to me by kissing her till she was physically incapable of leaving me, but we were standing at the Eastern Court bus stop at five thirty in the evening and we had already scandalized everyone by throwing our arms around each other.

'Bye,' I said.

I watched the 615 carry her away, her indistinct shape waving at me as it went.

On the ride home in the auto-rickshaw, just as we turned onto the bridge leading across the river to Mayur Vihar, O Mere Dil Ke Chain started blaring from the speakers.

'Music okay?' the driver asked.

I nodded.

'I can often pick myself up when I fall,' Kishore Kumar was singing. 'But if you hold my hand, I am strong enough to change the world.'

The retreating mugginess of early evening hits us as Bhats and I step out onto my corner of 29th and Charles.

'Shit, you're right, Rindu. We haven't met for more than five years. Too much, yaar,' Bhats is saying.

'Let's go this way,' I say, pointing west.

'Your building's awning is very cool. Makes it look like a street in New York,' Bhats says. This is the only awning on 29th Street for miles on either side but I decide to keep this fact to myself.

A young maple is turning by the dumpsters. Summer is near end. The dell across the street is still thick with green, blocking the view to the museum. On each floor of the rowhouse next to my building, diced into apartments long before I came to Baltimore, an air conditioner grumbles into the dying afternoon. At the end of the block a majestic magnolia stretches out over the street corner.

'Lot of kalloos here,' Bhats says, spotting two gangly teenagers waiting for the bus, dressed identically in purple Ravens' jerseys with the number 52 written large on them.

'Don't use that word,' I say. 'People understand what it means.'

We stop to cross Howard Street right in front of the housing project. On a street bench proclaiming Baltimore to be the greatest city in America sit old black men clutching their walking sticks, staring at us through rheumy eyes. I nod politely and smile. One of them nods back.

'52 is Ray Lewis, na?' Bhats says. 'That guy is too much, yaar. Best linebacker in the league. Without him your Ravens are nothing.'

'Well, the whole defence is really good and their offensive linemen are pretty decent too,' I respond, realizing that Bhats must spend a lot of time watching football on TV to know that 52 is Ray Lewis's number.

'Totally chutiya offence! Hardly scored anything through the playoffs,' he snorts. 'What a fraud team, yaar, won the Superbowl with no offence.'

'But they did win,' I say, feeling protective of the Ravens and puzzled at the fact that Bhats and I, friends since long before either he and I were aware that the NFL existed, are arguing about this.

'That was some night,' I continue, trying to resume my role as gracious host. 'People were driving up and down the streets and honking all night.'

We are out of Charles Village now, crossing Howard Street into the lower reaches of Hampden. The houses become smaller, lighter in colour, more compact. People sit on tiny stoops, or on plastic chairs placed by their doors: shapeless women, their thick thighs pockmarked with cellulite showing under their denim shorts; bored young men in plaid shirts, hair flowing out from behind baseball caps, their skin an unhealthy shade of pink. At the corners stand knots of teenagers, boys with very short hair and very wide trousers, girls in tight white tank tops.

'Yaar,' says Bhats in Hindi, 'whatever you might say, blondes are sexy.'

I nod in disapproving agreement, wondering whether I should point out that the words 'blonde' and 'sexy' are understood by English speakers even when they appear in a Hindi sentence.

On deck chairs two doors down from the crab house – crowded as usual – sits a black family, holding large foil wrappers full of something that smells fried, and delicious. The thought suddenly pops into my mind that Bhats is a brahmin, his nickname is a contraction of Bhattacharya. I look across him and, as if for the first time, notice how very fair he is. In a poorly lit room, I find myself thinking, he might pass for Caucasian.

The road dips now and we see the on-ramp for the 83, beyond which lies our destination, Druid Hill Park. Just across the street from the ramp stands a resolutely cheery white and red Burger King.

'How about BK?' I ask Bhats.

'Hain?' he says. 'Bee Kay? Listen, there was a TK in your class, a KK in mine. We had SK in the hostel who was two years senior to us and DK who was two years junior, RK who got into the IAS on his first attempt and JK who tried four times with no luck. And, of course, there was Lallu who would have been called LK if Lallu hadn't been a better alternative. But who the fuck is BK?'

Laughter expands into my ribcage, making it hurt. I can't control it, I don't want to. 'TK, KK, SK, DK, RK, JK,' I groan and another spasm hits me. Bhats is laughing too, he has spotted Burger King.

We turn right at the intersection and walk up to the old mill, now home to a silverware factory. There's a less travelled bridge here which leads to the park. As we walk towards it we hear the sound of a mighty river whooshing through a valley: the 83.

Face against the wire mesh I stand looking down at the highway. Cars erupt from under me: zoop, zoop, zoop. My toes tingle at the sound.

'What's the nala kind of thing on the right?' Bhats asks.

'That's the Jones River,' I say. 'They built the 83 on top of it.'

The river looks back at us, its gaze feeling like that of the old black men at the housing project. Its valley usurped, it continues to flow, translucent and calm, reflecting perhaps on that which has been.

'Yaar,' Bhats sighs. 'It's been a while since I went to India. Three years. Should plan a trip soon.'

'Wow,' I say. 'Three years. You're like a fucking camel, a ship of the fucking desert!'

We walk up the path past a large empty swimming pool. Outside its fence two orioles – black wing, orange breast like the baseball team's colours – hop, skip and peck their way through the grass. The row of trees on our left ends where the path ends and the reservoir comes into view beyond them. To our right a game is on in the basketball court. The players move with a television-inspired energy. They leap and crash like the people whose names are written on their clothes: Jordan, Pippen, O'Neal.

'Sisqo probably played basketball here,' I say.

'Thong Song Sisqo?'

'Yes,' I say and I feel pride fill my voice. 'He's from Baltimore. In fact the band he used to sing for was named Dru Hill after this place.'

Bhats looks impressed. Involuntarily he says: 'I played squash with Jadeja once.'

I have heard the story before, several times, of how Bhats had been playing squash at the Gymkhana Club in Delhi and how Jadeja had happened to be there and how Bhats had beaten him five games out of seven.

'Oh really,' I say, mock seriously. 'When?'

'Fuck off, Rindu.'

As we walk along the reservoir I think of the deep and intricate commonality Bhats and I share. Growing up Bengali and English-speaking in Delhi, we both absorbed the city's fine-grained, destructive notions of class. We knew, although we never talked about it, that for people like us who didn't have direct access to power and riches, the only way to gain status was to go abroad. What locked us into a perpetual understanding of each other was the recognition that the middleness of the life we had led in India was the definition of us, was the boiling pot from which the steam of our motives would always rise. Even when we were old men in exile, surrounded by American friends who would marvel at our success and be charmed by our accents and American children who would benefit from the former and be embarrassed by the latter, we would still be trying to prove something to someone back in Delhi.

'I talked to Kartik some time ago,' Bhats says. 'He bought a Corvette recently.'

'Corvette, haan? Good, yaar. Didn't the tech downturn affect him?'

'He sold his stock at exactly the right time,' he says. 'He made more money than anyone else in his company.'

'Wow,' I say.

'He lands on his feet, Kartik,' he says. 'He hits the ground running. He's a total Bond that way.'

'I was talking to him a few months ago,' I say. 'He was telling me about how his dad is really keen on building a house in their ancestral village. It's way out somewhere in the desert, the last few miles have to be done by camel cart. Kartik was complaining that his dad refuses to see reason, doesn't care how much effort or money it will take.'

'Does he want to live in the village?' Bhats asks.

'That's the thing,' I say. 'He doesn't. He just wants to build a big house there. Kartik was pissed off about it.'

'That's really stupid, yaar,' Bhats says. 'Really stupid. I hate that kind of materialistic bullshit.'

Bhats' judgement reflects my own, and a feeling of contrariness rises in me. The thought occurs that Kartik and his father are victims of their own insecurities, driven always towards some receding notion of unsurpassable success, destined never to be happy. And the difference between Bhats' judgement and mine, I realize, is slight. I feel trapped.

We reach the Moorish Tower which stands sentry over the junction of 29th Street and the Interstate. Asphalt strands ravel and unravel below us, old stone bridges mixing with new concrete structures. Small yellow daisies pepper the slope that leads down to the road. Across, on the other side, a shuttered railway station sits guard over rusted tracks, superannuated by the acrylic brightness of a Light Rail Yard some distance away.

And beyond these, laid out on the undulating contours of the Jones River Valley, lies the beautiful, battered city of Baltimore.

On our way home through the streets of Hampden we can see table lamps lighting up faded floral wallpaper. A pleasant evening breeze tinkles through dime-store chimes. Across the street from us a large man trudges along, back bent, a six-pack of beer hanging from his right hand. The workshop at the end of the block is closing down for the night, its hydraulic hiss winding down, an unattended hose leaking water into the gutter between the sidewalk and the street.

We pass a bar: 'Coca Cola! Packaged Goods Available.' Green-red light from neon signs proclaiming the names of various brands of beer spills out through the open door into the evening. The long wooden bar, smooth from several years of daily polishing, is occupied by three men who sit barstool-hunched over it. The jukebox is playing Hey Joe.

'How's your band doing?' Bhats asks.

'My band?'

'Yes, Pandit and company.'

'I don't know,' I say. 'Some years ago I met Pandit when I was in Delhi. He was in bad shape.'

'Drugs?' Bhats asks.

'I guess so. I didn't ask. He was going on about how he had gone to, come to, America and jammed with Prince or something like that.'

'Jammed!' snorts Bhats. 'With Prince! How did he get to America, anyway?'

'His sister lives in California,' I say.

'So is he here now?' he asks.

'No, he went back. Said it was not for him.'

'What a loser, yaar!' he says. 'In any case, here everyone can play the guitar, not like in Delhi where there are six good guitarists in the whole city. That guy we heard yesterday night, fucking awesome! No way that Pandit could ever be as good as him.'

I think of the old balding guy – his face marked with years of alcoholism, his teeth discoloured from smoking – who we had seen at a Fells Point blues place: a Stevie Ray Vaughan tribute act, destined to live the remaining years of his life emulating a dead man. 'Just love this music, man. There ain't much money in it.'

'I think Pandit could be as good as him,' I say. 'He could at least be good enough to get small gigs here and there even if he didn't become as famous as Hendrix or Satriani or whatever.'

'Ya,' he says. 'Spend your life wondering where your next drink is coming from. Bullshit!'

'At least he'd be doing what he likes,' I burst out, angry now. 'Better than hanging around stupid computer training classes to get a fucked up job debugging other people's code.'

'That's true, man,' says Bhats, conciliatory and reflective. 'That's the great thing about America, na? People here do what they love. In India if you try to do what you want to, you get fucked. Look at me. I don't even know what I want to do, I just do what everyone else does.'

The realization seeps into me that when our parents encouraged us to have 'hobbies' like music or dance or sports, they made sure that we knew that they were no more than pastimes, that they could not be careers. Pandit had missed Bhats' crucial insight: In India if you try to do what you want to, you get fucked. Pandit had made the mistake of knowing what he wanted to do and pursuing it at the cost of what everyone else was doing, and he had got fucked.

Suddenly I find myself thinking of Sheikhu and Neeraj, of the things they had wanted, of the things they want. A sentence floats through my head: We are what we want. It elaborates itself out and as it does I can feel my blood pumping with anger and helplessness. We aren't what we do or what we achieve or what we acquire or what we become, we are and we always will be what we want.

Hurrying past the Seven-Eleven, we walk across the bridge over the creek and emerge behind the medical centre. Bhats wants to see the campus, I show it to him. On our way home we reach the intersection of Art Museum Drive and Charles Street. I have known the man who stands there for five years, giving him a quarter every time I pass by.

'I'm jus' tryin' to get summin' ta eat,' he says, when he sees me, hobbling over to where we stand. 'Jus' tryin' to get a sandwich.'

I reach into my pocket and bring out a quarter.

'Always hit me with a quarter,' he says.

I smile guiltily. There is more change in my pocket but I pass by here twice a day and I am on a budget.

A man comes up behind us with a dog on a leash. The animal's discoloured brown skin hangs off its body, it drags itself along deliberately.

'Tha's an ole dog,' my panhandler friend says.

'Yes,' I say. 'It's too late to teach it new tricks.'

The panhandler is laughing hard long after the rest of us have stopped. Water streams out of his eyes. 'Too late,' he says. 'Too late to teach it new tricks.'

Finally, when he gets some control over himself he slaps his calloused hand into mine: 'I don't know your name, boy,' he says, 'but you really made me laugh.'

'We'll wait for you in the park,' Sheikhu told Pratap. 'Pick us up when you return.'

'Okay. I'll be back in an hour,' Pratap replied. 'Then we'll take Rindu to lunch.'

'Do you want some water?' asked Sheikhu. 'Jiten, two glasses of water.'

Jiten, a thin dark fellow with a pencil moustache came in to the basement carrying a tray.

'Thanks, yaar,' said Sheikhu, affecting a familiarity Jiten did not reciprocate.

'Nice place you have here,' I said, looking around the basement which housed the small software company that Sheikhu and Pratap were running.

It was the first time I was getting to meet Sheikhu since college. In the intervening years he had gone to IIM, then on to work for some big company in Bombay. Two or three years of doing that had bored him into a stupor, he said, so he joined forces with Pratap, found an uncle looking to invest some money, and Trikon Technologies had been born. 'We cover all angles and help you get to the point.'

'Nice-shice, yaar,' Sheikhu said. 'We are shutting down in a week.'

'Really? What happened?'

'Come, let's go and sit in the park, I'll tell you,' said Sheikhu, getting up peremptorily.

Malviya Nagar was busy with its late morning business when we emerged onto the street: steel rods were being unloaded from a blue lorry at a construction site; a saucepan was boiling over with milky liquid at the tea stall; buses were racing each other, their conductors slapping the sides of the bus as they went, like jockeys spurring horses. We crossed the road cautiously and got to the park, no more than a square patch of grass surrounding an old tomb.

'So, what happened?' I asked, flopping down on the grass.

'Still doing a PhD in Theory?' Sheikhu asked.

'Ya, what else?' I said.

'Are you really doing a PhD or are you just doing a PhD in theory?' he said and laughed. And then, turning serious: 'It's been quite a few years. Will you complete it soon?'

'It's been difficult,' I said. 'But I think I can finish up in six months. My advisor thinks I should.'

'What are you going to do then?' he asked.

'I don't know. I've applied for some postdocs, some faculty positions.'

'Come back to India, Rindu,' he said, taking me completely by surprise. 'We need people like you here.'

Then, seeing me speechless and quizzical, he continued: 'You know, all that we learned at IIT was total bullshit. Not one thing is of any use. All those pushdown automata and first order logic are good for nothing. All we need in India is a solid understanding of what is available.'

'What's available meaning what?' I asked.

'We don't need to be doing cutting-edge research, yaar, we just need to know what people have done and we need to know how to put it together for our own market. The real thing is to develop our own products. Everyone wants to provide services, but how long will this call centre nonsense last?

'But Sheikhu,' I said. 'How can we create intellectual property without doing research?'

'We need many other things before that,' he said. 'We need marketing, we need to create brand recognition. Most importantly, we need people who know technology but aren't just techies. We need people who can see the big picture.' He was pulling at the grass as he talked. It was green and soft and came out easily, bringing wet mud with it.

'You have that capability, Rindu,' he said, looking directly into my eyes. 'You should come back to India.'

'You have that capability' rang through my head, slowly turning into 'I have that capability'. Looking across at him, his gaze averted from mine as always, I thought of him sitting at the back of the van on our way back from Neeraj's house looking out of the window. I remembered us sitting in his room with him staring into the distance as I tried to explain my proof to him. And I felt the frustration of those moments melt away in that one moment when he showed me that, despite all the looking away, he had seen who I was and who I wanted to be.

'We need people who can figure these things out,' he said. 'And we need people who can explain what we are trying to do to others. Didn't someone say that you talk well, Rindu?'

He smiled finally as he spoke that last line, and I heard the laughter in his voice. It was a gentle laughter, free from derision, and it forever transformed Kanitkar's putdown into resounding affirmation.

It was nearing twelve now and small groups of people were trickling into the park. They sat in circles, opening their tiffin-carriers, separating the different compartments: roti, sabji and achaar. They shared their food, and when they were finished they brought out packs of cards and began the lunchtime ritual common to white-collar men all over the city. The women came out too, but their winter afternoon pleasure was knitting as they gossiped.

'What do you say, Rindu?' Sheikhu persisted.

'Ya, ya,' I waffled, trying to hide the commotion his words had set off within me. 'But tell me, why are you closing Trikon Technologies?'

'I am not closing it, yaar,' he sighed. 'We simply don't have enough money. Our business hasn't been growing.'

'What are you going to do now?' I asked.

'Just hang around for a while. Maybe some freelance consulting or something. Wait for a while and then see what can be done. I've made sure that all the guys who were working for us have been given long-term contracts by the clients whose projects they were working on. Pratap and I will find other things to do.'

'What will you do?' I asked.

'We'll find something.'

He had a plan, I could sense that, but I also knew that he wouldn't tell me what it was. Even when we had worked together, Sheikhu never thought aloud. I didn't press him. Like everyone else I would just have to wait and see.

'What research are you doing?' he asked.

'Some network-related stuff, little bit of graph theory, little bit of probability,' I said.

'You know,' he said, 'a couple of years ago I tried to read some papers, just generally some stuff I downloaded. I don't understand a thing any more.' His face was as inscrutable as ever when he said this, and I reflected for a moment on how the both of us were trying really hard to conceal the way we felt while knowing fully well that the other person was in the middle of a storm of emotion too.

'Ya,' I continued. 'Just some networks stuff. One or two papers are out, another couple are going to come out later this year.'

'Good, Rindu,' he said, and I could see he was trying to imagine me as the author of a paper.

There was something in his tone that made me want to tell him about what I had learned on St Patrick's Day a few years ago.

'Some time ago this guy in my lab, David, invited me over to his place for St Patrick's Day,' I told him. 'It's some Irish festival. David's wife is Irish. She had made cabbage and corned beef and we drank green beer. That's the ritual. He had also called this Romanian guy, Radu. Both Radu and David started a couple of years before me, they've both graduated now. This St Patrick's Day happens around the time when the graduate admissions committee makes offers. Radu was the student representative on the committee, so he had been spending hours sifting through applications. He was bitching away at dinner about all the stupid applications he was having to look at. He started ribbing me by telling me about how the Indian applicants always tried to save money by never sending originals of their GRE scores, just attaching photocopies. And, he said, sometimes it's even worse. There was this one Indian guy some years ago who had done research under Sridhar Kanitkar, you know, the three bistability guy. But this kid didn't have a recommendation from Kanitkar. We decided to make him an offer anyway, the chairman said that the letter was probably on its way.'

Several times before this meeting I had thought of the time I would tell Sheikhu this story. If there was one person who would understand that Radu's revelation had landed on my self-confidence like a rock on a windshield, it was Sheikhu, I had thought.

'What did you say?' he asked.

'What did I say? What could I say? I told him I was that guy. They all thought it was very funny.'

He half laughed. 'It is a little funny.'

'It isn't funny, Sheikhu,' I burst out. 'It made me feel like shit, like a total fucking fraud.'

'Look at it this way,' he said. 'At least you got the schol. Even if it was for the wrong reason.'

But that was not good enough for me, I wanted to tell him. It wasn't just the opportunity to do what I wanted that I needed, it was the recognition that I was worthy of it.

'Did you subscribe to *Science Today* in school?' he asked.

'Yes, I did. Why?'

'Do you remember they used to have one sci-fi story every issue?'

'Of course,' I said. 'That's all I read in *Science Today.*'

'There was this story once of this guy who is a famous batsman, modelled on Gavaskar. Do you remember that one?'

'No,' I said. 'What's the story?'

'It's the day before a big test match between the West Indies and India and this Gavaskar-like fellow is watching the news. They mention the match and show some footage of a cricket match. He recognizes himself getting run out on screen. There's a misfield, his partner calls for the second run and he is caught out of his ground. No matter how hard he tries he can't recall which match the incident is from. So he calls up someone at the TV station and asks them what footage they were showing and they tell him they didn't show any footage, just made the announcement. The more he thinks about it, the surer he gets that what he has seen is not from the past.'

'It's from the future,' I said, memory stirring in my mind.

'Yes,' said Sheikhu. 'And he goes to a physicist friend who gives him some mumbo jumbo about time-space.'

'I remember this story,' I cut in, as it all came rushing back. 'The next day he keeps looking at the scoreboard waiting for the moment that he saw on the screen. And then there it is. The bowler delivers, he hits the ball to the very fielder he had seen on TV the previous day, the man misfields. His partner calls for a second.'

'No, he shouts,' said Sheikhu. 'And he doesn't run. At the end of the over his partner comes up to him and asks him why he didn't run, there was a clear second run there and he says –'

'– I've never scored a century before lunch, have I? I think I'll do it today.'

The park was empty by now. Lunch was over. Pratap came in, helmet swinging on his arm. 'Come on behnchods,' he said. 'Lunch.'

Sheikhu got up, chucking aside the grass he had been playing with. His normally tight mouth twitched with a smile at one of its corners. I threw my arm around his shoulder the way I would have when we were in college. He tensed at first, then relaxed. Linking his own arm with mine, he passed it over my shoulder. Joined together like this we walked up to Pratap who took us to lunch and entertained us with stories of all the girls he had slept with in the last few months.

'Look over your shoulder,' Jatty-Jat said. 'See that mountain up there?'

I would have called it stubby, the feature he was referring to, except that it towered miles above anything else the landscape had to offer.

'That's Mount Rainier,' he said. 'I climbed it in jeans three weeks after I moved here.'

It was a few months after I had met Sheikhu in Delhi and I was on my way to a conference in Vancouver. Jatty-Jat was working in Seattle and so I bought a round-trip ticket to Seattle, planning to take the bus to Vancouver. He had picked me up at the airport and we were driving to the city when the massive peak had come into view.

'That! You climbed that? That's fucking crazy, Jat!'

He grinned his mischievous grin.

'Good to see you, yaar,' I said.

By the time we reached downtown, the sun had disappeared. My bus wasn't leaving for another two hours so we walked for a while in that grey city, stopping at times to look down at the steely waters of the bay below. Finally, a thin misty spray started floating down, forcing us to find a restaurant.

'Sure you don't want coffee?' he said. 'There's supposed to be good coffee in Seattle.'

'I've heard,' I said, charmed that he wanted to be a good host. Jatty-Jat had never touched anything with caffeine in it.

Over a soggy plate of french fries I filled him in on the news from those of our hostelmates who were my friends and he filled me in on the news from those who were his. He told me about his wife: 'She's athletic, like me. We go hiking every weekend. Nowadays she has less time because she's doing her masters in Computer Science, part-time from UW, and so she sometimes has to do programming assignments on the weekends. Don't tell her I said this when you meet her, but most of the time I end up writing her programs.' I told him about my research and how I was glad to be finally done with my PhD.

Jatty-Jat, I learned, had reached America the other accepted way. He had joined a software company in Bangalore that had sent him to Milwaukee on a project. While in Milwaukee he decided to look for a long-term job in the US but the project ran out before he could find one. Back in Bangalore he went to a bodyshopper: 'Remember Manocha, two batches senior, Chemical? He was in the bodyshopping business. Too much money in that business at the time. Not so much any more.' Manocha had sent him to Chicago, where he stayed for a few years before applying for the job he currently had in Seattle: 'That was a good job, but boring. Here I am part of a development team, there I was just a body. Half the time I was sitting on the bench.'

The drizzle stopped and a wet sun broke out. As we came out on to the street a thought struck me. 'Jat, while you were in Chicago did you meet Neeraj?'

'Of course, yaar,' he said. 'Neeraj helped me a lot when I first moved to Chicago. I used to hang out with him all the time.'

'How is he?'

'You should know,' he said. 'He's cracking the research scene, what else?'

I knew, of course, that Neeraj had become hot property in the world of Algorithms research. His very first paper, written with Kanitkar, had been a famous one, improving a result which had stood for a long time. His subsequent work, most of it solo, had established him as a superstar in the making. 'I know,' I said.

'He's with IBM Research now,' he said. 'In New York somewhere.'

'Ya, I know,' I said.

'He had applied to one or two of the top-ranked univs,' Jatty-Jat said. 'But they didn't hire him. Some politics, he said.'

'I heard about that,' I told him, but decided not to reveal what exactly I had heard – that Neeraj hadn't been offered the jobs because he was not thought to be a team player.

'You know what he's like,' said Jat. 'Says whatever comes to his mind.'

We were at the southern end of 2nd Avenue now. The Amtrak Station from where I was to take the coach lay to our left. In front of us was Seahawks Stadium, two large trussed arches built over its eastern and western stands making it look like a perverse bridge, a suspension without a roadway.

'The sun used to rise here six months ago, now it rises there,' said Jatty-Jat, his arm describing an arc through the sky.

'How did we reach this corner of the world, Jat?'

In the first few years after college I had mainly talked to Neeraj over the compguys' email list. The conversations followed a pattern: someone would post an article to do with Indian politics, or the Microsoft antitrust case, or the funding freeze at IIT Delhi; I would comment on it and Neeraj would attack me, or the other way round; others would come in on his side or mine; the thread would degenerate into imperfectly veiled personal attacks. I heard about his research achievements but never mentioned them on the list, my own PhD was in very poor shape.

As time had passed each compguy found success in some measure or the other – my PhD had also limped towards a satisfactory conclusion – and emails on the list lost their urgency, mainly speculating about impending marriages and, subsequently, children. In fact I had even talked to Neeraj on the phone a few times, polite professional conversations in which he had given me advice on applying for jobs to research labs and universities, and we had talked about each other's research like we were two strangers meeting for the first time between sessions at a conference.

'When did you last talk to Neeraj?' asked Jatty-Jat as we turned to walk towards the station. There was an hour left for my bus.

'It's been a while,' I said.

'So you don't know about what happened last year,' said Jatty-Jat, his normally cheerful face smoothening into solemnity.

'No, what?'

'Did you know Neeraj had a niece?' he asked.

'Yes,' I said. 'Chanda.'

He shook his head as if he wished I hadn't told him her name.

'What happened?'

'Yaar,' he said. 'It's horrible. It's hard to even think about it.'

'What happened, Jat?'

'Neeraj had told her to get a passport made,' he said. 'He had gone to India last year and filled out the form for her.'

'Ya,' I said. 'She must have turned eighteen, he wanted to bring her to America once she was eighteen.'

'The policeman came for address verification. Neeraj's father locked the girl in her room, told the policeman he had the wrong place. After the constable left he started beating her. He pushed her so hard that she she fell against the washing machine face first. The corner of the washing machine poked her in the eye. They took her to the hospital but the doctors said that there was no way her eye could be saved, it was crushed.'

'Oh shit, Jat! She's blind in one eye now?'

Smokers crowded the door of King Street Station: large men in plaid shirts and beards, women in high-heeled shoes wearing elegant coats, students. Jatty-Jat stepped past them and flopped his wiry frame onto a bench like an old man. I sat down beside him.

'How is she now, Jat?'

He sat with his chin on his chest like he was sleeping, or trying to solve an equation in his head. Finally, his eyes still shut, he spoke.

'She killed herself a month later. Hanged herself from the ceiling fan.'

Looking out of the bus window into the northwestern dusk as we rode up the highway to Canada, I thought of that little girl in her government school tunic, sitting on the empty floor of a burned room watching TV. The image of her sitting there became a pencil sketch of an empty room, with an empty window in the wall. I could see her smiling at Neeraj with Aparna stroking her hair. 'Chachi is beautiful, looks just like Smita Patil.' 'She's such a lovely girl, Rindu. It's so unfair.'

But then Chanda faded from my thoughts and, instead, I saw Neeraj at the dhaba on Mathura Road saying: 'Yaar, she's my niece. I love her. I can do anything for her.' The words rang in my ear – I love her, I can do anything for her – and, in that moment, I cried for Neeraj like I had never cried for anyone else. My head against the window, face covered with a sweater, I wept. Like vivid dreams on a tired night the images flashed in front of my eyes: at the Society, the night before registration, Neeraj sobbing, a train whistling in the distance; at the dhaba near the Happy School, 'Don't go, Rindu'; in my room at the hostel, 'That's not friendship, Rindu, that isn't friendship.'

And, then, just like that, I knew what friendship was. Suddenly I knew that Neeraj and I were linked by an unbreakable bond, that his pain would always be my pain, and my happiness would always be his happiness. If there had been a point in time when either of us had a choice in the matter, that point was long past. Our lives were ineluctably entwined. Whether we liked it or not, whether we met or not, whether we talked or not, we were each destined to suffer at the other's suffering.

I thought at first that I should write to him as soon as I got to a computer, then I thought better of it. At best I would say something like, 'Why didn't you tell me this had happened?' But it wasn't a petty exclusion I was feeling. 'I hope you are all right,' was pointless because I knew he wasn't, because he would know that I hoped that he was. 'I'm here if you want to talk to me,' was not true because I didn't really want to talk to him, neither of us knew how to say the several things we needed to say. I decided not to write to him because I realized that he already knew we were friends, he had known all along.

So I sat back in my seat, snuggled deeper into my coat, watched America change to Canada out of my window and wondered if what I had learned that day would change my life forever.

I didn't get a minute of sleep the last night I spent at IIT. The B.Tech project theses were due the next day and I spent all night reading and rereading my lemmas, theorems and proofs. Once I submitted this there would be no scope for correction, it would be bound in black and put away on a high shelf in the department's library, guarded for eternity by Mrs Sharma.

The end was near when dawn broke outside. I came out of my room wearing only my kurta. Leaving my door open I walked to the eastern stairwell, climbed it to the fifth floor and then went beyond to the roof of the E floor. The door was locked but a big panel from the bottom was missing. I squirmed out through it.

Stepping over thick metal pipes I went up to the boundary wall. Placing my elbows on it and cupping my face in my hands I looked down at the campus. The concrete was cool to my touch, I pushed more of myself up against it. I thought about climbing to the top of the stairwell, the highest point in the hostel. This was the last legitimate opportunity. So I disengaged from the wall and walked to the foot of the stairwell, put my chappaled foot into one of the grooves on the side and reached up with my hands. Immediately my foot slipped, my fingers scratched the side, I fell back.

Sitting on one of the water pipes, cool metal soothing my thinly clothed body, I looked up at the mountain I had decided to conquer. It was no more than eight feet of wall, grooved invitingly, an easy climb. The BSP's *Book of Records* held an entry in Jatty-Jat's name for this stairwell: he had climbed it all the way from ground level to the top. All I had to do was climb the last few feet.

I never thought of the danger of falling. All I thought of was how difficult it would be to explain why I was trying to climb the wall in case anyone got to know.

I stood up, determined to wriggle back into the stairwell through the hole in the door and go back to the last chapter of my thesis. But I couldn't bring myself to go. Just once, I thought, and if it didn't work I'd go back down to my room and I'd never think of it again. Positioning myself, I carefully placed my chappal on the wall. As my arm pulled weight onto the foot, I felt it stand firm. Some heaving and scraping later I was up. I was on top of the hostel.

The campus looked beautiful, green and quiet in the early morning light. Far below a doodhwala slowly pedalled his cycle down the road. I looked south, past the other hostels to the JNU hills and the yellow boxes of Vasant Kunj. There was a nip in the morning air. It travelled up my unclothed legs, giving me goose pimples as it went.

To my north was the green stretch where on weekends people in white would play cricket. In first year we would try and watch them from the fourth floor, even though we had exams to study for and the trees were in the way. Past the trees lay the rest of Delhi, ugly to many, beautiful to me.

I looked to where the sun was rising over the newly constructed flyover. There was a pink quilt of clouds in the eastern sky, just like there used to be when I would take the school bus early morning from Mayur Vihar, craning my neck as we hurtled across the river, twisting my body around to catch a glimpse of the morning light take over the sky with its oranges and reds.

On the flyover the streetlights were still on. I could see a few of them from here, a small arc of sodium orange lighting the road. The road lay hidden beneath the trees: the road which had taken me to my home across the river every weekend and brought me back every Monday for four years.

As I stood there drinking in each detail of this morning landscape, an aeroplane appeared in the distance, fixing course for the airport. I watched it approach till suddenly – it was still a few kilometres away from the campus – the streetlights went out with a sigh. It was time to get back to work.

Taking a deep breath I spread my arms out and turned slowly through three hundred and sixty degrees. For miles in every direction I could see the city I had been born in. As I whirled slowly, up on the highest point of the hostel, I could sense the desires and the aspirations of everyone who had ever lived here, in this city by the river: every Winky and Rocksurd and Pandit, every Bobby and Bagga, every Sheikhu and Neeraj, every Chanda and Bhavna and Abhilasha, every Aparna and every Arindam. I could touch the joy they had felt and the sorrow life had brought them, I could touch their fortitude and their despair, and, more than all of these, I could touch their hope. I wanted to embrace it all. I wanted to embrace them all.

Acknowledgements

I'd like to thank the following people for the various kinds of help and support they have given me over the years.

Rasna Dhillon, Anthony Macris, Bhavani Raman, Panchali Mukherjee, Prashant Billore, Dinesh Khanna, Arudra Burra, Andrew Warren, J.C. Hallman, Jennifer Smith, David Rosenthal, Ratika Kapur, Mukul Kesavan, Alok Rai, Amitav Ghosh, Manju Kak, Siddhartha Deb, Lokesh Gupta, Pankaj Mishra, Shormishtha Panja, Makarand Paranjape, Sameer Jadhav, Amitabh Chaudhary, Vijay Srinivas, Tripurari Singh, Sandeep Jomraj, Michael T. Goodrich.

My family: Indira Bagchi, Ajoy Bagchi, Anuradha Sural, Sumit Sural, Sonakshi Sural, Sanjoy Bagchi.

My friends and teachers at IIT Delhi and my neighbours in Mayur Vihar.

I'd also like to thank Nandita Aggarwal, P.M. Sukumar and Yogesh Sharma at HarperCollins India.

About the Author

Amitabha Bagchi is the author of the DSC Prize-winning *Half the Night Is Gone,* and *Unknown City*. He has also translated the ghazals of Muneer Niazi into English. *Above Average* is his debut novel, first published in 2007.

ALSO BY AMITABHA BAGCHI

Arindam Chatterjee—whom we first met in Amitabha Bagchi's bestselling novel *Above Average*—is now a nearly fifty-year-old novelist and professor. He revisits the relationships he had in his twenties during his years in America and after graduating from IIT—be it with history student Supriya, who wanted a companion to laugh with, not a partner demanding intellectual gratification; or with the activist Lisa, who sought an anchor, not a man unaware of her struggle with depression; or with the writer Razia, who wished to be desired, not summoned to mend a broken soul.

As Arindam looks back, he realizes that the unknown city that's the human heart felt unknowable to him because he was wearing the blinkers of his masculinity.

In *Above Average,* Arindam had said, 'It is a blessing to be understood, and an even greater blessing to be granted understanding.' Has Arindam finally been granted understanding?

HarperCollins *Publishers* India

At HarperCollins India, we believe in telling the best stories and finding the widest readership for our books in every format possible. We started publishing in 1992; a great deal has changed since then, but what has remained constant is the passion with which our authors write their books, the love with which readers receive them, and the sheer joy and excitement that we as publishers feel in being a part of the publishing process.

Over the years, we've had the pleasure of publishing some of the finest writing from the subcontinent and around the world, including several award-winning titles and some of the biggest bestsellers in India's publishing history. But nothing has meant more to us than the fact that millions of people have read the books we published, and that somewhere, a book of ours might have made a difference.

As we look to the future, we go back to that one word—a word which has been a driving force for us all these years.

Read.